FEBRUARY OR FOREVER

JULIET MADISON

BLOODHOUND
— BOOKS —

To my sister at heart, Alli Sinclair.

CHAPTER ONE

Chrissie Burns should have learned by now that white clothing and motherhood didn't mix. She rubbed a damp cloth at the smear of Vegemite on her Lorna Jane yoga top and wished she could also rub away the anxiety that had resurfaced since moving to Tarrin's Bay. It was known as *The Town of New Beginnings*, but for Chrissie, it was the town of bad memories.

'I won't go, Mum, I won't.' Her six-year-old son, Kai, planted his Vegemite-stained hands on his hips in defiance.

Chrissie sighed. 'Kai, you have to go to school. C'mon, let's wash your hands and clean your teeth.' She gave up on the smear and gently grasped her son's arm, but he yanked her hand away.

'Kai, please. You can't stay home.'

'But why, Mum, why do I have to go?' he whined, his freckled face creasing and blue eyes pleading.

'Mummy has to go to work, you know that. Kids go to school and parents go to work. Now c'mon.'

Chrissie led him into the bathroom and washed his hands on his behalf, and failing to get him to clean his teeth, left him crying in the hallway while she retreated to her bedroom and ripped off her stained top. She replaced it with a silvery-grey version of the same; a racer-back singlet with extra stretch, and returned to her red-faced son.

Kai sighed and trudged outside to the car, his backpack thumping against his little body with each step. Chrissie grabbed her bag and locked up, then dashed to the car and started the engine. She drove down Dune Road, past Serendipity Health Retreat where she'd be returning for work, and headed towards the school. She stole a glance in the rear-view mirror and her heart lurched at the sight of her son's blotchy red eyes and the sharp intakes of breath as his bottom lip quivered.

She clamped her lips tight and blinked hard, determined not to let a single tear fall in front of her son. She couldn't let him see that she was hurting too, couldn't add to his already excessive load of sadness at Daddy Not Living With Mummy Anymore. No, tears were for when she was alone. Crying was for the shower, when the stream of water could disguise it, and the bedroom, when Kai was asleep, and only the tear-soaked pillow was privy to her emotional state.

She didn't know what else she could do to make him happy. She couldn't be a stay-at-home mum or home-school him. They may have inherited a house right on the beach that would sell for a nice sum, but until the renovations were complete she still needed to earn a living and stick to a tight budget. Plus, this job was her saviour; she needed it for her sanity.

Chrissie pulled into the ten minute drop off zone outside the school and forced a smile as she unbuckled her reluctant child from his seat. 'It'll be fun, darlin', you wait and see. I bet Mrs Kitson has some super-cool activities planned for today.'

Nothing. No eye contact, no smile. Chrissie drew a deep breath and helped Kai from the car, his arms firmly crossed and glued to his chest.

'It's not fair,' he mumbled. 'You're so mean.'

Chrissie ran a hand over her head and gripped her ponytail, tightness clenching her jaw. With no time to argue, she raised her chin and marched Kai into the school playground. The bell had just gone and kids were lining up in their class rows. She nodded a hello to a couple of mothers, who looked like they belonged in the dictionary under 'happy' and 'perfect' and led Kai towards his Year One classmates. Mrs Kitson flashed a smile as they neared, and curved her hand towards Kai to encourage him to line up.

'He's a bit upset today,' Chrissie explained as Mrs Kitson's eyes narrowed in concern at Kai's red face.

'He'll be fine, you go. We're going to have a great day, aren't we, Kai?' She crouched to his level and he eyed her cautiously.

Kai unfolded his arms and grabbed hold of Chrissie's Lycra pants as she stepped away. 'Kai, I have to go now.'

'No,' he said, gripping the fabric tighter. It was so stretchy she could probably get all the way to the school gate before he lost his grip or she rebounded, or, heaven forbid, showed the entire school her three-dollar undies.

She wrapped her hand around his small fingers and peeled them away from her yoga pants, and Mrs Kitson grasped his hand gently but firmly. 'He'll be fine,' she whispered with a reassuring nod. 'I'll call you if there are any problems.'

He looked far from fine, but Chrissie stepped backwards, offering a feeble wave to her unimpressed child, before turning and walking away. She didn't dare look back. In another six hours she'd return and he'd probably act like nothing had ever happened, until the next morning when the struggle would begin all over again.

She got in the car and closed the door, paused for a moment to steady her breath, then turned the key in the ignition and drove around the corner onto Seaview Road. It sloped downwards, and

Chrissie's eyes scanned the ocean panorama, stretching across the horizon and wrapping around the town. She gulped, a lump of dread bobbing back up like a cork in water. To anyone else, the view might be called spectacular, and it *was* beautiful, but to Chrissie, the word that came to mind was deadly. Her chest rose sharply with fast, shallow breaths as she drove slowly down the road.

No, not again. Not after all this time.

Panic wound its way up her spine like a spiralling vine, tightening and gripping with each breath. Her heart pounded, each beat trying to outdo the previous one, until she gasped for breath. Chrissie veered off to the side of the road, slammed on the brakes and put on the handbrake. She placed her hand on her chest in an effort to stop the rising fear, as heat rose up her neck and sweat pooled at her lower back.

Oh God, oh God.

Her hand shook against her chest and she reached for her water bottle with the other, taking a quick sip.

Okay, I can handle this. Use the techniques, Chrissie. Remember?

She lifted her hands as she sucked in a long, deep breath, as though leading the air into her lungs, then turned her palms downward and lowered her hands with the exhalation. She repeated the technique her therapist had taught her years ago, until her breathing slowed. She didn't care whether any passers-by could see; she only wanted to regain control.

It'd been years since she'd had a panic attack. She'd thought they'd run their course, dying away along with the life she'd left behind. But being here again, where it all started, must have triggered something. Something she wished she could forget.

Chrissie glanced around the street dotted with a few cars, an elderly couple walking their dog, and mothers hand-in-hand with their toddlers who walked two steps to their one. Just an everyday

Monday morning. There was no reason to feel scared, everything would be alright. Chrissie talked herself around, and eventually put her hand on the key to turn the ignition. Before doing so, she clicked open the glove box and took out a CD, her favourite CD: *The Best of Drew Williams*. The Aussie icon's music always calmed her, made her feel grounded and positive; exactly what she needed right now to get this day on track. And the fact that he was as hot as the summer sun didn't hurt either.

She resumed driving and let the smooth, earthy tone of his voice soothe her senses. The pitch perfect notes gave order and structure to the chaotic thoughts in her mind, and soon the panic and fear dissipated.

Chrissie pulled into a spot in the staff parking area at Serendipity, even though she could easily park at the house, it being only a short walk away, but with her workday ending at 3pm she had to get to the school in time to pick up Kai. Reluctantly, Chrissie switched off the engine, along with Drew's delicious voice, and readied her mind for the day ahead.

Serendipity was a beautiful place to work; no busy, loud offices with endlessly ringing phones and chatter, unlike her previous job at the newspaper. Stepping through the doors here was like entering a sanctuary where the outside world didn't exist. Chrissie walked down the corridor towards the staff zone, breathing in the hint of orange essential oil wafting in the air. She nodded hello to one of the nutritionists as she passed the staff lounge and was about to walk upstairs to the yoga studios when someone called out.

'Oh, Chrissie, could you come in here for a moment?'

Chrissie turned to face her boss, and manager of the retreat, Helena Washington. Her thin glasses perched on her nose and white-grey hair falling in wisps around her face, she ushered Chrissie into the main office.

Oh no, am I in trouble?

She was a little late but hoped it didn't matter since she didn't have to teach a class till nine-thirty.

'How are you settling in?' Helena asked.

'Well, thanks. I love it here.' Chrissie smiled.

'Good, good.' Helena pushed her glasses further up the bridge of her nose. 'You met one of the other instructors, Rachel, last week...' Chrissie nodded. 'Well, the poor lass broke her leg yesterday. She fell from a horse and got trampled on, will be out of action for quite a while.'

'Oh no, is she going to be okay?'

'Yes, yes, luckily it was only her bones that got damaged and not her internal organs, otherwise it could have been a different story.' Helena shook her head.

Ouch. Chrissie felt for Rachel; she didn't really know her but couldn't imagine how painful it must have been, let alone the idea of being bedridden and not able to move around and stretch her body.

'And you'd like me to take over some of her workload?' Chrissie assumed.

'Yes, some, but Lisa and Damon can share the load as well. Mostly, there's another job I was hoping you could take on in her place.'

'Sure, as long as it falls within the school hours we agreed upon, I can do anything that's required.'

Helena's mouth curved up into a faint smile. 'Are you interested in taking on a challenge?'

Taking on challenges? Story of my life.

Chrissie widened her eyes and nodded.

'Good. It's just that with Rachel gone, you're the most experienced instructor we have here, and I need the best for this job.' She rested her hand on the edge of the desk and leaned closer. 'We have a V.I.P guest staying with us for the month of

February, arrived last night. He's requested daily yoga sessions — private sessions — and I assured him we could accommodate his request.'

Wow, only a few days in a new job and she was getting a promotion? Just what she needed; a chance to expand her experience and keep busy and focused on work. 'Of course, I can do that.' Chrissie thought it was probably some corporate guy on stress leave, needing a month of rejuvenation.

'Now, I know you can only do five days a week and the occasional Saturday, but he is fine with that. I said you would create a personal program for him to practise in his own time too, to get the most out of his stay.'

'Definitely.' Creating individual yoga programs was one of her favourite parts of the job. She loved selecting the poses to suit each person's needs and putting them together into an exercise prescription. Yoga was more than exercise; it was about unifying the body, mind, and spirit.

'Great.' Helena clapped her hands together. 'Now there's one other thing.' She picked up a manila folder. 'I'll need you to sign a legal document agreeing to keep the knowledge of his visit to yourself. His lawyer has requested complete discretion and privacy during his stay. Can I count on you for your professionalism?'

Man, who was this guy? Oh my God. What if he was some big-name politician... did politicians even do yoga?

She couldn't imagine the pollies taking a break during Question Time for a spot of downward dog.

'I won't say a word to anyone,' Chrissie replied, her brows drawing together. 'Who is the guest?'

Helena opened her mouth but closed it again, then led Chrissie to the corner window of the office which had a snippet of a view into the V.I.P garden. 'See for yourself.'

Curiosity tingled inside as Chrissie peered out of the window. Her heart beat faster in anticipation then skidded to a halt at the sight of the man. There, sitting on the garden swing, swaying back and forth with a guitar on his lap, was none other than the owner of the voice that had permeated her car only minutes before.

CHAPTER TWO

'Drew Williams?' The words almost choked her as they catapulted out of her mouth.

Am I seeing things?

'The one and only,' Helena replied. 'You a fan?'

His biggest.

'Um…' She gulped, running her hand down her long blonde ponytail. 'He's ah, very gifted.'

In more ways than one.

Chrissie stole another glance in his direction. His tanned face appeared to glow under the sun's rays, his eyes squinting, but he didn't seem bothered. He strummed his guitar, then put it aside and jotted something down on a piece of paper. Writing a song?

'He grew up here in town, did you know that?'

'I knew he came from somewhere down this way, but wasn't sure where.'

'Yep, Tarrin's Bay, born and bred.' Helena swivelled the rod hanging from the Venetian blinds, reducing the sunlight to thin horizontal slits, signalling the end of Chrissie's spying opportunity. 'He's asked for a session this morning, can you do that?'

'Now?'

'No, after your morning group class. 11am'

'So, Damon will take over my other class?'

'Yes. Consider Mr Williams your top priority from now on. Well, until he leaves the country on the first of March. I told him we could arrange afternoon sessions in addition to or in place of the morning class if he prefers, but he'll see how he goes.'

Chrissie nodded with a little too much enthusiasm, or perhaps nerves, and wondered if this was some kind of dream and she hadn't even left the house yet. Maybe she was still tucked up in bed and she'd wake any minute and laugh at the fantasy she'd created.

Chrissie looked at the forms that Helena placed in her trembling hands. A lot of legal mumbo jumbo, but the gist of it was that she would not tell anyone that Drew Williams was staying at Serendipity, or that she had anything to do with him.

This was no dream. Her favourite celebrity was right outside and she'd be meeting him in less than two hours. She wanted to call her friend Melinda in Sydney and brag, but couldn't. She would be the envy of every woman her age, and she couldn't tell a single soul.

Thoughts bounced through her mind as Helena ducked out to make a call, leaving her alone to peruse the document and add her signature, which would probably look nothing like her real signature on account of the shaky hands. She read and re-read the document, her mind not really taking in the information, but she knew what it meant. She took a deep breath and put the tip of the pen to the paper, and scrawled *C Burns*, complete with the little flourish at the end of the 's'.

There. Done. I can keep a secret.

'Yes, of course, see you then. Bye.' Helena ended her call and placed the phone on the desk, raising her eyebrows to ask if Chrissie was done.

'Signed, sealed, delivered,' Chrissie said, handing over the forms.

'Fantastic. Thanks, Chrissie. I'm so glad you've joined us here at the retreat. Perfect timing, huh?'

That was yet to be determined. Such an important role so soon after starting a new job, in *this* town of all towns. She had no idea if she could handle it. But, somehow, she had to.

'Now, you had a look through the V.I.P quarters only recently during your staff orientation, so you should be familiar with where everything is?'

Chrissie nodded. 'I hadn't expected anyone to be staying there so soon.'

'Me neither. Usually we have a fair bit of notice, but this was a spur of the moment arrangement, apparently. Luckily Ms Kidman didn't happen to be here at this time.'

'Nicole Kidman stays here?'

Helena smiled, then unlocked a drawer under her desk. 'This is a bit different to teaching in the hall above the dry-cleaners, I bet?'

Hell yeah. Chrissie had spent a good five years running classes there in Glebe, both before and after Kai was born, and had only been at a slightly more upmarket fitness centre for just over a year before the opportunity at Serendipity came along. The fitness centre's own V.I.P program had given her experience in one-on-one sessions and program design, but the V.I.P's were mostly well-paid execs and spouses of the well-off rather than... famous people.

'I'm really happy to be here.' Chrissie smiled.

'Here you go.' Helena handed her a key card suspended from a lanyard. 'The key to the V.I.P quarters — the general rooms that is — obviously the sleeping quarters have a separate key.'

Sleeping quarters. Bedroom. Drew Williams... naughty thoughts crept into her mind and, her cheeks becoming hot, she willed them to disappear. She had to remain completely and utterly professional at all times. But you wouldn't be a woman if you hadn't at least imagined *Mr Williams* in a more personal nature at some stage in your life.

Then another thought crept into her mind.

How will I teach him without... touching him?

Stop it, Chrissie!

She took hold of the key card, its cold, hard plastic cooling her heated fingertips. This was the key to the most exclusive part of Serendipity and, symbolically, the key to a new world which, although temporary, would no doubt be challenging, exciting, scary, amazing, and unforgettable — all at the same time.

CHAPTER THREE

Chrissie put the remaining wedges of orange in the fridge of the staff lounge. She'd only eaten one after her morning class and couldn't eat another. Her nerves were in no state to tell her body how to digest food. Besides, yoga was best on an empty stomach. Although, when you taught three or four classes a day, you couldn't exactly go without food all day in order to follow the recommended principles. At least the lunch break allowed enough time to have a decent healthy meal — all cooked by award-winning gourmet chefs too.

'I'll have that, if you're not going to eat it?' Damon asked before Chrissie could close the fridge door.

'Sure, go ahead. I'm not that hungry.'

'Nerves will do that to you.' He winked, and bit into an orange wedge. 'All ready to meet your special student?'

'Oh, you know who it is?'

'Yeah, all the main staff have been briefed. I signed my legal doc. I just hope Lisa can keep her mouth shut, she likes a bit of gossip.' He held a hand below his chin to catch any drips of juice.

'I guess she'll have to,' Chrissie replied.

'Are you going to ask for his autograph?'

'Autograph? No!' Chrissie flicked her hand as if the idea was ridiculous. She wasn't an obsessed teenage fan. At least, not anymore.

'Well, you'll have something better: one-on-one time with the star. Pretty good perk for your first week on the job.' Damon's grin added a sparkle to his dark eyes.

'Yeah, I never expected this.'

Damon ate the remaining orange wedge, rinsed his hands under the tap, and turned for the door. 'Adios, Chrissie, enjoy!' He waved and disappeared around the door.

Chrissie chuckled. After he'd finished his shift last Friday he'd said, "Sayonara." Which language would he embrace next?

The good thing about working in a health retreat was that everyone was happy and friendly. The atmosphere was laced with a calm, positive buzz. Of course, like Chrissie, people had their bad days, but it gave her comfort that she was in a supportive environment for the duration of her workday.

Chrissie raised her wrist and a fluttery sensation in her belly increased her heart rate a notch. Ten minutes to go. Should she head up there now? What if he wasn't ready yet? What if she looked too keen? Maybe she should wait till five to eleven. But what if the key malfunctioned and she had to call the reception staff to help, and then she'd be late and things would get off to a bad start with him?

Okay, I'll go up at seven minutes to eleven.

She focused on her watch and willed her heartbeat to match the ticking of the second hand on the clock face, when in reality it was more like double the speed.

Breathe, Chrissie, breathe. He's just like any other student, he's only human, he's... Oh who am I kidding? He's Drew freaking Williams!

Chrissie used the same technique she used for her panic attacks and hoped for the best. She took a quick glance in the mirror and tightened the elastic on her ponytail, lifted her singlet to wipe the sheen of oil from her nose, and grinned wide to check her teeth.

Right, time to go.

She grabbed her bag and hooked the lanyard with the V.I.P key around her neck, then exited the staff lounge and walked down the inconspicuous corridor behind the café. She passed the door to a storage room and turned the corner to face another door.

'STAFF ONLY' the sign read, but it was really the secret entrance to the V.I.P quarters. Drew had his own private entrance that led outside the building, but this was how he could get in and out from inside, if he wished, and how the necessary staff could get in.

Chrissie's hand poised above the electronic lock, and she plastered a smile on her face.

Hi, Drew, I'm Chrissie,' she practised.

Urgh. Too casual.

Good morning, Mr Williams. It's a delight to meet you.

Too serious and old-fashioned.

Drew Williams, what an honour. My name is Chrissie and I'm absolutely thrilled to be your yoga instructor. I'm here to help in any way I can.

Strike three.

Oh c'mon, Chrissie. What are you trying to do, convince him to put you in his will?

She pushed out a breath and slid the key card down the slit in the lock. It lit up green and she pushed open the door, letting it close behind her slowly.

Suddenly aware that now, beyond this door, it was only herself and the multiple Grammy award-winning artist, she felt a tad underdressed in her Lycra outfit and comfortable rubber slip-on sandals. An occasion like this should call for a nice dress, or even trousers and a classy top, and definitely heels. But no, she'd be meeting her favourite singer in the clothing she wore every day. At least the requirements of her job had allowed her figure to regain its sculpted firmness after the birth of Kai, combined with eating a healthy diet and doing circuit sessions at the gym.

Why am I worried about how I look? Yoga is not about appearances, it's about the unity and oneness of everything. Aesthetics don't matter when we're all the same on the inside.

Chrissie tried the whole 'talking herself around thing', but couldn't help feeling exposed, vulnerable, uncertain. Was she really cut out for this job in her sensitive emotional state of late?

A sound from above yanked her back to the present moment, and she realised there was no time or point to pondering such things. She had a job to do, and she had to get on with it. Now.

She straightened her shoulders, convinced her facial muscles to relax into an 'everything's cool and I do this all the time' expression, and walked past the V.I.P dining and lounge area which opened-up and merged into the private garden. She turned the corner and walked slowly up the stairs. Each footstep seemed too loud, obtrusive, like the floor was warning its resident of an unfamiliar visitor. She made it to the top of the stairs and breathed deeply. Luckily Drew wasn't standing at the top, or she might have tumbled backwards and ended up sharing a hospital room with Rachel and her broken leg. The hallway was encased in rich, inviting, earthy red walls, and a warm, yellowy glow formed arches on the wall above each light fitting. The yoga studio was on the right, and around the corner to the left were the sleeping quarters; requiring, as Helena had mentioned, a different key. This place was practically a prison. Albeit a luxurious one.

Is he in there waiting? Or is he yet to come out of his room?

Chrissie prepared herself just in case, easing her mouth into a soft smile and pushing open the door to the studio.

The light flooding the room washed over her eyes, and she blinked a few times to adjust to the brightness. Empty. Her shoulders relaxed and she set her bag down on the table in the corner and placed her key inside, then withdrew a couple of high-quality floor mats from the storage shelf, and placed them on the floor. She eyed their closeness, bent down, and moved them further apart. Satisfied she had the most appropriate distance calculated between the two, she turned and took her class notebook out of her bag, writing the day's date at the top, followed by the words, *Drew Williams, private session #1*. She didn't know what level he was at in terms of ability, but his sculpted physique assured her he was no stranger to exercise. Not many men admitted to being fans of yoga, but Drew seemed different. From what she'd seen of him in the media, which wasn't much since she'd left her career as a journalist ten years ago, he was very much an outdoorsy, earthy, natural type. No fancy hairstyles, multiple piercings, or excessive tattoos covering his body like third-degree burns; he was just himself. The boy next door, blessed with natural good looks, no accessories required. Drew Williams was the true-blue Aussie superstar the whole country — hell, the whole world — adored.

'I should have brought my sunglasses.'

Chrissie spun around at the sound of his voice, and her breath halted at the sight of him in the doorway; his hand shading his eyes from the glare of sun invading the room, and a small smile arching into his cheek and peeking behind the shadow his hand had created.

Ba-boom, ba-boom, her heart pounded. 'Oh, I'll adjust the blinds for you.' Chrissie scurried over to the windows and swivelled the rods.

'It's okay, might help me stay awake and shake off this jet lag.' Drew stepped into the room and walked towards her, each step he took making Chrissie's heart beat faster in anticipation. 'You must be Chrissie?'

'Yes. And you must be Drew?'

Oh God. Duh, Chrissie!

He smiled and held out his hand. Chrissie hoped hers wasn't sweaty and held it out to meet his. He grasped it gently but firmly, his warm skin sending a shot of adrenalin up her arm.

I just touched Drew Williams!

Inside she had succumbed to fan-girl hysteria, while on the outside she hoped she appeared nonchalant but friendly. 'It's great to meet you,' she said.

'Likewise.' He withdrew his hand, his eyes still fixed on hers. 'So is Chrissie short for Christine?'

'Christina, actually.'

No one had called her Christina since... well, since she didn't want to be called that anymore.

'Nice name,' he said in a deep, soulful tone as hypnotic as his singing voice. 'Funny, how we like to shorten our names. No one calls me Andrew anymore except my mum.'

'Mums are like that.' Chrissie smiled, even though the word *mum* shot a painful arrow through her heart. She'd never hear her own mother call her name again. Chrissie scratched her arm even though it wasn't itchy. 'Do you have family in this neck of the woods?'

Did that sound too nosy?

What was she supposed to do; forget the pleasantries and go right ahead and tell him to drop and give her twenty salutes to the sun?

'Sure do, my parents have lived in Tarrin's Bay all their lives.'

As he spoke, the sunlight reflecting off his face made the hint of stubble framing his jaw sparkle. He was the type of guy who looked even better with a sprinkling of facial hair. He had just the right balance of hair to skin; enough to accentuate his features and give him that masculine look, but nowhere near enough to make the thought of kissing him akin to a trek through the Himalayan jungle.

Hang on — kissing him? *What am I thinking? Get your mind out of the jungle — er — gutter, Chrissie!*

'I could have stayed with them, of course, but sometimes you just need a bit of time on your own, don't you?' he said.

Chrissie nodded. She'd probably agree to anything he said at this stage... he could tell her that toothpaste on toast was a delicious breakfast and she'd still nod.

Chrissie, you're thirty-seven, not seventeen. Be professional.

'Well, there's no better place to have some down time than Serendipity.'

'I'm looking forward to it, and can't wait to get my body limbered up after that long-haul flight.' He swung his arms forwards and backwards. 'I'll definitely be taking advantage of some massage too, while I'm here.'

Oh wow, those massage therapists would be in their element.

'That's a good idea.' Chrissie cleared her throat. 'So um, how much yoga experience do you have?'

'I did an intensive retreat in Bali a few years ago, learned the ropes. Continued to practise through an instructor in L.A., but after a while I got out of the habit. Life, especially in this job, can be all over the place at times,' he said.

'I can imagine.' Well, not really. Chrissie had no idea what living the life of a world famous musician was like, but she did know what motherhood was like. It was often 'all over the place' too, in a different, domestic kind of way. 'All the more reason to make it part of your life,' she added. 'Yoga can be a constant. Something you can count on to ground yourself when things get chaotic.'

'Exactly the reason I'm here.'

'Well, I hope you have a relaxing stay.' Chrissie offered her best smile.

'I hope so too.' His gaze fell to the left before connecting with hers again. 'Though I'm not overly proficient at taking holidays. I can't go a week without playing my guitar or working on a song.'

'I guess it's just part of who you are,' Chrissie said. 'Something you can't cast aside.'

Like her ex-husband who couldn't cast aside his propensity for angry outbursts. "It's just my personality," he'd said. "I'm a feisty, passionate person. Take it or leave it." And leave it she did. She'd loved his exciting nature when they'd first got together, but after marriage and a child, domestic responsibility and commitment didn't agree with him.

'True. My guitar is like a limb to me. I feel naked if I'm not carrying it.'

Why did he have to say that word? Another image flashed in Chrissie's mind, one she certainly shouldn't be indulging in. 'Unfortunately you'll need both hands to be *guitar-less* for the next hour or so.' She attempted a laugh.

It wasn't that funny, but he seemed mildly amused. 'I think I'll survive.'

'Right, well let's get started.' Chrissie clapped her hands together like she did when it was time for Kai to go to bed.

Geez, can I stop acting like a mother for once?

'Ready when you are, boss.' He grinned, and placed his hands loosely on his hips, awaiting her instructions.

Boss? She chuckled, flicking her hand. 'The only boss here is the one downstairs. In this room, we're equals. I'm simply the facilitator.'

He held out his hands wide. 'Facilitate away. I'm all yours.'

His eager openness sent a tingle of excitement through her nerves. He might just turn out to be the perfect student: positive, uncomplaining, and willing to be challenged. Oh, and bloody hot.

'Right, well, first of all I need to know if you have any significant medical conditions or injuries?'

'Nope. Perfect health. As far as I know. My only issue is I get a bit of neck pain and stiffness, here...' He rubbed the side of his neck. 'And down that side of my back.' He twisted and pointed. 'Maybe from the way I hold my extra limb?'

'Ah yes, the tension of your left arm as it holds the guitar could create some stiffness down that side.'

'Thought so.'

'Regular stretching should help that, and massage when needed.' Chrissie wished she was also qualified in massage.

Drew nodded. 'Apart from that, I'm all good.'

'Good.' She nodded.

'Good,' he said.

Chrissie turned away and lit the floating candle in the bowl atop the small table that sat between the two large windows. 'Not that we need any extra light in here, but I always like to light a candle for my classes.'

'I like candles,' he said. 'Electricity is overrated.'

Her lips eased into a smile and she gestured towards the yoga mat in front of hers. 'If you'd like to take your position, we'll start with some breathing as you stand in *Tadasana*.'

Drew stood straight, his feet shoulder width apart, hands by his side, relaxed but firmly in position. Even in track pants and a T-shirt he looked good.

'Now, make sure your weight is evenly distributed, and feel a sense of lifting up from your knees and thighs and hips, lengthening the spine.' She walked around him, assessing his posture, and feeling slightly guilty that she was glad her role allowed her eyes free rein over his body. His shoulders were slightly hunched forwards and she brought her hands up to touch them, warmth from his body reaching her before she got to them. 'Bring your shoulders back and downwards, but don't tense them.' She grasped his rounded deltoid muscles and encouraged them gently backwards, rolling his shoulders back and down. God, they were hard. His muscles tensed ever so slightly at first touch, then relaxed into the correct position. 'That's better,' she said softly. 'When you're playing guitar your shoulders roll forward, so you need to counteract this regularly.'

'Sure, I can do that.'

Yep, perfect student. So, so perfect. She smiled as she stood behind him, a natural, masculine scent circling around her as she worked. 'Make sure your core muscles are gently drawn inwards, and activate and tuck under your, um...' She glanced down at his...

'My arse?'

'Um, yes.' She cleared her throat.

'Or my *ass*, as they say in the States,' he put on his best American accent. 'My previous teacher always used the term buttocks, but it's too fancy schmancy, don't you think?'

Chrissie remained behind him with her hands on his shoulders, ensuring he wouldn't let his upper body posture drop while concentrating on his lower body, and that he couldn't see the red heat crawling over her face at his uninhibited honesty.

'It does sound a bit... formal. I'll be sure to use your preferred term from now on,' she said, holding back a grin.

She walked around to the front of him, and pointed to the circular painting on the wall above the floating candle, its symmetrical patterns and balanced colours having a calming effect. 'Keep your focus on the mandala over there, and breathe slowly and deeply.'

His chest rose and fell.

'When you inhale, feel the air fill your lungs and expand your ribcage. The middle of your torso should move outwards, rather than just your upper chest or belly.'

He adjusted his breath and his body followed. She breathed in and out along with him, then took position on her floor mat. She expertly took the *Tadasana* stance, slightly off centre of the mat so he could stay focused on the wall behind her. 'Keep breathing in... and out.' Chrissie could imagine the air between them being sucked into opposing lungs, each exhalation merging together in front of them in a curly, sinuous haze.

After ten deep breaths Chrissie locked eyes with Drew. 'Now, let's get the blood flowing with *Surya Namaskar*, otherwise known as Sun Salutations. You'd be familiar with that?' She raised her eyebrows.

'Yes. Hopefully I can remember the order everything goes in. Can you show it to me first?'

'Sure.' Chrissie inhaled and stretched her arms above her head, focusing on her hands as she pointed them to the ceiling. Exhaling, she lowered her arms and bent at the waist, placing her hands on the floor either side of her feet. Even though she wasn't fully warmed up yet, her body moved with the ease and flexibility of years of practice. Her body she could control, her personal life — not so much.

She jumped her legs back into a plank position, the deep muscles in her core kicking into gear, and her body heated up at not only the movement, but the knowledge that Drew Williams was watching her. She pushed her hands against the floor and her torso upwards, a rewarding stretch elongating her stomach muscles, then opposed the movement by pushing her 'arse' in the air as she eased into downward dog. Each change of movement was accompanied by a change in breath — inhale, move, exhale, move. She jumped her feet forwards to meet her hands, straightened up to repeat her stretch to the ceiling, then lowered her arms into the pose of *Tadasana*.

Clap, clap, clap. Drew was clapping? She'd never had a round of applause for yoga before. The sound woke her from her yogic focus, and warmth flushed her face. Hopefully he would think it was from the effort of saluting the sun.

'Perfect,' he said. 'I wish I was as flexible as you.'

'By the end of the month you'll be a lot more flexible.'

'I'm glad you'll be here to keep me on track.'

'I'll do my best.' She smiled. 'So, let's see what you've got,' she challenged him.

Drew took a deep breath and stretched upwards, then lowered his torso down. 'I can really feel that at the back of the legs.'

'Bend your knees if you need to at first.'

He continued with the sun salutation, and Chrissie watched the position of each movement. When he pushed back into downward dog, his posture was a bit off.

'Try to keep your heels on the floor, and don't hunch your shoulders,' she said, hoping she didn't sound too picky. It was only his first lesson, but it was important to get the posture right from the get go, rather than force the body into a deep stretch that wasn't correct. 'Remember, shoulders down and back, so your spine can elongate.'

She had to do it, she had to touch him. She'd do this with any other student, so she shouldn't make an exception for fear of coming across as too keen. Chrissie placed her hand on the small of his lower back, her fingers coming into contact with skin as his T-shirt fell away a little. She pushed gently against it, encouraging proper alignment of the back.

'Ah yes, I see what you mean,' he said, his voice slightly thick from his head being upside down. His body eased further into the stretch and she released her hand, though a tingle of warmth remained on her fingertips. He stepped his feet towards his hands and rolled his body up to standing, stretching his hands to the ceiling. 'Ooh,' he said, after returning to *Tadasana*. 'It has definitely been a while!'

'It'll get easier,' Chrissie replied. 'You're off to a good start.'

Drew's gaze paused on hers, and they both released a small laugh. '*A Good Start*, eh?' He smiled. 'You know the song?' He eyed her curiously.

Every. Single. Word. Backwards even.

'Yes, I do.'

Drew appeared genuinely flattered. 'It wasn't even a number one hit, was really only on the album to fill it up. But it ended up being one of my favourites.'

'Sometimes it's the unexpected things that turn out to be the best.' Like this. Today. Him.

'Serendipity indeed.'

Chrissie grinned. 'You like a good pun, do you?'

'Can't pass up a perfectly appropriate pun opportunity,' he replied. 'Careful.' He held up his hands. 'They may sneak into conversation a little too often and you'll probably end up rolling your eyes by the end of the month.'

If she rolled her eyes, it would more likely be from utter bliss than irritation. 'Oh, I doubt it.' She held out her hands to mimic what he'd done earlier when he told her to "facilitate away". 'Go for it. Pun away!' she joked.

He laughed, a beautiful ripple of delight decorating his face. He pointed gently towards her. 'Don't say I didn't warn you.'

Her earlier nerves had transformed into something else. What was it? She was more relaxed, yet still sort of wired to be in his presence. She felt more... awake. And it was a feeling she could certainly get used to.

After guiding him through ten more sun salutations, the rest of the class was spent re-learning some of the basic yoga poses, and before Chrissie knew it their time was up. It had gone so fast, and although she desperately needed to go eat something and take a break, part of her didn't want to leave the room.

'Here,' she said, handing Drew her business card. 'This has my details on it should you have any questions during your stay. Helena said you're welcome to change to an afternoon session if you prefer, or even have two a day.'

'Thanks.' He took the card and glanced at it, her smiling photo on the front. 'Yes, I'll see how I go. If every class is as enjoyable as this one, then that's a tempting offer.' He slipped the card into the pocket of his track-pants and grinned.

Chrissie glanced at the floor as heat flushed her face. 'Oh, shucks,' she said with a chuckle. 'You're too kind.'

'As are you.' He held his hand towards her, taking her by surprise. 'Thank you, Chrissie. I'll see you tomorrow.'

She shook his hand and he held it a moment longer than expected. 'I'll be here.'

One day down, twenty-seven to go.

____

CHAPTER FOUR

Twenty-seven and a half days to go. Would that be enough? Enough to take some time off, yes, but enough to let the media scandal blow over? News and gossip moved fast, especially in L.A., but once a reputation was tarnished it could be hard to redeem.

Drew left the dining room after the kitchen staff cleared the table of the lunch remains, and walked upstairs to the sleeping quarters, the month ahead on his mind. He grabbed his guitar and sat on the king-sized four-poster bed, resting the instrument on his lap, filling the mould his body created for it like a lock and key. The strings vibrated as he ran his thumb across them, the perfect graduation of tones calming his mind. There was nothing more he could do right now — short of going on a talk show and telling his side of the story, but that wasn't in his nature. Why should his personal life be public entertainment? His music, yes, his life, no. Unfortunately, the industry didn't see it like that.

He'd have to try to forget about it, let his legal and publicity people back home do their jobs, so he could be free to do his: work on some new songs.

He reached across to the bedside table and grabbed the pen

and piece of paper he'd scribbled notes on. With any luck, if he managed to create a new song before his tour next month, he could perform it to his fans as a bit of a bonus. A sneak peek at what might be on his next album. *If* he still had fans after all this.

Tightness pinched at Drew's chest and he tossed the paper to the floor in frustration. One minute he was okay and the next he wasn't.

Why couldn't she have left things alone?

Why did she have to mess things up for me?

He should never have got involved with Jolene, should have seen that she was trouble the moment she got upset when he'd gone to a simple function without her. It was a quiet industry function with a few associates important to his career, not a wild party with all the high-flyers she loved rubbing shoulders with and paparazzi queued out front snapping pictures. He'd tried to make it up to her by planning a romantic dinner, but pretty soon nothing was ever good enough for her, and he couldn't be with her every second of every day. When he'd broken it off, it had also broken off her connection to the limelight — something even worse in her books. So what did she do? She worked her way back into the spotlight and garnered sympathy by spreading false rumours about him and tainting his good guy image.

Drew picked up his phone and his finger hovered over the internet browser, unsure whether to check the latest public comments about the scandal. He wanted to get on there and leave his own comment, tell everyone she was a liar, but he was advised not to indulge the hype. He tossed the phone onto the bed and clenched his fists, clamping his lips together. Letting go was difficult, but he had to try. Starting now.

He closed his eyes, and an image of Chrissie flashed in his mind. She was pretty, and with her golden skin and natural blonde hair, she looked every bit the Aussie, beachy woman. Her soft, clear voice echoed inside his head... 'Let the air fill your lungs and expand your ribcage.'

Drew breathed in deeply, his chest expanding, then released the air through pursed lips. In... and... out. He opened his eyes and brought his attention to a painting on the wall, a calming scene of a beach at sunset with an effortless blending of colours. Kind of like the notes he liked to play — each one blending easily into the next, creating one perfect melody that was like a sunset to the ears.

Chrissie had told him to focus on the mandala on the wall in the yoga room, so he decided to do the same here with the painting. With each breath, he imagined the waves rolling in on the shore, then washing back into the ocean with each exhalation. The ocean. He'd have to go for a walk on the beach later on. As long as he kept to the more secluded north end, he shouldn't be spotted. He'd love to go for a surf sometime too. But if the waves were big the crowd might be big, and then so much for laying low. As for eating a takeaway lunch in Miracle Park and kicking a ball around like he'd done with his mates as a teenager, well, that was completely off the cards. If word got out he was here, the media might camp out at Serendipity. And even worse, Jolene might find out where he was.

He shook his head, trying to shake away the constant interruptions to his peace.

'Keep breathing in... and out.' Chrissie's voice returned in his mind, and he allowed her gentle instruction to bring him back to the present. As the sunset painting blurred under his gaze, he yawned, his body telling him it was time to go to bed, even though it was only 2pm in Australia. It would be best if he could stick it out and stay awake till at least nine, to adjust his body clock to the new time zone. He was no stranger to long hours and late nights, but now that he was getting older, he couldn't bounce back as well as he used to. His life was changing, and he had to change with it. And this was the time to make a start. A *good* start.

He grinned as he remembered Chrissie's words, and how they'd laughed at the fact that it was also one of his song titles. He was surprised she knew it. *A Good Start* didn't get much air time on radio, so she must have listened to the album it was on. If she was a fan, she hadn't made a fuss about it, and that impressed him. It was nice to meet someone who treated him like a normal guy. A lazy smile eased into Drew's cheeks, and her image flashed in his mind again. Chrissie. Yoga would be his 'constant' for this month, as she'd advised. Something he could turn to, to keep his mind from straying into unwanted territory. Which meant — Chrissie would be his constant too. He decided right then that whenever Jolene's face intruded into his mind, he'd replace it with Chrissie's. And by the end of the month, he hoped, he would barely even remember what Jolene looked like.

Drew whooshed out a heavy breath and laid back on the bed, fatigue weakening his body, the image of Chrissie's face the last thing he saw before sleep claimed him.

CHAPTER FIVE

'I'm exhausted.' Kai practically fell through the front door after school and kicked off his shoes, leaving one in the hallway and one in the living room.

'Kai, can you please put your shoes away in your room?' No sooner had the words left Chrissie's mouth than Kai had flopped on the couch, his face squished sideways into a cushion. Chrissie sighed. 'Kai, shoes first, then you can rest.'

'Oh, but Mum. You don't understand. You don't know what it's like to be this tired.' He strung out the last word with dramatic emphasis.

'Oh for heaven's sake.' Chrissie bent and hooked the heel of one shoe on her finger, then the other, and flung them into her son's room. At least they were out of the way; he could put them in the wardrobe himself later. Chrissie picked up Kai's school bag that he'd dumped next to the couch, and chuckled. *Don't know what it's like to be this tired?* She shook her head at her son's naivety. Granted, he was only six, but if only he knew. Getting up five times a night on average for the first year of his life? That was the definition of tired.

She plonked the bag on one of the dining table chairs whose

seat cushion was tearing at the seams and exposing a chunk of foam, and zipped it open. She withdrew a drawing of what resembled a nasty looking angel and a few school notes; parent information night, curriculum summary and expected academic outcomes, and what do you know? A lice outbreak already and it was only the fourth day into the school year. Great, she'd have to get out the fine-tooth comb and magnifying glass and examine Kai's head for the little critters. Why did school have to feel like a whole second job? Chrissie longed for the calmness of Serendipity, the peace inherently present within its walls, and the exhilarating buzz of being around...

'Mum?' Kai yelled.

'Kai, I'm right here, no need to shout.'

'Can you get me a drink?'

'Magic word?'

'Pleeaase.' When she didn't reply immediately, Kai added, 'Pretty please, with sugar on top?'

'Sugar's not healthy.'

'Well, um, with...yoga on top?'

Chrissie tipped her head back with a laugh. Kai was well versed in the health benefits that yoga provided. Although, when he was in preschool, she'd had to clarify her profession to him after he'd told a classmate that his mum was a 'yoghurt teacher'.

'Well, that wasn't *exactly* what I had in mind,' she replied, an image of *Drew on top* flashed in her mind before she flicked it away, 'but since you asked so nicely.' She left the school bag and opened the fridge, pulling out a carton of milk and a tub of *yoghurt*, then grabbed a box of frozen berries from the freezer. 'One smoothie coming up.'

'Yum.' Kai pressed the remote on the television and a wildly colourful cartoon blared from the screen.

Glossy white milk seeped in between the clumps of berries as Chrissie poured it in the blender, followed by a couple of dollops of yoghurt. She held the cover closed as the blender whirred, whipping the ingredients up into a purple-pink liquid.

'Here you go,' she said, handing Kai a plastic cup full of the mixture and placing a coaster in front of him on the coffee table. 'Be careful though, no spills.'

Like that would prevent any.

Chrissie remembered the time they'd had lunch at a friend's house in Sydney. She could see that Kai was about to spill his drink so, in a split second, she'd flung her hand out to grab it but in the process knocked over her own glass, the drink soaking the pants of her friend's daughter, seated next to Kai.

She placed her own smoothie on the dining table and continued extracting things from Kai's bag. 'Oh, no wonder you're thirsty, your water bottle's only half empty and you haven't had your popper.' Chrissie held up the small juice box.

'I forgot,' he said.

'And what about your banana?' She held up the browning squished fruit that had been compressed at the bottom of the bag by the lunch box and a couple of picture books.

'I didn't feel like it.'

'Oh, Kai. You really must try to eat what I've packed for you, otherwise it's a waste.'

Just as she'd thought, only half his lunch had been eaten too. She brought the half-sandwich over to him. 'You can eat the rest now, please.'

'But I want something fresh.'

'What do you call that?' She pointed to the smoothie.

'But that's drink, not food, silly.'

'Kai, it has fruit in it, and fruit is food. So drink up, eat up, and I don't want to hear another complaint from you today.' She gave him the 'Don't mess with Mum' look and hoped it would last at least the next half hour so she could finally sit down for a bit.

Chrissie downed the smoothie in about thirty seconds, then opened her notebook. Not the yoga one, the other one; the one that would eventually lead to her financial freedom and hopefully her dream of starting up her own rural yoga retreat.

She re-read the list of priorities on the first page:

1. Go through Aunt Felicia's things.
2. Renovate house to maximise sale price.
3. Sell house for top dollar.
4. Buy a new house on a large acreage.
5. Create a stable life for Kai.
6. Plan yoga retreat business.

She'd almost added: and finally be happy and settled.

She turned the page and divided the second page in half by drawing a line down the middle. At the top of the first column she wrote Big Jobs, and at the top of the second she wrote Small Jobs. Would she need a Medium Jobs column, or would that be taking things too far?

Her deceased aunt's house — now *her* house — could have been sold as is for quite a decent sum, considering its solid structure and breathtakingly beautiful and sought after beachfront location that marked the beginning of the Tarrin's Bay township. But it would go for so much more with some renovations and revamping, and the more money the better. She wasn't greedy, just wanted to get the most she could for her aunt's property. She had to do it; there was no one else in the family left but her. Besides, if she left it as is there was a slight chance the buyer might knock it down and rebuild. Felicia would have hated that; this house was — had been — a part of her. And even though Chrissie's last memories of being here were ones she'd rather forget, she couldn't sit back and let someone tear it down. No, she'd bring it back to its former glory, and more. She'd use the equity to get a loan for what needed doing; building a garage to replace the weathered carport at the side of the house, extending the L-shaped veranda around the other side of the house and expanding it into a large covered deck and entertaining area, and replacing the tiled roof with something more robust and hardy to deal with the constant salt spray from the ocean.

The five-bedroom house was too large for only her and Kai, but it would be their temporary home until the work was done. Besides, her therapist had told Chrissie that it would be good for her — a chance to face her past and come to terms with what happened here during the summer she turned thirteen. She'd been given the name of a new therapist in Tarrin's Bay, but with getting Kai settled in a new school and starting her new job, unpacking their things and sorting through Felicia's, there hadn't been a spare moment. Maybe she wouldn't need one anymore. Maybe the act of cleaning out the old and revealing the new would somehow heal her of its own accord. She could only hope. And maybe the whole Drew thing would be a welcome distraction after all, instead of something she feared she couldn't handle. Chrissie tapped the pen against her chin as her gaze wandered around the white interior with beachy decor, while her mind wandered back to her yoga session with Drew.

Kai laughed hysterically at something on the television, breaking her daydreaming, and she brought her attention back to the list. The kitchen; it would need a complete overhaul. A good kitchen would make it easier to get a higher price. People wanted state of the art appliances, not rustic equipment that had seen decades of use. She'd get a few quotes and plan to have it done during the April school holidays when she'd secured a week off from work. For the other week, Kai would be at his father's house, making it easier for Chrissie to get to work. Although she hated having to share him with her ex-husband in this way, like a parental tug-of-war, it did have its advantages. It was nice to get the odd break from her role as a mother and spend some time alone. She could even go back to Sydney and spend a night on the town with Melinda if she wanted to. Then again, she was sort of past all that. A nice dinner and conversation with a friend beat living it up on the dance floor in a crowded, sweaty nightclub by far.

Chrissie's thoughts returned to the kitchen with its homely look and she wondered what sort of bench-tops and cupboards to get. A brief laugh escaped as she eyed the clock on the wall that said 'time to eat', remembering her aunt's voice calling out to her and her sister as children, telling them to stop playing in the sand because it was getting dark and was 'time to eat'. Chrissie and Danielle would play for hours outside, their backyard being their own private section of beach. She shook away the memories which, although happy, only led to those that were unhappy.

Chrissie eyed the colour scheme of the house — baby blues, rustic whitewashed furniture, and splashes of sandy-coloured wicker in the backs of the dining chairs, legs of the coffee table, and the magazine holders bursting with craft magazines. Various ornaments were displayed haphazardly; a shell sculpture sat on a bookcase underneath a decorative anchor displayed on the wall. Everything cried out, 'I'm a beach cottage', even though the house seemed too large to be called a cottage. It was nice, comfortable, but it would probably be best to go for a more modern, minimalist style: off-whites, caramels, and earthy tones to blend in with the natural environment surrounding the property. She had an eye for detail, but could always call in a colour consultant and interior designer, if necessary, to get things right.

Kai released another belly laugh and Chrissie smiled. He may be a little difficult, but it was these moments that gave her hope; reassured her that everything would be okay, that *he* would be okay. He would be, wouldn't he?

CHAPTER SIX

<hr>

If the next morning was anything to go by, Chrissie was about ready to take Kai out of school, leave her job, and move into a tent somewhere far away where they could live off the land and forget about rules and schedules and timetables and expectations. How would she cope with another day of this, let alone the whole year, and every year till he finished school as a teenager? Late again, and just as grumpy and upset as he'd been yesterday, Kai had reluctantly stood by Mrs Kitson in the playground as Chrissie scurried off before he could run after her and find a way to permanently attach himself for the rest of his childhood. Anyway, it was out of her hands now. He was at school, she was at work. *Focus, Chrissie.*

'Off with the fairies?' Drew asked.

'Huh? Oh, sorry, I must have been a bit zoned out. All this yoga, you know.' She shrugged and pressed her lips together in a small smile. 'So, ah, let's try *Trikonasana* again. This time, focus on opening up the chest and keeping the hips from tilting forward.'

'Okay, let's do it.'

Drew widened his legs and pointed his right foot out at a

ninety-degree angle, then held his arms out straight to the side. Chrissie stood behind him. 'Remember, reach and lengthen to the right first before bending sideways.' She guided his arm with her hand as he stretched out. 'Good, good. Now bend, keeping your torso facing the front.' He followed her instructions well. He was a little stiff, but nothing that regular daily practice couldn't loosen up. As his left arm reached high, the sleeve of his T-shirt fell down around his shoulder, circled around it in a kind of embrace, and his shoulder blade bulged beneath the fabric of his top. She adjusted his arm's position slightly, aligning it with his right arm that reached down and rested on his leg. 'Imagine a metal rod is connecting your left hand with your right, keeping both arms in a perfect straight line.' He didn't speak, simply adjusted and breathed, and for a few moments there was silence. A sense of peace washed over Chrissie. It was always rewarding watching the human body bend and twist and support itself in positions that weren't part of normal daily life. Especially the human body in front of her now. It really was a beautiful sight...when a student got the pose just right. 'Fantastic, now inhale and engage your core as you come up.'

Drew stood straight again, then repeated the pose on the other side.

'Okay, let's try a variation of that pose, with the knee bent.' Chrissie went to demonstrate when a jingling sound came from her bag. 'Oh, I thought I turned it off. Sorry!' She continued to set up for the pose.

'It's okay, go get it. I don't mind.'

'Oh that's okay, I never answer phone calls during class.' The ringing stopped as it went to voice mail. She stretched her arms out to the side and bent her right knee, when the jingling sounded again.

'I'll grab a sip of water, you take your call.' Drew walked over to the side table and picked up his bottle as Chrissie got her phone and swiped the screen to answer.

'Hello?'

'Mrs Cavanaugh?'

'Um, it's Ms Burns, actually.' She was used to being called Mrs Victor Cavanaugh, but had hoped people would get used to her returning to her maiden name after the divorce. She'd kept the surname for Kai, though.

'Oh, right, Sorry. It's Jenny from the school reception—'

'Is everything okay?'

'Yes, well, there's no need to worry, but Kai has been in sick bay for over an hour.'

'What's wrong? He doesn't have a fever or anything?'

'No, no fever. But he's been complaining of a tummy ache since recess.'

Great. Probably didn't eat his morning tea and his ache is actually hunger, or he's dropped it and eaten it anyway, along with a clump of dirt or bugs or something.

'Oh, well, could you check if he's eaten anything today? Or maybe he just needs some water and a bit of a lie down for a while. I'm sure it will pass.'

In other words, I can't possibly leave work right this minute to pick him up.

'Well, he's eaten, had some water, and has been lying down for an hour. He says he still feels sick. It's our policy that if there's no improvement after an hour we have to request that he be picked up from school.'

Chrissie swore under her breath.

'I'm sorry?'

'Oh, nothing. It's just that I'm at work. I'm not sure I can leave yet. Can you keep him there for another half hour or so?' She added a hint of desperation to her tone of voice.

'I am sorry, Mrs Cav — Ms Burns, I understand it's an

inconvenience, but I really must insist. I have other work that needs doing and I can't watch over him constantly, I'm afraid.'

Chrissie hung her head, then glanced at Drew who mouthed, 'It's okay, go,' and gestured to the door. Bless him.

'Ms Burns?'

'Yes, of course. I'll leave now.' She ended the call and placed the phone in her bag, then looked at Drew as he approached her. 'I am so, so sorry. My son's feeling sick and the school wants me to pick him up.'

'No worries. Family comes first.'

'If only they'd watch over him for another half hour I could complete your session. Oh, this is such an inconvenience for you, I really am very—'

'Chrissie.' He grasped her hand lightly. 'Seriously, it's okay. We've already had half an hour. I'll do a bit on my own for now. I'll manage. You go take care of your son.'

His touch relaxed her tense muscles yet heightened her senses at the same time. She smiled apologetically as he ushered her to the door. He may be okay with the interruption, but how would Helena react? Leaving work early on her second day teaching the V.I.P. guest? She'd probably replace her with Lisa, and this would be the last time she'd ever see Drew Williams.

'I'll see you tomorrow, if your son's okay for school, that is.' Drew smiled.

I bloody hope so. 'Of course. Thanks for your understanding, Drew.'

She scurried down the stairs and into Helena's office, who although agreed that she had to go and collect her child, also suggested she start searching for a short-notice babysitter to call on when needed.

Chrissie dashed to the car and drove towards the school.

Perfect timing son, perfect timing.

Bad timing, but Chrissie had to go and be with her son. It didn't faze Drew, he only felt sorry for her feeling so bad.

That's parenthood, I guess. Lots of unexpected twists and turns.

Not that he'd know. At thirty-seven he hadn't even come close to settling down. When his career skyrocketed in the early days it was the furthest thing from his mind, of course, but now, almost twenty years later, it was starting to feel like every day was *Groundhog Day*. He needed a change, some sort of life reinvention, but first, he needed peace and quiet. Time to think, to rejuvenate, and to work out what to do next in the journey of Drew Williams' life and career. Away from the prying eyes of the media.

It must be hard, having to think about someone else all the time, putting them ahead of everything. Hopefully her son was okay. Drew was looking forward to seeing his niece and nephew on the weekend; it'd been a good year since they'd met up at Disneyland when the family had flown over to the States — his shout of course. Money was no issue, and he'd rather spread it around. The charity he'd set up to provide instruments and teach music free of charge to sick and underprivileged kids was a success. So many kids never got to learn an instrument because their parents couldn't afford lessons or the instruments themselves, but the work of Star Sounds was putting an end to all that. It was great to give back when the public had given him so much.

Drew took another swig of water and stretched his arms towards the ceiling, the rewarding pull on his muscles lengthening his spine. He sat on the floor mat and crossed one foot over his bent knee, swivelling his torso sideways and relaxing into the spinal twist. He took five deep breaths and twisted further with each one, then repeated the stretch on the other side. As he stood, he thought he could smell a hint of Chrissie's perfume, or maybe it was something she used in her hair. Either way, it was fresh, sweet, and he breathed in deep to try to get another whiff of it. Funny how it was easy to miss things like the scent of a person when they're in front of you, but the moment they leave, it becomes noticeable. Maybe because his other senses had been hogging the spotlight; his ears listening to her concerned voice as she spoke on the phone, his gaze gliding over her petite frame and the way her clothing moulded effortlessly to her body.

He walked over to the window and glanced outside into the V.I.P. garden. Sunlight speckled the grass and leaves wafted gently in the breeze. He'd never really stopped to notice such things before. His life was all about getting to the next event or meeting, always moving forward. Now, the only way he'd be able to move forward was to back up a little and press the pause button. If only he could press stop on the scandal he'd run away from.

Yawning, Drew returned to his yoga mat and lay on his back, shifting his body into the correct alignment for *Shavasana*; legs slightly apart, arms relaxed by his side with palms facing upwards, and eyes closed. A yoga class always finished with this relaxing pose, and he often found when the time was up he didn't want to move. Sometimes it would take a while to switch his mind off to relax, but once he did, it was like he'd entered a whole new world, a new realm he didn't want to leave. Peace. Stillness. Calm. When he was younger those things were plain boring, but now he craved them.

Refreshing breath filtered into Drew's lungs as he inhaled deeply, and he imagined each breath curling and swirling inside and nourishing his body with a boost of oxygen. Colours formed in his mind, swirls of blue and purple, with a tinge of pink, like the sunset picture in his room. A melting sensation warmed and softened his muscles until he could barely feel his body against the mat, as though he was floating, and with a few more deep breaths he succumbed to the delicious, enticing invitation of sleep.

Drew's eyelids snapped open, sunlight streaming into his eyes. Instinctively he checked his watch. Almost one o'clock. He'd slept for an hour, damn. So much for trying to settle into a new time zone. Bloody jet lag. He eased himself up and yawned, stretching his mouth wide and his body high as his arms reached up. A subtle recollection of a dream narrowed his eyes. *What the?* Dreams were weird things. He sculled some water as he remembered what he'd dreamt — his own goddamn funeral. What kind of morbid thing was that to dream about? He'd heard a voice conducting the ceremony at the gravesite, but there was nobody around, nobody at all. Geez, he wasn't exactly Scrooge and this was no *Christmas Carol*, but the only attendant at his funeral was his beloved guitar. It was resting against his grave, although weakened and unable to stand tall and proud without its owner. Would that be all he had at the end of his life, a freaking guitar? Of course he had family, but his parents wouldn't last forever, and as for friends, well they were all back in L.A. If you could call them true friends; they'd only got to know each other by being in the industry and who knows what they'd be if they didn't have music to bond them. Would they still be mates if he wasn't a singer? He'd left his good mates behind at age eighteen when he'd won Australia's *Search for a Star* contest on television: they'd all gone their separate ways.

Drew pushed out a heavy breath and swivelled side to side, uncertain what to do next. He was so used to being on the move he'd forgotten how to just be. Lunch? He probably should eat, but he didn't have much of an appetite. Nah, he needed to get out in the fresh air, wake himself up, get moving. As long as he didn't get close enough for anyone to recognise him, it'd be okay.

He closed the door behind him to the yoga studio and went to his room, grabbing his sunglasses from the bedside drawer and plonking a baseball cap on his head. The usual celebrity camouflage. At least the weather was warm and the sun was strong, he'd need them anyway. Winter's camouflage was a beanie and scarf, and growing a bit more stubble than usual.

He jogged down the stairs, his feet barely touching the floor, and exited through the private entrance that led out to the side of the building. He walked quickly along the pebbled pathway that curved around a row of trees, his bare feet dimpling with hundreds of tiny round stones, until it opened up into a grassy area. He jogged along to the left until the grass merged with sand, and he traipsed across the sand dunes and onto the flat sand below. A handful of people were on the beach further south, gradually minimising as he went in the opposite direction.

The north end was more rugged a landscape; long stems of sand grass shot up from the ground, twigs and shells scattered themselves around, and jagged rocks traced the back of the beach, curving into a huge mound as the shore narrowed to mark the end of the beach. He jogged up to this point, then dropped to the ground and did as many push-ups as he could until his muscles urged him to stop. *One more,* he told them silently. He liked to push himself a little further each time, that was how he kept his body in top condition, never letting his muscles adapt or get out of a challenge. Spontaneous, organic exercise outdoors was his favourite, though he often only had time and opportunity for sessions at the gym. Drew stepped onto a low rock, lumpy but not hard enough to cut his feet, and rapidly stepped on and off it like he was in a step class. Up, down, up, down, his thighs burning with each step. *Ah, that's what I'm talking about.* Yoga was great, but nothing beat a bit of hardcore working out. He knelt down and placed his toes on the rock, pushing his arms into a push-up position again, and went in for another set. His raised feet put extra weight on his upper body, and he pumped up and down, sweat trickling off his face and forming tiny blobs on the sand.

He stood, hands on hips, panting, and glanced at the rock formation next to him. *Yep, I can do that.* He grabbed hold of some protruding rocks and pulled himself up, placing his foot on a concave part, then his other foot higher up, gripping and grabbing and pulling. He reached the top and scanned the magnificent stretch of horizon from his vantage point. Man, he missed this. Missed getting out in nature and going with the flow. He turned to the left, his focus resting on the old double-storey beach house that'd stood the test of time. Its white weatherboard exterior, faded and peeling from the salty air, like an elderly person whose wrinkly skin had seen many summers. The house was in a prime secluded location, with its own backyard pocket of beach as the rocky hill gave way and opened up to let the sandy shore spread up towards the house.

He glanced at the ocean, its rippling waves hypnotising him for a moment, then turned back to face the house where someone sat on the veranda. A woman. Her head was buried in her hands, and a long blonde ponytail dangled over her shoulder.

Chrissie? She lives there?

Drew felt suddenly self-conscious, like he was intruding, even though technically he was standing on public property. *Is she okay?* He hesitated on the rocky ledge, unsure whether to go over and talk to her or leave before she noticed him. Before he could decide, she turned to the left and picked up a phone, bringing it to her ear. She got up and tucked a strand of hair behind her other ear, and walked around the side of the house, obscuring his view.

Intrigue wound its way around Drew's spine as he climbed back down the rocks.

What's her story?

He had twenty-six days to find out.

Chrissie wandered around the other side of the house, careful not to let Kai hear her speaking. 'Thanks for calling me back, I know you're busy.'

'Are you kidding? Talking to my best friend takes precedence over research any day. I'm neck deep in work here and my brain was starting to fry, your call was just what I needed to give me a break from the daily grind,' said Melinda. 'So, what's up? Your voice message sounded... strained.'

Chrissie had been close to tears, but as usual, held them back in front of Kai. 'Oh, it's just Kai.' Chrissie glanced through the side window at her supposedly sick but totally faking it son as he lay on the couch and listened to an audio book. 'I don't know what to do. He hates going to school, every morning here is like PMS on steroids, and today he pretended to have a tummy ache so I'd pick him up early from school.' She rubbed her palm against her forehead as a headache formed. 'I had to leave work early, and there's no way I can keep doing that. He's so grumpy when he has to do anything he doesn't want to do.'

'That's kids for ya.' Melinda chuckled. 'But Kai has been through a bit of stress lately, he's probably just feeling insecure.'

'He's not the only one.'

'Have you talked to his teacher?'

'Only briefly at school drop off and pick up. She says he's quiet but goes along with everything okay. I wish they'd watch him better at lunch though, he hardly eats anything.'

'Let me guess, you pack apples, healthy sandwiches and raisins?'

'Of course.'

'Sometimes you've just gotta chuck a packet of chips in there, Hun, if only to make sure he eats something.'

'I don't want to get him used to eating junk, I can't bribe him with treats all the time.'

'What about once a week? Tell him if he goes happily to school every day he'll get chips in his lunch box on Fridays.'

Ever practical, Melinda. She had to be, working from home as a freelance journalist with a four-year-old and a two-year-old as office colleagues.

'I guess that's not a bad idea.' Chrissie nibbled on her bottom lip. 'So rewards, not punishment works best, huh?'

'I think so. Give them something to look forward to.'

Something to look forward to... Chrissie knew what she looked forward to; the day when Kai smiled and waved at her at school drop off, the day when she could leave the beach house and move somewhere not so close to the ocean, and of course, tomorrow, when she'd see Drew Williams again.

'Also, tell him how grown up he is when he does something good. Give him a bit of extra responsibility — that'll raise his self-esteem.'

'Have you turned into Dr Phil?'

'I wrote an article on it last month. Haven't you read it?'

Chrissie hadn't had the time or concentration to read lately, her mind provided enough drama as she lay in bed mulling over things. 'No, but I'll have to. Send me the link.'

'Already did, last month. Don't worry, I'll send it again in case it drowned in the deluge of emails that is your inbox.'

'So, rewards *and* responsibility. Should I have him cook dinner once a week?' Chrissie added a hint of sarcasm to her voice.

'Worth a try! Nah, seriously, it doesn't have to be big, just something new. What about... does he catch the bus to school?'

'Nope. It comes by the far corner of our street, but he won't do it. I have to drive him, and even that's a struggle.'

'Try and build up to it. Take him to the bus stop and let him see the other kids get on, then get in the car and follow the bus so he can see where it goes and the kids arriving at school. Do that a few times until he's used to it and then see if he'll get on. Tell him it's what big kids do.'

'I think he's quite happy to be a little kid at the moment. But I'll try.'

'That's the spirit.'

Thank God for Melinda. She was so go-with-the-flow and down to earth. She was like the sister she... the sister she... well, the sister she *once* had. At least, that's what Chrissie imagined her sister would have turned out like had Danielle lived beyond the age of eleven. Would they have stayed close? Maybe she would have had her own kids by now, and Kai would have cousins. But it wasn't to be. Kai would never know his aunt, nor his grandparents. There were Victor's parents of course, but they weren't the grandparenty types. They were all 'don't touch that' and 'keep your voice down' and 'don't interrupt the adults when they're talking' kind of people. They were about as warm as a winter's morning.

If only Mum was here to talk to, to ask her advice on motherhood. Chrissie's mind wandered, remembering her mother's soft eyes and sweet voice. Unfortunately, along with those memories came memories of the bags under her eyes and her voice straining to speak through the weakness of her final days. Hot tears threatened behind Chrissie's eyes and she clamped them tight.

'Chrissie?' Melinda asked.

'Yes, I'm here. Sorry, was just thinking.'

'Look, I know you've been through a ton, but just take each

day as it comes. You can do this. You're strong. You're a great mother.'

Chrissie's heart doubled over at her friend's kind words. She didn't feel strong sometimes, and if she was such a great mother then why was Kai so difficult and whingey?

'And,' Melinda continued, her tone lightening. 'You've got a damn good figure. I'd kill for your legs!'

'Oh, stop it!' She giggled, walking around to the back of the house, her gaze wandering across the horizon over the large rocky hill.

'So, plan of action: chips on Fridays, give him responsibility, and give him some kind of reward here and there to look forward to. Got it?'

'Got it.'

'Good.'

Chrissie wouldn't have been surprised if her friend typed up an action plan with tick boxes and emailed it to her.

'So, how's the new job? Any cute guys there?'

Chrissie's toe caught on one of the loose floorboards on the veranda and she stumbled forward. 'Um...'

'Well, is there?'

'There's a male yoga teacher, Damon, but he's, um, well I guess he's okay but I haven't really thought of him like that. He might even be gay, I'm not sure.'

'And?'

'And what?'

'There's only *one* guy working in the whole retreat? What about the massage therapists? The chefs?'

The guests?

'Well, there are a few other guys, but...' God, she so wanted to tell her. The words hovered on the edge of her tongue, tingling and twirling and desperate to be spoken. Maybe she could just mention there was a celebrity and not say who? *No, Chrissie! You signed a legal form, for crying out loud!* And Melinda was a journalist. Not that she'd betray a friend's trust in order to sell a story, but Drew obviously wanted his visit to Tarrin's Bay to remain private for some reason, and Chrissie had to respect that and stick to her agreement. 'No. No one of interest.' God that was painful. The one person she was dying to tell and she couldn't even hint at it.

'Oh well, keep an eye out, you might meet someone around town. And if you do, I'm the first to know, right?'

Chrissie hated being dishonest, but what could she do? Anyway, it's not like she'd 'met someone'. She was just teaching him for the month, and then he'd be gone. Back to the States, out of her life, like he was never in it. She might not even be allowed to tell anyone about it, ever. 'Sure, yep. Anyway, how are you going?' Her voice became high-pitched. 'Kids well?'

'All's good here. Nothing new to report. Just the usual chaos.' She laughed. 'Damn, someone's at the door. Can I call you back?'

'Don't worry, Mel. You better get back to your research. I'll be fine.' *And I can't handle talking to you another minute without spilling the goss.*

'Well, if you're sure. Text me if you need me.' Footsteps sounded through the line. 'And I'll try to come down for a visit in a few weeks.'

'Sounds good.'

'Bye, Hun.'

Chrissie ended the call and stepped back into the house. She held a hand to Kai's forehead to double-check he really wasn't sick, then took her laptop from its bag and placed it on the kitchen table.

She sat and opened up the search engine. Hopefully Google could find something for Kai to look forward to as a reward. The local paper would be out tomorrow and might have some ideas for kids' activities in the town, but she never usually read the papers. Not since leaving her journalism career. It was too easy to get sucked in again, and she couldn't risk that.

Her fingers hovered over the keyboard. Without thinking she typed *Drew Wil,* then gasped. *What am I thinking?* She tapped backspace eight times, erasing her stupidity. She'd never succumbed to celebrity gossip and wasn't about to start now. If she wanted to know anything about Drew Williams she could bloody well ask him herself. Chrissie glanced around and shifted in her chair, as though she was a schoolgirl doing something naughty when the teacher wasn't looking. Then she typed *Fun activities for kids in Tarrin's Bay.*

'Mum?'

'Yes?'

'Do we have any packets of chips?'

Chrissie rolled her eyes and sighed. *Kids.* 'No, and even if we did I wouldn't let you have any right now, young man. I'm either going to take you back to school or you can eat the grapes I put on the coffee table. What'll it be?'

Kai tentatively reached over and plucked the grapes from the plate, slinking back down behind the backrest of the couch as though pretending to be invisible.

She scrolled through the search results then clicked on a link. *Aha! This might be just the thing.*

CHAPTER SEVEN

C hrissie walked up the stairs, each step in time with her heartbeat, then took a deep breath as she travelled along the hallway. She plucked her phone from her bag and turned it to silent. There was no way Kai was interrupting today's work. Besides, with any luck the bribe she'd offered him would do the trick and there'd be no morning dramas. At least for the rest of the week. She'd have to come up with a new bribe for next week. Chrissie returned the phone to her bag as she entered the yoga studio, then looked up to find Drew standing at the window.

'Oh, good morning. You're early,' she said.

He turned to face her. 'Glad you're here. I wasn't sure if you'd make it in today. How is your son?'

'He's fine. All good now.' She would feel silly if she told him the truth.

'That's a relief. Glad he's okay.' Drew stepped closer, genuine concern on his face.

Oh man. Who was she kidding? She didn't have a dishonest bone in her body. 'Actually, he wasn't really sick. He was putting it on to get out of school.' Warmth flushed her face.

Drew's mouth opened and he tipped his head back a little. 'Ahh, I see. A future actor, perhaps?'

'Could be.' She grinned.

'Well, he's not the first kid to pull the old "tummy ache" trick. I think I did that at least a dozen times when I was a little critter.'

'Really?' Chrissie had never faked illness. She was always the good girl, going along with everything. 'You don't seem like the type to try to get out of hard work.'

He chuckled. 'Music and yoga are one thing. Mathematical equations and memorising the periodic table are a whole other matter.'

'True.' She plonked her bag on the corner table. 'Although I think I did have the periodic table memorised at one point. Not that I remember it now. I clearly didn't need it for my career.'

'I'm impressed. I think I got as far as Lithium then forgot the rest.'

'Beryllium. That's the next one, then...' What was she doing? Why act like a complete know-it-all nerd? *You're here for yoga, Chrissie. Do your job!* 'Um, some other element.' She released a laugh.

'See, you didn't forget. It's amazing what we can remember years later. Let me guess, you still know all your times tables?'

Was he teasing her? The slight crease at the corner of one of his eyes glinted and that warm feeling rushed onto her face again.

'I guess so. I haven't tried to recall them. Though I'm sure I'll be helping my son soon enough.' She absolutely did remember them all. Plus, she had a times tables magnet stuck to the fridge, ready and waiting for Kai when the time came. Maybe it would filter into his subconscious in the meantime and help the process along. 'But I do remember my yoga terminology and poses, luckily.'

'I would hope so. Otherwise you could be feeding me a ton of gobbledygook and I'd be none the wiser.' Damn that glint in his eye, it was doing weird things to her insides.

'Don't worry, you're safe with me.' She smiled, and thought she noticed a hint of something serious in his expression, like her comment had triggered a memory. He looked away, then back again, his gaze dropping subtly to her left hand.

'So, does your son have any brothers or sisters?' Was that an indirect way of asking if she was married? Though if he'd overheard her talking to the teacher on the phone and correcting her last name, he probably suspected she wasn't.

'No. It's just Kai and me.'

'Nice name.'

'Thanks, I think so. Short and sweet.'

Drew slipped his hands into his track pants pockets. 'Does Kai see his father?'

This was one nosy celebrity, but Chrissie didn't mind. In fact, talking to him eased her mind. It was comfortable. Nice. She could just as happily forget the yoga sessions and chat instead. 'Yeah, every second weekend and half of each school holidays. Probably more often than when we were actually together.' She snorted, then to distract from the fact she was probably sharing more than appropriate, she lit the candle on the small table underneath the mandala. The wick glowed to life, and the familiar scent relaxed her shoulders.

'Well he has a great mum by the looks of things.' Drew smiled.

Chrissie flicked her hand. 'I doubt he thinks that sometimes. I'm the mean mother who sends him to school and gives him healthy lunches he doesn't eat,' she mocked.

'Ah yes, I had one of those. I mean, have. I *still* have one, but unfortunately she doesn't make my lunches anymore!'

Chrissie laughed.

'He'll realise what he's got one day, don't worry.'

'I hope so.' Chrissie withdrew a yoga mat from the storage shelf, then went to grab another but Drew beat her to it. They placed them on the floor, slightly closer than in the first two classes.

'Have you thought about rewarding him for good behaviour?'

For someone without kids, Drew seemed knowledgeable about family life. Unless he had a child somewhere in the world and she didn't know because she'd boycotted the media in an effort to recover from her panic attacks.

'Funny you should ask. I was talking to my friend on the phone yesterday and she said the same thing.'

'Ahh.' Drew glanced towards the ceiling for a moment as though he was remembering something. 'Well your friend gives good advice. A bit of bribery never goes astray, especially with us weak-minded males. Dangle a carrot and we'll do whatever we need to do to get it,' he joked.

'Good to know! Although I figured it would take more than a carrot to get him to be a good boy and go to school, so I opted for something a bit more enticing.'

'Do tell.' Drew crossed one foot over the other. By the sounds of it, Drew was more than happy to replace the yoga session with a chat session too.

'I searched the internet for kids activities in the area, and turns out there's a country fair on this Saturday at Tarrin's Bay Hills.'

'Ooh, I used to love those country fairs! Can I come too?' He laughed. 'Just kidding.'

What must it be like, not to be able to go out in public without getting mobbed? Stardom was nice for the money and ability to do what you loved, but it did come at a price. She actually felt sympathy for Drew.

'I remember they had pony rides, toffee apples, lucky dips, and—'

'A jumping castle, chocolate wheel, and baby animal farm,' Chrissie chimed in.

Drew grinned. 'If I'm right, I think you're as excited as Kai.'

She tilted her head forward, then up again, her thumb and forefinger pinched together. 'Just a tad.'

'He'll love it. If you go there in the afternoon, it won't be as busy. Mornings were always packed, but a lot of the locals head off to watch the football in the afternoon.'

'Thanks for the heads up.' That would give her time to do the grocery shopping in the morning, and maybe sort through a box or two of Felicia's belongings, before heading to the fair.

'So Kai went off to school happily today, I take it?'

'For the most part, yes. He started out with his usual grumbling and huffing, but as soon as I reminded him of his reward at the end of the week, he put all his effort into behaving. I had to hold back a few laughs as he volunteered to put his lunch in his schoolbag.'

'Problem solved, then.'

'Until next week. I have no idea what I'll do for another reward!'

'Take it one week at a time. One *day* at a time. Sort of like yoga, right?'

'Exactly. You're learning well.' She smiled.

'I have a good teacher.' He held her gaze, and a feeling that everything would be okay washed over Chrissie. *Yes, one day at a time. I can do this.*

'But maybe you'll have to bribe me if I slacken off in class, huh?' He playfully nudged at her arm. 'A piece of chocolate for every correct pose?'

'Hmm, that could work. Though I don't think chocolate is allowed in here.'

'You could smuggle some in. No one has to know.' He winked.

This man was an absolute delight. He was like the cheeky, cute Corey from high school all over again. Only suaver and without any acne.

'Actually, I do recall that the kitchen makes a delectable-looking dark chocolate, almond, and coconut mousse.' She gave a brief, satisfied nod.

'Oh yes, I think I've seen that on the menu. I'll have to order one up. Or two, if you'd like to join me for a post-yoga indulgence.' His lips practically twinkled with cheekiness, it was all she could do not to grab them with her own and eat them all up. This talk of food combined with Drew's delicious appearance had her salivating, and she turned her lips inward to quench the moisture.

She smiled and shrugged, as if saying, 'maybe, one day.' 'Well, before I succumb to your offer in a moment of weakness, I think we'd better get started.'

'Whatever you say, Burns, you're the boss.' He grinned. 'Sorry, I often call my mates by their last names. Just a habit.'

Did that mean he considered her a mate? Could they actually end this month as chummy friends who'd text each other and send Christmas cards?

Chrissie twisted her lips to one side. Two can play that game. 'In that case... on the mat now, Williams.'

Drew quickly jumped onto the mat and eyed her with amusement. 'I think February is going to be a very enjoyable month, Burns, whadd'ya reckon?'

'I reckon you're absolutely right,' she replied, then raised her arms up to begin their salutes to the sun. If there was a yoga sequence for salutes to Drew, she'd opt for that instead.

CHAPTER EIGHT

Well, she'd done it. One week done and dusted, and Kai going to school without so much as a whimper — no packets of chips required. Chrissie downed the rest of her glass of water and left it on the wash up tray to be collected by the kitchen staff this afternoon. That was another bonus of working at Serendipity; food was provided, and no taking turns with staff to wash everyone's glasses and mugs.

Damon entered the staff lounge and sunk into the sofa. 'Ahh, that feels nice.'

Chrissie stood in front of him. 'Lisa, there's something different about you. If I could only put my finger on it.' Chrissie tapped her chin.

'Haha, very funny.' Damon put his feet up on the coffee table. 'Lisa's sick, so I'm taking her classes today. Double shift for me. Takes a bit of strength to do that, I tell ya.'

'Oh, I'm sure. By the looks of things you're handling it very well.' Chrissie eyed him as her voice conveyed sarcasm.

Damon shot up from the sofa. 'Yes. I am. No problems at all here.' He swung his arms back and forth. 'The 3pm slump's got nothin' on me, even if I have been up since four-thirty this morning.'

'Ouch.' Chrissie scrunched up her face. 'And when do you clock off?'

'Eight o'clock tonight.'

'Double ouch.'

'Meh, I can handle it. Mind over matter and all that.'

'Well, good luck!' Chrissie flung her bag over her shoulder and stepped towards the door.

'Piece of cake.' He waved her away. 'An organic, gluten-free, fruit-filled cake, that is.' He winked as she turned the door handle. *'Ciao, bella.'*

Chrissie turned back. 'Italian today, huh?'

'Seems so.' He grinned, his dark skin glistening with the sheen of an intense yoga class. 'Though I'm nothin' but Maori through-and-through.' He gestured a hand down the length of his body. 'I just like to challenge my vocabulary.' A yawn stretched his mouth open wide. 'And my body.' He raised his eyebrows and chuckled.

'Let's hope Lisa is back on deck tomorrow. We can't have you falling asleep in the middle of *Parsvottanasana.*'

'Ha!' Damon laughed. 'No, definitely not. *Padottanasana* would be better, at least my head could rest on the floor for a few moments. My students might not even notice.'

Chrissie laughed, imagining her colleague snoring in the pose where the body bends at the waist and hands reach through the legs to touch the floor. 'True, true.' Chrissie checked her watch. 'Well, hope you get through the day, see you tomorrow.'

'*Ciao!*' Damon waved as she walked out the door, and she wouldn't have been surprised if he fell asleep thirty seconds later.

The school bell rang and two dozen children filtered out of the classroom, accompanied by many more from the adjacent classrooms, their sizes gradually increasing in height. Before she knew it, Kai would be one of those taller kids in Year Three, and before too long, Year Six, and heaven help her, Year Ten. If he was a challenge now, what would he be like as a teenager? The thought was enough to make her instantly sprout a thousand grey hairs.

Kai approached with schoolbag perched high on his back, a triumphant and self-satisfied grin on his face. 'So can we go to the fair tomorrow, Mum?'

She ruffled his hair. 'Yes, we can. Good work.'

He grinned wider and they walked out of the building and towards the school gates. 'Can I have a toffee apple at the fair, and ride a pony, and get a lucky dip?' He had an even greater memory than her.

'That's the plan.'

'Yippee!' He ran the rest of the way to the gate, crashing into a mother on her way in.

'Careful, Kai.' Chrissie glanced at the woman. 'Sorry,' she mouthed.

The mother flicked a dismissive hand. 'It's fine.'

She helped Kai buckle into the car and got into the driver's seat. 'Right, home we go. You'll have to get to bed early tonight so we can have lots of energy for tomorrow, okay?'

'Okay.'

Plus she wanted to curl up on the couch and watch a movie on her own, preferably one that wasn't animated and didn't have talking animals. And definitely one with a rating higher than PG.

They drove down Seaview Road and turned left into Willow Street, which ran through the town centre. As she slowed at the roundabout, Kai said, 'Mum, can we stop at the park for a while? I want a go on the playground.'

Chrissie eyed the corner of Miracle Park, where people wandered in and out, and children climbed and swung and slid on the equipment. Would this be too much of a reward, the park *and* the fair? What the hell, it was the start of the weekend and right now she just wanted Kai to be happy. Plus it might tire him out and help him get to bed early. 'Okay, then. Hang on till I find a parking spot.'

'Yay!'

Chrissie slowed and pulled into a spot opposite the historic terrace shops and next to the cute Willow Lane, like a step back in time with its unique gift and candy shops with decorative railings and awnings.

Kai slammed the door shut with enthusiasm and dashed over to the playground in Miracle Park so fast Chrissie thought he might crash into it as he'd done to that poor mother. Chrissie jogged to catch up, then glanced across the main road. Café Lagoon stood out with its busy assortment of people and fancy swirling lettering. Her stomach grumbled. 'Ah, Kai?' Her son looked back as he was about to climb the slippery slide. 'I want to go across the road and get a coffee first, come with me.' Chrissie didn't usually drink coffee; it was just an occasional treat. And right now, she decided, Kai wasn't the only one who deserved a reward for getting through the week.

'But Mum!' He sighed.

'No buts. C'mon. We'll come straight back.'

He trudged over, all joy drained from his face.

'I'll watch him if you like, you go,' a woman's voice said. Chrissie turned to the left to see the woman Kai had crashed into earlier.

'Oh, that's okay. Thanks.'

'Seriously, it's no problem. I've got to watch my own anyway.' She pointed. 'I'm Sam's mum.'

Chrissie looked at the dark-haired boy that she'd seen Kai chatting to at school drop off this morning.

'Your son's in my son's class.' The woman smiled, tucking a clump of sandy hair behind her ear as the breeze wafted it around.

'Oh, hi.' Chrissie smiled, then glanced at Kai.

'Can I go back and play with Sam?' Kai looked up at her with pleading eyes.

Pleased that he'd appeared to have made a new friend, she patted him on the back with her blessing. 'Well, thanks,' she said to the woman. 'I'll only be a few minutes, I'll just pop over to the café.'

'No worries. I'm not going anywhere,' she said.

Chrissie turned to walk away then turned back. 'Oh, can I get you anything? Coffee, tea, cake?'

'I probably shouldn't.' She patted her stomach. The woman was curvy but by no means fat.

'I'm happy to shout you something. It's the least I can do for watching my child, who so carelessly ran into you earlier!'

She laughed. 'Ah, it was nothing. But okay. That would be great, thanks. I'll have a decaf skim cappuccino.'

Chrissie nodded then dashed across the road. She entered the café and was greeted by a blast of cool air conditioning. *Ahh...* The décor matched the café's name and cooled her even more; walls of swirly blues and greens, and a tree painted in the corner, like she was stepping into an actual lagoon. She studied the menu on the wall. Not that she was here for a meal, but her grumbling stomach piqued her curiosity.

'What can I get you today?' someone asked. She lowered her gaze from the blackboard to meet the hypnotic eyes of a strapping young man, maybe in his early twenties, his smooth hair swiped over the side of his face in an arc.

'Um, I'll get a decaf skim cappuccino to take away, and a

regular cappuccino too.' Forget decaf and skim. If she was going to treat herself she'd go all out.

'Coming right up.' He winked, and if Chrissie was fifteen years younger, she'd probably giggle and twirl a strand of her hair.

'You new in town or passing through?' he asked while he automatically made the coffee, as though he was so used to it he could do it blindfolded.

'I'm new.' Chrissie smiled. Everyone was so friendly here. 'Not sure if it'll be for good, but I'm here for now.'

'Ah, the bay will draw you in. Always does. It's *The Town of New Beginnings* you know.'

'So I've heard.' Chrissie adjusted her bag strap on her shoulder. 'And I certainly need one of those, so we'll see what happens!'

'Well I hope you'll visit Café Lagoon again. We often have live music on Friday and Saturday nights if you're interested. Depending on whether there're any local musicians available we can round up.'

'Oh, right.' She cleared her throat. She could round up a musician, not that he'd be able to attend such a public place. 'I've got a six-year-old son, so unfortunately I don't get out a lot, but I'll try and drop in on one of the nights he's at his father's.'

'Sounds like a plan.' He smiled, and tapped the cup on the counter twice then added a decorative smiley face to the froth. He did the same to the other one, put a lid on each, and placed them in a cardboard holder, handing them to Chrissie.

'I hope you get your new beginning,' he said.

'Thank you...' She eyed his name tag, '...Jonah.'

'My pleasure. Enjoy your afternoon.'

With service like that she should make a habit of having coffee more often. The guy was a total charmer; no wonder the place was busy. She sipped her coffee as she walked out. *Mmm...* Okay, the fantastic coffee probably played a role too.

Chrissie looked along the length of the street, memories of old times rolling through her mind. Good memories; getting fish and chips from the takeaway shop, an ice-cream from the parlour, and getting lost in the whole other world that was Mrs May's Bookstore. It was great that it still existed, although she guessed Mrs May herself would be retired by now. Chrissie wondered if the puppet shows still ran in the store. That could be another future reward for Kai.

Chrissie crossed the road and walked past the Wishing Fountain. She'd made a wish in it at one of the Wishing Festivals during summer holidays when she'd stayed with Aunt Felicia, but now, she couldn't even remember what she'd wished for. Whatever it was it probably hadn't come true.

'Here you go,' Chrissie said, handing the coffee to Sam's mum.

'Oh, thanks, that's kind of you.' She blew through the little mouth hole then took a slow sip. 'I'm Sarah by the way.' She held out her free hand and Chrissie shook it.

'Chrissie. Chrissie Burns. Kai has a different last name, just so you know.'

'Oh, right. I know all about that. Sam is my second child, we share my husband's surname, but my teenage daughter has a different father and hence a different surname.'

'Do you find people sometimes call you Mrs So-and-so, as in the wrong name?'

'Yes, when Gemma was younger. It can get confusing with all these blended families!'

'It sure can.' The women sipped their coffees while the children climbed and slid down the slide repeatedly. Sarah waved at a couple of other parents walking past, and Chrissie noticed the beaded bracelet on her wrist. 'That's nice. I've never seen one like that before, it's unique.' She pointed at the multicoloured glossy beads interspersed with metallic shapes and dangling charms.

'Oh, thanks.' Sarah held it out and twisted her wrist. 'Actually, I made it.'

'Wow, you're talented. I know who to go to for my jewellery needs then.'

'Thanks. I often set up a stall at the local markets. I have a website too, but it's more of a hobby. I just make what I can when I can. It's something I've always enjoyed.'

'I'll have to come and check out your stall sometime.'

'That'd be great,' Sarah said. 'So how long have you been in Tarrin's Bay?'

'Since the second week of January, so almost a month now. You?'

'My whole life.'

'Wow.'

'Yeah. Never even left, except for the odd trip.'

Sarah looked to be a similar age to Chrissie. She might have even gone to school with Drew Williams. But she couldn't ask, it would be silly and she couldn't risk letting others know he was here.

'You must love it,' Chrissie said.

'I do, I can't imagine living anywhere else. I mean, I could have, but we just got settled and stayed put. What made you decide to move here?'

'My aunt left me her house when she died. I'm going to live in it for a while and get it fixed up and ready for sale.'

'Oh, I'm sorry about your aunt. But that's great, you wouldn't consider staying in the house yourself?'

Live forever in the house that only reminded her of her sister's death? No thanks.

'No. I'll get something else later on, maybe up in the hills, or further south.'

'Well, all the best with the renovations. Have you got a handy hubby?'

Chrissie tipped her head back with a laugh. 'Nope. And even when I had one he wasn't particularly handy.' She glanced toward Kai to make sure he couldn't hear her.

'Oh well, who needs 'em? You look strong, I bet you can handle a lot of things around the house better than any guy.' Sarah smiled.

'Oh, I don't know, but thanks. I'll be getting the experts in for sure, but I will do some of it myself, like the painting, and gardening.'

'Well, my husband's a builder if you need one.'

'Really? That's good to know.'

'And maybe Kai will give you a helping hand too.'

'Ha, he'll probably sit around and watch me make a mess of things!'

'Or if he's anything like mine, he'll make his own mess of things.' Sarah looked at her son who was clambering up the ladder of the slide, passing a younger child who'd barely placed one foot on the rung. 'Sam! Hop off, please. Let the other little boy have a turn.'

Sam leapt off and landed with a crouch on the ground, the younger child watching him and then copying him by jumping off himself and giggling. The child stepped onto the ladder again then jumped off with a squeal of glee. Who needed the slide when they could make their own fun?

Kai gestured for Sam to join him in the cubbyhole that had circles cut out of it where kids peeked through and climbed in and out. 'They seem to get along well,' Chrissie said. 'I'm glad he's found a friend.'

'Sam's mentioned Kai before. Said he's good at making scary faces.' Sarah grinned.

'Oh no, really?' Chrissie hoped he wasn't making faces at other kids in a menacing way.

'Apparently. Sam showed me one but said Kai does it better. It was something like this...' Sarah contorted her face into a demonic-like expression with wide eyes and lips stretched downwards with bottom teeth biting her top lip.

Chrissie spluttered some of her coffee and she wiped her mouth.

'Sorry!' Sarah said.

Chrissie waved her apologies away and wiped her mouth again. Another laugh escaped and Sarah joined in. 'I can't believe that's what my son will be known by his peers for — scary faces. Oh, dear God.' Chrissie shook her head. 'If only the teachers thought of that as a commendable skill.'

'It probably gives them some much needed comic relief.'

So Kai was probably having *some* fun at school, in his own lets-see-how-much-I-can-scare-people kind of way.

'Hey, we should get the kids together for a weekend play date sometime. What do you think?' Sarah suggested.

'That would be great, thanks. Kai's been having a bit of a rough time settling into life without his father in the house, so anything to help him enjoy being here would be great.'

'Kids are resilient beings. I'm sure he'll be fine. So, when and where?'

Chrissie squinted, and pursed her lips as she thought. 'Actually, I'm taking Kai to the country fair tomorrow. Would Sam like to come with us?' That way she could keep them occupied with fun things and not risk the child getting bored around Felicia's house, or heaven forbid, having to supervise him near the water.

'That would be fantastic. I was thinking of taking him but I have so much to do at home I was hoping he'd forget! Isn't that terrible? Anyway, if you're sure that's okay, he would love it.'

'I'd be happy to take him along.'

'Hey Sam!' Sarah called. 'How would you like to go with Kai to the country fair tomorrow?'

The child's eyes opened wide. 'Without you? Just me and Kai?'

'Well, and Kai's mum.' She chuckled.

Kai looked at Chrissie with inquisitive eyes as if to check that this strange woman had her facts right. She nodded and he smiled.

'Yay!' Sam pumped a fisted hand up to the heavens. He looked at Kai. 'What will we do first?'

Kai narrowed his brows in serious thought for a moment. 'Pony rides. Then lucky dip.' The children continued to discuss their itinerary for tomorrow's Fun Day Out as they walked towards the swings.

'I was thinking of going after lunch, say, 1pm?' Chrissie said.

'Sounds good.'

'I can pick him up and drop him home. What's your address?' Chrissie opened her bag to find a pen but Sarah plucked a card from her own purse.

'Here are all my details. One o'clock would be great.'

Chrissie looked at the business card; it had a picture of a cartoon superwoman character on the front and the words, *Sarah McAdams – mother of Sam and Gemma, and overall domestic goddess.* It listed her phone numbers, email address, and home address. Mothers were supposed to have business cards these days? Chrissie looked in her bag for one of her yoga business cards but there weren't any left, or she'd left them at work. 'Here, I don't have a card but I'll write down my mobile in case of any problems.' Chrissie scribbled on a scrap of paper and handed it to Sarah.

Maybe she should get her own personal card too? Her lips curved into a hint of a smile as she imagined what it could say:

Chrissie Burns (not Mrs Cavanaugh) – stressed out mum to Kai and overall undomestic goddess. Call at own risk.

And as though sensing her thoughts, her own phone beeped with a text message. She took it from her bag and excused herself to Sarah.

Oh my God. It was from Drew.

CHAPTER NINE

C hrissie normally deleted her text messages after they'd served their purpose; it was a symbolic way of trying to stop the past from keeping a hold on her. But this one, she decided to keep. After all, it wasn't every day that one received a message from the singer they'd fantasised about almost twenty years ago, and still had a massive crush on.

As she unplugged her phone from its charger the next morning, she re-read the message:

> Hi Chrissie, just wanted to say thanks again for a great first week of yoga, and I'm enjoying the individual program you worked out for me. I even had a brainwave this afternoon during one of the meditation exercises you set for me — a new song! I'm playing around with the lyrics as we speak. Enjoy the weekend with your son, I look forward to seeing you on Monday. Until then, Adios, Sayonara, Farewell. Drew.

Chrissie laughed. She'd told him how her colleague, Damon had a propensity for cultural diversity. Chrissie wondered what Drew's new song would be like. Would she be lucky enough to even hear a sample of his sweet singing voice face-to-face? Maybe that was too much to ask. She was there to provide a service to him, not to be entertained by someone clearly needing a break from the spotlight.

Chrissie kicked off the ballet flats she'd worn grocery shopping and replaced them with running shoes for the country fair this afternoon. She opened the dresser drawer and chose a headscarf to go with her denim capri's and watermelon-coloured top, wrapping the white and blue patterned scarf in a thin band over her head and tying it in a knot at the nape of her neck. The ends trailed down her back, peeking through the lengths of blonde strands, poking out a few centimetres at the bottom. She ruffled her tresses then glanced back in the open drawer. It was only a country fair, but since her work meant she could rarely wear any jewellery or accessories for the fact of them getting in the way, she opened a cardboard gift box that housed a selection of items. Her fingers rifled through the tangle of chains, hooks, and beads, until they lifted a tear-shaped pendant necklace with a vibrant pinkish stone to match her top. Something else was caught in the chain. She shook it gently but it didn't unravel, so she picked it up and her fingers hovered near the culprit — the silver charm bracelet that had belonged to her sister. It was one of a pair, with only one half of a heart-shaped charm, but Chrissie's bracelet with the other half had gone missing years ago. It had never seemed right to wear Danielle's bracelet, but she'd kept it as a memento of their sisterhood. If only she hadn't lost the other half she could store them together. It would be a way of saying they would always be together, somehow, even if only through a piece of jewellery.

Chrissie gently thread the bracelet under and over to release it from the necklace, and placed it back in the box, curled up in the corner. She'd have to sort through all of her stuff, it was still jumbled up after moving house. She hooked the necklace behind her neck and, approving her reflection in the mirror, closed the drawer and left the bedroom.

'Kai, you ready to go?'

'Yep, but I don't know which hat to wear, this one or this one?' He held up his two choices: a car racing hat and a *Shrek* hat. Oh dear, was she raising a little Chrissie? She wasn't overly fussed with fashion but liked to dress in her own unique style and paid careful attention to accessorising, depending on her mood. Sometimes choosing something as simple as the colour of a top became a difficult decision. Her therapist had said it was to do with needing to feel a sense of control over our actions, and also that because our past decisions may have affected the outcome of something significant, a person would subconsciously be scared to make the wrong decision in case something bad happened again. That made sense. She'd made the wrong decision all those years ago on that terrible day and something bad *did* happen. Her decision-making was more thorough now. She couldn't bear the thought of making another mistake.

'How about the car racing one? They might even have a car ride you can go on.'

Kai popped it on his head. 'I hope so. Mum, when am I old enough to drive?'

Chrissie laughed. What had she told Melinda, that Kai was happy being a little kid for now? Maybe that phase had come to an end. 'You've got quite a few years to go yet. When you're about seventeen or so.'

'Seventeen?' He raised his upper lip in disappointment. 'But that's way old.'

'To you, maybe. To me? I'm more than double that age.'

Kai gasped. 'You are?'

'Yes, I'm thirty-seven remember?'

'I think it'll take me hundreds of years to get to thirty-seven.'

She laughed. 'Well, to be exact, it'll take you about thirty-one years, but who's counting?'

'You are, Mum.'

Chrissie shook her head in amusement. He was like two different children — cute and unknowingly funny on weekends and defiant and stubborn on weekdays. If only weekends lasted longer than two days.

'Right, then. Let's go pick up Sam, shall we?'

Fifteen minutes later Chrissie was officially responsible for the lives and wellbeing of two six-year-olds. She waved to Sarah who stood smiling on the porch of her rendered brick two-storey home. It was a great place; lots of room and open plan living, with a wonderful landscaped backyard with mature trees providing areas of shade and privacy. Her husband, the builder, must be doing alright by the looks of their living environment. Chrissie didn't think Sarah's casual handcrafted jewellery business would be enough to pay for such a place. Then again, she could have inherited it like Chrissie had her aunt's place. People could think the same of her; how she could afford a beachfront property, even if it was a bit run-down, being a single mother teaching yoga classes? Although she hadn't stayed with Felicia since Danielle's death, she'd seen her here and there when her aunt had come to Sydney to visit. But that fateful day had driven a stake through both their lives and sense of security. Each blamed themselves; Felicia for not keeping a better eye on them, and Chrissie for leaving her sister alone, even if it was only for a few minutes.

Sam straightened up in the back seat and Chrissie eyed him in the rear-vision mirror.

'My mum said I have to be extra good today, and if I am, she'll give me extra ice-cream for dessert tonight. So I'm going to be extra good and you have to tell her if I am extra good, okay, Chrissie?'

She'd told him he could call her Chrissie since she was no longer Mrs Cavanaugh. And to make it even, Sarah had told Kai she could call her by her first name instead of Mrs McAdams so he didn't feel different.

'I will be sure to tell her,' Chrissie said with a smile in her voice.

'Can I have ice-cream tonight too?' asked Kai.

'Um, I don't think I have any Kai, and we just went shopping today. It'll have to wait till we need to go to the supermarket again, okay?'

'Oh, but Sam is having some.'

'Kai, you need to be on your best behaviour too, as we have a guest with us. And anyway, if you're lucky I might make some choc chip cookies for dessert.'

'Yum!' Kai seemed happy enough with that. Kids. Food and fun were all they wanted.

Chrissie drove the chatting youngsters up into the hills, passing some impressive properties on the way that had panoramic views of the ocean in front and the rural landscape behind. The best of both worlds. If the speed limit wasn't seventy and there weren't cars filling the road she would have slowed down to look at some of them. She passed a property called Honeydew House and stole a glance at the long driveway swerving down to a magnificent home. It would make an ideal location for a yoga retreat. She'd have to have another look on the way home, and maybe take a drive next weekend when Kai was at his father's. It'd be nice to see more of the area, get a feel for where she could move to later on. Maybe there was something already on the market, or maybe she could put an expression of interest down with a real estate agent. Honeydew House, even if it would be for sale, would probably be way too expensive, even with the large sum she knew she could get for Felicia's house. It was possible she could get a loan, but she didn't fancy the idea of being tied to a large mortgage if she didn't have to be. She'd have to stay within budget and find something a bit more modest, but still with enough scope to house a few guests for her future retreats. But it was nice to dream, and driving past all the beautiful properties only inspired her to work on the beach house and prepare it for sale. It might be painful now, but the rewards would be great. She had to be patient and keep her eye on the prize.

The traffic slowed near the turn-off to the tiny township of Tarrin's Bay Hills, and as cars filtered out, probably leaving the fair behind, more cars filtered in along with her. She passed a group of rowdy teenagers with football jerseys getting into a car. Perfect timing; as Drew had said, many locals would be off to the footy.

'Look, Mum, a huge slide!' Kai pointed to the right as they turned into the street alongside the reserve where the fair was held. A humungous yellow plastic slippery slide stood proud in the corner, and Chrissie spied a couple of kids slipping down the length of it, no doubt grinning all the way down. Maybe Kai would forego his strict itinerary and opt for a few slides before the pony rides.

Chrissie pulled into one of a few available parking spots and had barely put the handbrake on before the kids had unbuckled their seatbelts, clambering to get out and into the fun.

'Whoa, hang on kids.' Chrissie tugged on Kai's T-shirt. 'Here you go, keep these in your pockets. It's got my phone number on it in case of emergencies.' She handed them each a scrap of paper. She really should get one of those 'mother cards'. 'Also, let's organise a special spot to meet up in case — and I don't mean it would be likely to happen — but just in case anyone gets lost.' The reserve was large but not too expansive, but the lack of barriers surrounding it meant that it would be easy for kids to wander off. You could never be too careful.

'How about the big slippery slide?' Kai asked.

'Great idea. Why don't we head over there now, and remember, if you get lost, go straight to the slippery slide. Okay?'

'Okay,' they echoed.

The queue was almost as long as the slide itself, clearly the attraction of the day. Luckily, it moved quickly as it took mere seconds for someone to slide down the thing. It reminded Chrissie of cooking — spending ages preparing a meal, only to have it wolfed down in minutes. So unfair. Especially when it was met by an 'I'm still hungry' comment from a growing child.

'Are you having a go too, Miss?' asked the slide attendant, a short chubby man of about fifty.

'Oh, um...'

'Yes, you go too, Mum! We'll see you at the bottom.' Kai curled around behind her and pushed her forwards, then scooted in front of her again. Whatever happened to ladies first?

'I guess I am,' she said to the man.

'Here you go.' He handed each of them a mat to sit on. 'Only two at a time, kids, take a spot near the red markings.' He pointed to two places at the top of the slide. 'Sit on the mat and lean back a little. Steve will give you a little push.' He pointed to another man, younger, who stood at the top of the slide.

'You ready, boys?' Chrissie asked.

'Yep.' They took their places and Kai's eyes lit up on looking down.

Whoosh! They both slid down the wavy slide, Sam tipping slightly sideways and for a moment Chrissie thought he might topple off the mat. When they reached the bottom, Steve ushered her and a child behind her to the two allocated spots.

What am I doing? It'd been years since she'd been on one of these. Maybe it would be good for her to do something fun and childlike. Maybe it was just what she needed to loosen up and deal with—

Whoosh! *Whoa!* Fresh air pushed past Chrissie's face and lifted her hair from her shoulders like a cape. She couldn't help but grin, and the air had helped pushed her mouth back into a wide smile too. She slowed to a stop at the bottom, Kai cheering from the sidelines.

'That was awesome fast, Mum, how come you went faster than me?'

Because I'm a tad heavier than you, my darling. 'Who knows?'

She handed her mat to the attendant and adjusted her pants.

'Ooh look! There are the ponies. Let's go on them!' Kai pointed, then tugged Sam's shirt.

'Stay with me, boys, don't run off.'

Sam slowed down and walked alongside her, obviously conscious of being a 'good boy' so he could get his extra ice-cream tonight.

They walked to the cordoned off riding area, the ponies appearing to move in slow motion compared to the speed of the slide.

'Are you going to go on one too, Mum?' As was the case with an only child, Kai always expected his mother to be his playmate.

'No, I think I'm too big. I'll just watch you two.'

Sam and Kai were helped up onto the back of the calm animals, and a guide held onto a rope attached to the reigns and led them around the circle.

'I'm a cowboy,' said Kai as he rode past Chrissie. He turned back to Sam riding the pony behind him.

'Me too,' said Sam. 'I'm Cowboy... Cowboy Warrior!'

Kai laughed. 'I'm, um...' He let go of the reigns with one hand and tapped his chin. '...Cowboy the Great!'

Chrissie laughed and plucked her phone from the small

knapsack she'd strung diagonally over her body for easy carrying. She clicked a few pictures, one of Sam with a 'thumbs up' sign and Kai with his fist powering into the air.

'That was cool,' Kai said on dismounting the pony.

'Way cool,' said Sam.

'Where are the lucky dips, Mum?'

Chrissie scanned the fair; people dawdling along, kids licking toffee apples, chirpy sideshow music filling the air... 'Um, should be somewhere over there I think.' They walked in the direction of stalls selling arts and crafts. She eyed her surroundings and homed in on a group of kids standing near one of them.

Lucky Dips ~ $2 each or three for $5, the sign said.

I think one will be plenty. Chrissie remembered the boxes of Kai's toys she had yet to unpack at the beach house. 'Two lucky dips, please,' she asked the woman behind the stall, handing her four dollars.

Kai and Sam crouched in front of the large box on the ground, eyes moving all over trying to ascertain which wrapped package would contain the most desirable prize.

Kai plunged his hand in and rummaged around.

'Maybe this one.' He pulled one out, feeling it with his fingertips. 'Nah.' He dropped it, picking up another. 'This one instead.' He ripped the paper and revealed a yo-yo with a smiley face on it. Fantastic. A toy he'd probably struggle to learn to use. Might be one for Victor to teach him, as Chrissie didn't know if she had the patience.

'Cool,' Kai remarked, clearly unaware he'd scored something almost as tricky as the Rubik's cube.

Sam chose his prize and unwrapped it, holding up a silver whistle on a ribbon. 'Oh, a whistle!' he said, hanging it around his neck and wrapping his mouth around it, releasing a loud blow. Kai blocked his ears.

I bet Sarah will be over the moon with that. Chrissie chuckled.

'Here, Kai, I'll keep the yo-yo in my bag so you can try it out at home.' She took it from his hands.

'Can we get a toffee apple?' Kai pointed to a display of glossy red things on sticks.

'How about we wander around a bit first, go on a few more rides, and then we can sit down and have one, yeah?'

The kids agreed and they spent the next hour or so enjoying the sights, amusements, and activities on offer, including petting the cute baby animals.

Chrissie headed over to the public toilets and waited at the entrance of the men's for each child to go, then ushered them into the ladies bathroom. 'You boys wait right here, okay? I'll just be a couple of minutes.' It was hard knowing what to do with a growing boy when it came to public bathrooms. When Kai was younger she'd bring him into the cubicle with her, but now he was older it was a bit weird, and even now, if she left him waiting near the sinks some women would scoff at her for letting her male child be in the ladies room. What was she supposed to do? She wouldn't dare leave him outside, vulnerable to being taken by some weirdo. At what age was it okay to start doing that? She couldn't bring him in with her forever. She wondered how fathers of daughters managed; it would be even trickier to have to bring a female child into a male bathroom with the risk of seeing a lot more than one should at a young age.

Chrissie finished up and washed her hands, then peered around the corner to where she'd left the boys standing near the entrance. *Oh no.*

She dashed outside. 'Kai? Sam?' Her heart pounded and blood pumped rapidly through her veins. 'Kai! Where are you?' she yelled.

'Boo!' Chrissie jumped as Kai leapt from behind the toilet block and flashed one of his award-winning scary faces, Sam giggling.

'Kai!' She crouched and pulled him in close. 'Don't you ever do that again! I didn't know where you were. When I tell you to stay put I expect you to stay put, young man.' She held a hand to her chest to steady her heart, and glanced at a guilty-looking Sam.

'I'm sorry, Mrs Chrissie, it was Kai's idea.' Ha, the consequences of ratting out one's mate were obviously nothing compared to not getting any ice-cream.

Chrissie looked at Kai.

'He's right, it was my idea. I thought it was a good one.'

'Well it wasn't. At home maybe, but not in public. I need to know exactly where you are at all times.'

Kai hung his head. 'Sorry, Mum.'

'Okay, well you're forgiven, as long as you've learned your lesson.' She eyed both the boys.

'Yes,' they agreed.

Sam held up his whistle. 'Would you like to keep my whistle? You can have it if you want.'

She smiled. Prepared to give up his whistle for a shot at extra ice-cream. This kid might have a serious case of dairy-dependence.

'No, that's okay, Sam. But thank you, it was kind of you to offer.'

Sam let the whistle fall to his chest.

'Okay, now that you've learned your lesson, let's get back to the fair.'

'You mean we can still have fun? We're not going home early for punishment?' Kai asked.

Chrissie feigned seriousness. 'Well, it did cross my mind, but as long as you promise to be extra good we can stay a while longer. Deal?'

'Deal.' The kids held out their hands and Chrissie shook them, sealing the agreement.

'Now, who wants a toffee apple?'

'Meeee!'

Chrissie paid for the teeth-rotting sweet treats and took them over to a seating area to watch some side shows. There was a juggler, a ventriloquist, and, *oh no*. Not one of those things. Chrissie looked at the transparent tub filled with water and the tall structure with a seat on it. One of those ridiculous dunking games. 'Dunk a firefighter!' the sign read. Apparently if you could hit the button hard enough with a rubber hammer it would let the clasp loose and the victim would fall into the water below. All this to raise funds for the Rural Fire Service. Couldn't they have taken donations instead? Or made a raunchy calendar, surely that would bring in the big bucks? She'd buy two copies, one for her, one for Melinda as a Christmas present.

'Can I have a go at that?' asked Kai, pointing to the firefighter sitting atop the chair.

'Ah, no, I think we'll leave that one, it's a bit tricky.'

'I'll just watch then.' The boys licked their toffee apples and focused on the dunking game. A teenager with hammer at the ready hit the button. Nothing. He hit it again, and still nothing. He gave it one final enthusiastic hit, and suddenly the man had dropped through the gap and a flurry of water whooshed around him in the tub. His arms and legs flailed, and although he was putting on a show, Chrissie's heart raced. *Come up, come up,* she chanted to herself. The man rolled around under the water, his body visible through the clear tub apart from the froth created by his movements. *Oh God, just get out of the water!* Heat crawled across Chrissie's back and her chest tightened. She clutched at it, twisting her top into a knot. She swallowed a heavy lump in her throat and as the man surfaced with a big grin on his face she let go of her top, forcing herself to take slow deep breaths.

It's okay, it's just a game. He's okay, no one can get hurt here, it's not deep enough. She kept bringing her thoughts back to reality. Just because she never saw Danielle resurface didn't mean that every person who ventured underwater would be destined to suffer the same fate. But still, it was easier, safer, not to take the risk. Humans didn't need to swim; it wasn't a necessity for a full life. She knew how of course, had learnt as a child, but so had Danielle, and that hadn't saved her.

'Are you still angry at us, Mum?' asked Kai, eyeing her with concern. It was only then Chrissie realised her turmoil must be apparent to the youngsters and she forced a smile and casually leaned back in the seat. 'No, I'm not angry. Everything's okay. I'm just a bit puffed out from all this fun!' She ruffled his hair and Sam's concerned expression relaxed.

'As soon as you're finished eating those apples, how about a few more goes on the slippery slide before we head home?'

'Yes!' Kai said, then munched on his treat at twice the speed. 'Mum, you could watch us at the bottom of the slide and tell us who goes faster.'

'I will.'

And she did, making sure they both got equal opportunity to be the Slide King to avoid any disappointment.

As they walked to the car, happy yet tired, Chrissie's mind went over her near panic attack at the dunking game. She couldn't risk those things happening when she had children under her care. Not that anything bad would happen, except a bit of hyperventilation, but she didn't want to scare them, and certainly didn't want to risk Sarah not allowing Sam to play with Kai on the impression that his mother was a complete basket case. She'd have to get around to going back to therapy with a new practitioner. Or be stricter with her techniques and use that hypnosis recording the psychologist had given her to deal with her fear of water. Maybe living near the ocean would eventually help her desensitise and come to grips with it. Either that, or make things ten times worse.

CHAPTER TEN

Kai and Sam talked nonstop on the drive back about what the best parts of the fair were, while Chrissie took in the surrounding properties again, taking an extra glance at Honeydew House. Something about it calmed her. Maybe it was the fruit trees lining up alongside the driveway, or the fancy lettering of the house's name on the sign out front, or maybe her mind was fixating on something for no particular reason in order to deflect from the beach house.

Minutes later, she pulled into the driveway of the McAdams residence and Sam cleared his throat. 'Thank you, Mrs Chrissie, I had the best time ever and you are really nice.'

She turned in her seat to face the overly complimentary child and smiled. 'Well, thank you. I enjoyed the day too, and you are really nice as well.' He grinned and looked at her hopefully. 'And I'll let your mother know I think you deserve that extra ice-cream tonight.'

His face eased into a wider grin and he leaned back, pleased with himself. There was no point harping on about the toilet block incident; it was just one of Kai's cheeky tricks, and she was sure he'd learnt his lesson. Sam was just an innocent bystander.

They got out of the car and Sarah must have seen them coming because the door opened before they got to it.

'Hi there! How was the fair?' She bent down to welcome Sam home.

'It was extra cool, and I was extra good, so can I have—'

'Extra ice-cream?' Sarah stood. 'If Chrissie says you can, then yes.'

Chrissie nodded.

'Yes!' Sam said. 'Can I show Kai my toy car collection?' The kids were already in the doorway.

'Um...' Chrissie scratched her head.

'You're welcome to come in for a bit if you like, you probably need a seat after all that. Here.' Sarah led the way and pulled out a chair for Chrissie at the casual kitchen table setting.

'Thanks, Sarah, we won't stay long.'

'Cuppa?' Sarah raised her eyebrows. 'Tea, coffee, hot chocolate...'

'Yes thanks, do you have any herbal teas by any chance?'

'I do. Peppermint, green tea, chamomile...'

'Peppermint thanks.'

'Coming right up.' She flicked the switch on the kettle and took two mugs from the high cupboards above the dishwasher.

'Thanks again for taking the boys, it looks like they had a great time. Sam wasn't any trouble I hope?'

Chrissie flicked Sarah's concerns away with her hand. 'No, he was great, and polite. Although he did get a whistle from the lucky dip, so I hope he doesn't make too much noise for you!'

'Ah, no worries. I have a teenage daughter; she makes more noise than Sam.'

Phew. Chrissie remembered when someone had given Kai an electronic toy drum set for his birthday. The cymbals it came with were so high-pitched and irritating she accidentally-on-purpose took the batteries out and told Kai it was broken. It was either that or throw the bloody thing out the window and hope it got crushed by a passing car.

'So, ready for another week of lunch-making and school runs?'

'Does it ever end? The weekends go by so fast.'

'Oh, I know. Just when you've recovered from the previous week the next one creeps up on you. I really think school should be on weekends and weekdays should be free, don't you?'

'Absolutely. A two-day week sounds much better.' Chrissie smiled, and Sarah placed the steaming tea in front of her and took a seat opposite.

'So, how long have you been in this house for?' Chrissie scanned the room. It was well-lived in, but tidy.

'Seven years. Moved in when I was pregnant with Sam. Liam, my husband, built it.'

'Really?'

'Yep. We'd not long been married when we bought the land. Liam was in his element working out the plans with the architect. It's great to have a place that's built with the way you live in mind.'

'It's a great place. You're very lucky.'

'I sure am. What about your place, where is it?'

'Fairly close to Serendipity, and the beach.'

'Wow, great spot. You must love it.' Sarah sipped her tea. 'But you're going to sell, right?'

'Yep.'

'Let me know when you're house hunting and I'll see if I can go with you. I love looking at houses.'

A sense of gratitude flooded Chrissie. Sarah was so nice, so accommodating. Maybe being away from Melinda wouldn't be too hard after all. 'Actually, that'd be great. I could do with an objective eye.'

Sarah's eyes widened and she clicked her fingers. 'Oh, I'm

taking Sam to the aquatic centre tomorrow, Kai's welcome to join us if he likes. My way of paying you back for looking after Sam today.'

Crap. She always dreaded these types of invitations. How could she tell another mother that she'd never taken her own child to swimming lessons? She'd have to eventually, but not yet. There was still time. She just had to wait until she'd dealt with a few things first.

'Oh, thanks, that's nice of you, but there's no need to pay me back. And Kai and I still have some boxes to sort through and unpack. I'd like him to help me, give him some extra responsibility to raise his self-esteem, you know?'

'Of course, yes, he needs to be involved. I think it's a great idea. Boys love to be helpful and strong, lifting boxes and making decisions about where things go.'

Chrissie nodded.

'But if you change your mind, let me know. We'll be going sometime late morning.'

'Sure thing.'

The muffled sound of a guitar vibrated through the wall nearby.

Sarah glanced to the right. 'Oh, that's my daughter. Been in her room all day.' She rolled her eyes.

'Teenagers, huh?'

'You just wait,' Sarah said with a mischievous grin, pointing her finger playfully. 'Sometimes I think the whole changing nappies and night-feeding business is easier than this.'

'Oh dear. I'm trying not to think about it yet. Must be challenging for you with both a child and a teenager.'

Sarah plumped her lips together and nodded. 'I love 'em but they know how to test me. One minute they don't want to leave your side and the next, they can't wait to be away from you. The way my daughter talks, anyone would think I'd raised her in a prison or something. The girl can't wait to leave home, and unfortunately, in a few months time she'll legally be able to.'

'That's tough. I'm sure you've taught her well though, she'll learn how much you've done for her once she's out on her own.'

'I'm hoping. She's still my baby, I want her to stay here a little bit longer!' Sarah pinched her thumb and forefinger together and squinted.

The guitar strumming became louder, and a soft voice wafted through the walls. It kept stopping and starting, like she was practising something and trying to get it right before continuing, then she resumed. A rhythmic melody got Chrissie's foot tapping, and when the girl's voice sang along, perfectly in tune, and hitting a few notes Chrissie's voice would no doubt crack if she attempted, her hand flew to her chest.

'Wow, your daughter is amazing.'

Sarah smiled, a pink glow emanating from her cheeks.

'Really, really amazing.' Chrissie leaned forward on the table.

'I know,' Sarah replied. 'Takes after Uncle Drew.' Sarah's hand flew to cover her mouth as if she didn't mean to let that slip.

Uncle Drew? Chrissie's foot stooped its tapping and her breath halted. 'You don't mean *Drew Williams* by any chance, do you?'

'Oops.' Sarah sunk into her chair. 'All the locals know I'm his sister but I try not to let the cat out of the bag too early with new friends.' She raised her palms up in an 'oh well, too late' gesture.

'Wow, he's really your brother?'

'The one and only.'

'Sorry, it's just such a coincidence, because...' Oh, she wasn't supposed to say anything to anyone. But she *was* his sister; surely she knew he was staying here? But what if she didn't and there was some kind of family feud going on, and by letting her know she was working with Drew she put her foot in it and made things worse?

'Because what?' Sarah asked.

'Oh nothing, it's just...' Surely Drew would have chosen to go somewhere else than Tarrin's Bay if he didn't want to see his family? No, they must know. They had to know. 'I know him.'

'You know him?' Sarah's eyes bulged.

'I met him only recently.'

'Recently... as in this month?'

'Maybe.' Chrissie narrowed her eyes to suss out the situation. She wouldn't be breaking her contract by revealing what someone already knew.

Realisation dawned in Sarah's face and she leaned back in the chair. 'You don't *work* at Serendipity do you?'

Relief flooded Chrissie's bloodstream. 'Yes, I do!' She made a show of wiping her brow. 'I didn't want to risk it getting out in case you weren't aware he was here, I'm under strict instructions to keep things quiet.'

'So I hear, yes. Poor bro, not being able to walk down the street without being mobbed. So what do you do at the retreat?'

'I'm a yoga instructor.'

'Are you *his* instructor?'

Chrissie nodded and smiled.

'He told me he was having private lessons, I had no idea it was you!' She shook her head. 'Small world.'

'It sure is.' Chrissie couldn't believe it. A week ago she didn't know these people, and now she was getting up close and personal with not only her favourite celebrity but his sister too? So much for this being a sleepy small town.

'No surprise you're involved with something physical, I was going to ask you how you keep your figure looking so good. I'm totally jealous.' She winked.

'Oh, stop it. I still have some lovely stretch marks courtesy of my son.'

'Aren't they the worst?' Sarah scrunched her face up, and

Chrissie smiled at the bond developing with this down to earth woman.

'They are indeed. And nothing — nothing — gets rid of them, even those organic oils I've been told work wonders. Nup. Stuck with the damn things.' Chrissie said, and Sarah laughed.

'Well if I knew you and my brother were pals I would have asked you over for dinner. He's coming over tonight.'

Chrissie gulped.

'Would you like to stay? We're a friendly bunch, I'm sure he wouldn't mind, he mentioned how great his yoga teacher was.'

He did?

Dinner with Drew Williams? The thought was exhilarating and terrifying at the same time. Yoga was one thing, having conversation over a home-cooked meal was another.

'Oh, no, I don't want to intrude. He's probably looking forward to catching up with you. I'll leave you to have some family time.'

'You sure?'

Definitely. Absolutely. This would be too much excitement for one day. 'Yes, you enjoy the night with your brother. Kai's probably tired anyway, I'll try to get him to bed early so we can start the sorting at the break of dawn.'

That's if she'd be able to sleep tonight. This detour in her life was turning into movie-worthy material, and even though it made her nervous, she couldn't wait to see what the next scene had in store.

CHAPTER ELEVEN

The sun glowed orange as it hung low behind the hills, outlining them in a long curved line, much like a heartbeat on an ECG. Drew could almost feel the beat of the landscape itself, the low, earthy hum he sensed as his eyes absorbed his surroundings. Nature had its own song. It wasn't audible, just a feeling, a knowing, and it inspired him. *No place like home*, he thought, remembering Dorothy's line from *The Wizard of Oz*.

He lifted off the seat of the bike as he pedalled uphill, blood pulsing through his veins and muscles heating up. Serendipity had provided use of these wheels, and he revelled in the freedom to move and get where he wanted to go without having to hire a cab or limo, and to zip through the streets in town without anyone recognising him. After cycling up into the hills, he stopped for a moment and took a swig of water, then adjusted his cap and sunglasses, gazing over the huge expanse of ocean. The water too, had its own rhythm, a constant ebb and flow of energy, pulsing in and out, under and over, and he could never tire of watching the waves roll in to shore.

He hopped back on the bike and turned around, waiting for a lull in the highway traffic to cross to the other side, conscious of needing to keep moving to avoid being noticed. It wasn't far to get from Serendipity to Sarah's house, but he'd wanted some time to just ride and feel free, get the wind in his face and be out in the open. He rode into town and swerved into the cul-de-sac where his sister lived, excitement at seeing his niece and nephew bubbling away inside.

He leaned the bike against the porch and stepped onto the welcome mat, tapping the door with his fist.

'He's here!' Sam called from inside, followed by quick, muffled footsteps. 'I'll open it!'

The door opened and Drew glanced down at his nephew. 'Oh I'm sorry, I'm looking for Sam, but you're much older and bigger. Maybe I've got the wrong house.' He made a show of turning away.

'No, silly! It's me, I'm Sam!'

'Get outta here! Really?' Drew bent down and grasped him by the shoulders. 'You're practically a man now.' He pulled his nephew in for a rough-and-tumble hug with lots of wriggling and back-patting.

'I'm six and a half.'

'So I hear.' He stood. 'Great to see you, buddy. Where are your parents and sister?' Sam yanked him inside and Sarah walked in from out the back.

'Hey, stranger, welcome to our humble abode!' She kissed his cheek and wrapped him in a hug.

'Good to see you.' He pulled back and noticed the pink glow of her skin. 'You're looking well.'

'Thanks, not looking too bad yourself.' She ran her hand across his head, sending little tingles across his scalp. 'Where did all your hair go?'

'I decided to go for easy maintenance,' he said. 'Plus, if I start going bald it'll be less noticeable.' He winked.

'Gemma, look who's here!' Sarah called out, and a few

moments later the bathroom door down the hall opened and his niece emerged, her hair all wavy and styled, eyes lined with black, lips a glossy fuchsia. How could she have grown that much since the last time he'd seen her? She looked about twenty-five.

'Drew!' She ran into his arms. 'I can't believe you're here! You look so cool, how's L.A.? Are you ready for your tour? I wish I could go back with you!'

'Hey, hey, one question at a time.' He kissed her cheek. 'Don't forget to breathe.' His mouth turned up into a smile, remembering those exact words he'd written as part of a new song he'd been working on. Who would have thought that emptying one's mind during meditation could actually fill one's mind with great ideas? Or maybe Chrissie was his muse. He should take time off more often.

'Let your uncle settle in a bit, I'm sure he doesn't need you acting like a journalist after what he's been through.'

'Sorry, I'm just so excited. I can't wait to show you my new songs. You're still coming back over tomorrow to help me out, right?'

'Of course, wouldn't miss it. Might even show you some new stuff I've been working on myself.'

'Really? Awesome!'

'Uncle Drew, look what I got today.' Sam covered a whistle with his lips and blew, his cheeks becoming round, like a puffer fish.

'Oh, Sam!' Sarah covered her ears. 'That's a bit of a loud way to welcome our visitor.'

Drew laughed. He'd missed this family chaos. 'It's nothing, my ears have been immune to loud noises for years now. Where'd you get that?'

'The country fair. I also rode a pony, and went on the huge slide, and ate a toffee apple, and—'

'Sam, there'll be plenty of time over dinner for filling Uncle

Drew in about your day.' She turned to Drew. 'Come on outside, can I get you a beer?'

'No beer for me, thanks, taking a break from alcohol for a while. Anything else you've got is fine.' Drew walked through the living room, Sam hanging at his side, and stepped outside to the patio.

'Hey mate, how's it goin'?' Sarah's husband, Liam, said, stretching out his hand and when Drew shook it, giving him a man-slap on the back.

'Good, yourself? How's business?'

'Busy as always, but great.'

'I see you've put on a new deck.' Drew gestured to the raised area a few steps above the patio.

'Yeah, took me long enough. Have to fit in our own home improvements around my schedule.'

'Well it looks great, I think Sam likes it.' The boy was on the deck, playing air guitar and making guitar noises with his voice. Another musician in the family?

Sarah handed Drew a mineral water and he took a welcome sip, bubbles fizzing down his throat.

'What do you think, too much?' Gemma came outside and held out her arm, multiple silver bangles jingling around it.

'It might be', 'No, I like it', Sarah and Drew said at the same time. Oops. He should know to always get the mother's permission before giving his opinion on something relating to fashion.

He bit his bottom lip and glanced at his sister who shook her head and mumbled, 'Men.'

'So should I wear them or what?' Gemma asked.

'Whatever your mum thinks, Gem.' Drew held up his hands in defeat. 'Probably best as a female decision.'

'Okay, wear them. They do match your earrings, I guess.' Sarah said.

Gemma nodded a smile. 'Cool. Just wanted to make sure.' She glanced at Drew. 'Sorry I won't be hanging around, I wanted to take the opportunity while I had it.'

'No worries, I'll see you tomorrow. You go and enjoy your gig with your dad.'

'Thanks, it's gonna be awesome. The last one we did someone even stood and clapped, I couldn't believe it.' The girl was beaming. He knew that feeling of performance euphoria all too well. The moment he realised he'd won *Search for a Star* at age nineteen was the most incredible moment of his life, one he'd shared with a huge percentage of Australian television viewers. Not much had been private since then; he'd grown used to living life in the spotlight, but he'd also grown tired of it. Not tired of doing what he loved — writing songs, making albums, and performing — but the judgement and lack of privacy that came along with that.

'It's only the beginning for you. I'm sure tonight will be just as great.' He tapped her on the arm.

'I'll get my guitar,' she said, walking back inside.

'Drew,' Sarah said, sidling up close. 'I was hoping tomorrow you could have a bit of a talk with her, you know, tell her it's not all fun and parties? She's got it in her head that she's moving to the city as soon as she's eighteen, but I don't think she's ready. She's got stars in her eyes. She needs to know what it's really like, from an insider.' Sarah's face relayed concern.

'Sure, I'll talk to her. But I don't think I should flat out tell her to hold off, otherwise she'll rebel. I remember what it was like at her age, having musical skills and feeling like you have the world at your feet. It's pretty empowering. I don't want to dampen her enthusiasm.'

'I know, but just sort of give her an idea that it's hard work and that not everyone is as nice off stage as they are on stage.'

'I'll be honest, sure, but I think it's good that she wants to go for her dreams. Look what it did for me, for our whole family. We've never had to worry about finances.'

'I know, I know, and I'm so grateful for everything you've shared with us. I just...' She hung her head and clamped her lips together, and Drew suddenly realised what this was about. His baby sister was losing her baby. She'd only known motherhood, and from a very young age, and now everything was changing. If Gemma left, it would be like a part of her had gone too. She'd practically grown up alongside her daughter, became an adult while becoming a mother. Mostly on her own in the beginning too. She didn't know how to be anything else now. Sure, she had Sam, but Drew imagined it must be different, that mother-daughter bond, plus the fact that Gemma was her first born.

'You want her to stay a child a little bit longer, right?' He rubbed her arm.

Sarah looked up, red rims framing her eyes. She nodded. 'All of a sudden she's a young woman. I don't know how to deal with that. When I was her age I was pregnant.'

'It's a bit of a culture shock, eh? You'll handle it fine, just like you have all these years. You're the strongest woman I know.' Well, apart from the woman who encouraged his body to form strange shapes and postures every weekday this month, but that was a different kind of strength.

Sarah flicked his compliment away. 'Oh, I just did what had to be done. Took it one day at a time.'

'Exactly, and you'll do the same now. Your daughter has a talent, a talent that should be used. Sure, encourage her to take her time while she's young, but as soon as you try to force her to hold back, she'll do the opposite, you know that.'

'Yeah, I know. Mum was so strict with me not going to parties until I turned eighteen, and the one night I snuck out... well, we all know what happened after that!' She laughed. 'And here I am now.' She held out her arms. 'Life certainly goes in unexpected directions sometimes.'

'Tell me about it.' Drew hugged an arm around his sister and dawdled over to the barbeque that Liam was prepping. 'So, what can I do? Want me to grab the meat from the kitchen?'

'Oh, yes, thanks. It's all in the fridge. I better get onto those salads.' Sarah said, wiping the corner of her eye with her middle finger. 'Sam, don't climb the railing, honey!' she said as she walked back inside.

A knock on the door sounded and Drew turned to face the entrance. A lump formed in his throat.

'Gemma, your father's here!' Sarah called out, walking to the door.

She opened it to reveal a slightly overweight Barry who, ironically, had been called The Stick by other kids in school owing to his long lanky frame, which had more than filled out with age. His desk job probably hadn't helped.

'Hey, Baz, she's ready I think.' Sarah welcomed him in then returned to the kitchen, like he was just part of the furniture. They'd gotten over their issues years ago and were like old mates now, but for Drew, Barry still made his muscles tense and his stomach turn. It was hard to get over a grudge when the other person had one of their own against you.

Drew gave a curt nod. 'Barry.'

'Drew.' He nodded back.

'It's been a while.'

'Yeah, it has. How's L.A.?'

'Oh, you know... same old, same old.'

'Actually I don't. Never been there.'

Damn. Foot in mouth.

Drew scratched his head. 'Well, nothing beats Tarrin's Bay, I can tell you that.'

'You haven't been back for a while. How long you stayin'?'

Barry's hands slipped into his pockets. He obviously didn't want to shake hands.

'Going home on the 1st of March.'

'Right.' He nodded.

A clicking of heels on the floor became louder as Gemma emerged from her room, guitar in hand. 'Hey, Dad. Ready to go?'

'Absolutely.' He leaned forward and pecked her on the cheek. 'We're going to rock Café Lagoon tonight, aren't we, huh?'

'For sure.' She smiled.

'It's not quite Wembley Stadium, but there's something great about a small, intimate crowd, don't ya think?'

'I'd be happy with any type of crowd Dad, and Wembley Stadium? Oh man, I so hope I get there one day!'

'There's no rush, honey.' Sarah came over and hugged her daughter. 'But have a good night.'

Barry ushered his daughter to the door. 'You can achieve whatever you want, sweetheart. You've got what it takes, that's for sure.'

'Thanks Dad,' she said, walking outside, then turning around briefly to wave. 'Bye Drew. See you tomorrow. Shame you can't come tonight.' She pouted and turned away again.

'Yeah, shame. But that's the price of fame, eh, Drew?' Barry said when Gemma was out of earshot.

His stomach turned again. There was definitely a double meaning in Barry's words. He knew how to make him feel guilty for what he did all those years ago, and even though Drew knew he'd done what any of his other band mates would have done, given the same choice, it still gnawed away at him.

'Don't listen to him,' Sarah said, when Barry and Gemma drove off.

Drew chewed on his lip. 'After all these years, he's still mad at me.'

'Well, aren't you still a little mad at him too?' She raised her eyebrows.

'Well, yes, but that's different. That's about a big brother wanting to protect his little sister.' He pinched her cheek.

'I don't need protecting now, Drew. I'm not seventeen any more. I'm a thirty-five-year-old mother of two, and I'm finally happily married. What's done is done, don't keep blaming Barry for something I played a fifty percent role in.'

'Sorry, can't hold back those brotherly instincts, I guess. But you wanted to travel and see the world, and then he — my mate — goes and gets my little sister pregnant. I was so angry at him at the time; I didn't even know he had the hots for you. Explains why he always wanted to do band practice at our house instead of his.'

'Yeah, well, he was a teenager. Hormones and all. And it was almost twenty years ago, let's just forget about it.'

'I would if he would — he's never forgiven me.'

'Well maybe February will be the month for forgiveness. You two should talk while you're here, sort things out once and for all.'

'We'll see. I have a few other things on my mind to deal with too, you know.'

'Yes, I know. Sorry, how is it all going?'

He rubbed the back of his neck. 'Actually, let's not talk about it now. Let's just enjoy a nice dinner, hey?'

'Sounds good.' Sarah plonked a bag of spinach leaves into a salad bowl, then glanced up. 'Oh, I almost forgot. Your yoga teacher is very nice, isn't she?' Sarah grinned.

'What?' Drew gulped. 'You met her? How did you know? Did she say something?'

'No, no, of course not. I opened my big mouth, that's all.'

Drew leaned on the kitchen bench, curious.

'Her son, Kai, is friends with Sam. She took them both to the country fair today. I invited her in for a cuppa afterwards and she heard Gemma singing.' Sarah tipped a container of cherry tomatoes into the bowl. 'I blurted out that she takes after Uncle Drew and the poor woman's jaw practically dropped to the floor.'

A grin slid into Drew's cheeks.

'Even then she didn't say anything, but was acting strange, so I eventually got it out of her that she was teaching you for the month. I think she was scared of breaking her contract, but obviously I already knew you were here.'

Drew straightened up. 'She mentioned she was going to the country fair with her son, I didn't know he was bringing a friend. That's great, might help him be happier about going to school.'

'It was a last-minute thing... hang on, it sounds like you know a whole lot about Chrissie and her son. Have you been spending time together outside of the yoga studio?'

'Of course not. We do yoga, we talk, nothing else to it.'

'She's nice, I like her. Sounds like she's been through a bit though — divorce, her aunt's death...'

'Yeah, I think there's something else going on beneath the surface. I can tell she's trying to be strong, but... I don't know, just a feeling.'

'You and your feelings. Always the intuitive one, aren't you?'

'I find people interesting, that's all. Probably why I get caught up with ones like Jolene, I get this idea in my head that I can help them.'

'Maybe you can. Chrissie I mean, if she needs it that is, not Jolene.'

'Something tells me she doesn't want any help. I think she wants to keep putting on a brave face and pretending everything's okay.'

'Don't we all?' She tilted her head to the side and smiled softly.

'True.' Drew picked up the tray of meat and walked out of the kitchen. He'd been putting on one of those faces for a long time. Even when he thought he was alone, you could never tell if anyone was hiding in nearby bushes with a camera rolling. At least at Serendipity he'd have a chance to relax and be himself, have some much needed privacy, and prepare himself for the media attention when he returned home. But after enjoying his first week back in the bay, part of him was wondering if he even wanted to go back to L.A.

CHAPTER TWELVE

C hrissie's phone beeped as she got out of her car in the Serendipity parking lot.

Please don't be the school, please don't be the school...

She eyed the text message:

> Hi Chrissie, how's Kai? Did you try out the reward thing with him? More importantly, how are you? Mel xx

She closed the car door with a flick of her hip and keyed in a reply:

> I'm good. Thanks for advice, Kai went happily to school rest of last week, took to a fair as a reward & he made a new friend. As for today... he kicked up a fuss again, can you believe it? Will have to think up new reward, or get his dad to come up with one. Gotta go, have a good week xx

She pushed open the door to the staff entrance and tried to push away the image of her son's face this morning. He'd had the whole 'but Mummy, I want to be with you and cuddle all day' look going on, which always tugged at her heartstrings. At least he hadn't used superhuman six-year-old strength to glue his body to the spot where no amount of tugging or lifting would move him. He was too big now, too heavy. When he was younger and he pulled that classic childhood trick she could still pick him up and heave him to where he needed to go, but now, she'd probably end up with a slipped disc or a hernia.

'Chrissie, hi,' Helena said, gesturing her into her office.

'Morning, Helena. How are you?'

'I'm great, how are you going with Mr Williams?'

Helena remained standing, indicating this was to be just a quick meeting.

'It's going really well. He's a pleasure to teach.' She hoped that didn't come across too keen. If she showed any indication of being smitten Helena would no doubt get Damon to take over the role. Not that she *was* smitten, she barely knew the guy. If she felt anything, it was purely an appreciation of his incredible musical skills and entertaining ability. Wasn't it? But somehow, after knowing him only a week, and meeting his sister, it felt like she'd known him a lot longer. Yoga did that. It stripped away the surface stuff and opened people up to simple, human, connection: with themselves, the universe, and with the people in the class. A room full of meditating people was quite powerful; you could sense a lifting of energy, like a positive vibe, wafting through the room. With only two people the effect, although less, was more palpable. Chrissie was comfortable around Drew now — most of the time. When she was doing her thing, in her element, she could relax and be herself without all the baggage that she came with.

'He says you're a pleasure to be taught by.' Helena smiled.

'He does? Oh, well that's good. I'm glad he's enjoying the lessons.'

'How's your son going? No more tummy aches?'

'No more, thankfully.' Chrissie tapped her knuckles on the wooden desk.

'Good. Well, your morning class awaits. I'll let you get organised. And keep up the good work with the private lessons. Let me know if I can help you with anything.'

'Will do, thanks Helena.' Chrissie walked out, waving at Damon on his phone in the staff lounge.

Despite Kai's reluctance this morning to attend school, maybe this week would turn out just fine. A sense of anticipation bubbled inside, not for the group class she was about to teach, but for what would come afterwards.

'Hello, hello,' Drew's energetic voice said as he entered the studio. 'Ready for an awesome week ahead?'

Chrissie shook the flame away from the match she'd used to light the candle, and smiled. 'Yes indeed. You look like you've had a good night's sleep. Recovered from your jet lag yet?'

'Pretty much. But I'll have to un-recover as soon as I get home next month.'

'True.' There it was again, the reminder that Drew was only here for a short time. In three weeks, he'd be gone. Out of Tarrin's Bay, Australia, and her life. The thought twisted uncomfortably inside her head. 'So, how is your new song going? I'm glad the meditation helped.'

He rubbed his hands together. 'Yes, it's turning out well. I'm playing around with some variations in the melody and still have to write the second and third verse, but I like it.'

'I hope I get to hear it one day.'

'I hope so too.' He smiled. 'I might have to dedicate it to you and the beautiful place that is Serendipity for inspiring me.' He walked to the window and looked out over the garden.

'Oh, I bet it was just that you'd quietened your mind, that's all. Relaxation puts your brain into an alpha state, which can open up the well of creativity and intuition. That's why you often think of things or get ideas right before falling asleep, when waking up, or even in the shower.' Why was she trying to rationalise his creativity and downplay his compliment? She should just say 'that's lovely of you, thanks', and smile like a normal person, but instead she was talking about alpha brain waves and getting ideas in the shower? *Settle down, Chrissie.*

'Ahh, I often get ideas in the shower. If they're good ones I can be in there for ages. Good for my creativity but not so good for saving water.' He grinned.

Why did he have to mention showering? Hang on, I was the one who brought it up, and now all I can think of is Drew in the shower... steam... water dripping down his skin... stop!

Chrissie cleared her throat. 'I guess you've got to go with the inspiration when it strikes.'

'And it often strikes when you least expect it.'

'Most things do.'

He nodded slowly. 'They do, don't they? Life is one long journey with unexpected twists and turns. Bit like yoga, though the twists and turns are expected.'

'Yes, and they can be controlled, unlike life.'

'If only life was like one long yoga class... time to warm up, prepare, know what's coming, and time to rest and recover here and there.'

Chrissie admired Drew's analogy as she took the mats from the shelf. 'Sounds perfect.' That was exactly why she loved yoga; it empowered her and gave her strength. If a pose was difficult she could ease back a little, try again later, if one was easy she could fully embrace it and enjoy the moment. With yoga she was in the driver's seat, with life she was a worried passenger clinging to the seat as life swerved her around corners and leapt over bumps, knowing there could be a collision at any time and constantly bracing herself for impact. Panic attacks had taken her sense of security, made her live in fear, and although she had mostly recovered from them, their resurgence recently had rattled her confidence. But she would get through it all, somehow. She had to. There was a young man depending on her, and she couldn't let him down. She wanted nothing more than to give Kai the long happy childhood she didn't have. At least, she *did* have one until it had been cut short. She was determined not to let that happen to her son. Whatever it took, she would take care of him, guide him, and keep him safe.

'I heard Kai had a great time at the country fair.'

Chrissie dropped one of the mats. 'Um, yes. He did.' She eyed him with a questioning look.

He smiled. 'My sister told me all about it.'

'Ahh, so she told you that we... that I... that we're...'

'That she knows you're my fabulous yoga instructor, yes.' He bent down and picked up the fallen mat, placing it in the middle of the floor, Chrissie placing hers nearby.

'You're the most complimentary person I've met.' Chrissie tucked a loose strand of hair behind her ear.

'And you're the most *complimentable* person I've met. If that's even a word?'

'Well it is now.' She grinned.

'I'll have to speak to those Oxford people and see what they can do about adding it to the dictionary,' Drew said.

'For sure. And while you're at it, see if they can add "healthious". Kai made that one up, for food that is both healthy, and—'

'Delicious?'

'Yes.'

'Healthious.' He nodded. 'I like it.'

'I'll let him know you said that,' Chrissie replied. 'Oh.' No she wouldn't. Couldn't. Not that a child would leak to the media the news of a celebrity in town, but you couldn't be too careful with schoolyard gossip. 'Don't worry, I won't really tell him. He doesn't even know about you. I mean, he knows about *you*, he's heard your music when I play it in the car, and...' *Oh God, save me now.*

Drew held up a hand. 'It's okay, really. I know what you mean.' He took a few steps closer. 'You play my music in your car?'

Heat rushed up her spine, encircling each vertebra like a spiralling tsunami of fire. 'Um, yes. Sometimes. Not that often, just when I feel like it. Not that I don't always feel like listening to your music, just when the mood strikes, and—'

'Chrissie. He placed a hand on her arm. 'I'm flattered. Thank you.' Sunlight rebounded off his eyes and landed on hers, and she blinked twice, the variations of blue hues in his irises resembling the ocean.

'Sounds like your niece has taken after you,' Chrissie said, hoping she didn't appear to be prying into his personal life. 'I heard her sing. She's fantastic.'

A subtle glow emanated from Drew's face. 'Isn't she? I spent a few hours jamming with her yesterday. She's got some great ideas for songs, and plays the guitar like it's an—'

'Extra limb?'

He turned the palm of one of his hands upwards. 'Exactly. Though I can't take all the genetic credit; her dad's got some mean musical skills too.'

'Really?'

'Yeah, he plays a few local gigs, even took Gemma to one on Saturday night.'

'Not at Café Lagoon by any chance?'

'Yes, actually. You been there?'

'I was there on Friday. The young barista mentioned they had live music on occasion. He was quite the salesman, made great coffee too.'

'So you do drink coffee? You're not one of those diehard vegetarian organic free-range natural yogis?'

She laughed. 'Not exactly, a bit hard to be one when your child wants sausage sandwiches and potato chips. I do follow a clean diet, but there's room in life for treats in moderation.'

'Good to hear. I thought maybe my yoga teacher would force me to eat nothing but fruit and vegetables and tofu. But you, well, you're my kind of yogi.' The way his lips moved when he spoke was hypnotic.

'Well, I really should be advising you to follow the yogic way of living, but I also know that we live in a world where sometimes we just have to do the best with what we've got. Some people can get so obsessed by what they eat, the stress causes more problems than not eating the unhealthy food!'

'I'd choose me some pizza over stress any day.'

'Stress is much worse for the body.' And didn't she know it. It had taken years to get off painkillers for her headaches, but thanks to natural medicine and consistent yoga practise, she only got them occasionally now.

'I can imagine.' Drew glanced to the side, and Chrissie sensed that he was holding in some stress of his own beneath his cheery, positive persona.

'So do you think your niece will follow in your footsteps to a career in music?

His gaze returned to her. 'Yes, I think so. Though Sarah's not too keen for her to jump in at the deep end. Gemma, of course, wants to get started as soon as possible. Now that she's finished school and nearing eighteen, well, the world is at her feet.'

'She's lucky to have you to help her.'

'Thanks, I love seeing how far she's come. I do try not to step on her father's toes though, it's better if he can be the one to guide her.'

'I'm sure he'd be wrapt to have you give her some inside knowledge of the industry.'

Drew frowned. 'Hmm, not so much.'

Chrissie narrowed her eyes.

'We used to be mates. When we were teenagers,' Drew said. 'We set up a band and practised on weekends and after school. He also plays guitar and sings, though he always said he had more of a back-up singer's voice. Anyway, long story short, he's never really forgiven me for leaving the band in favour of a solo career.'

'Oh, that's tough. But surely, I mean, that was so many years ago, he hasn't let sleeping dogs lie?'

'Tried to. We've seen each other occasionally of course, on account of my niece being his daughter, but unfortunately, when I left our friendship went down the gurgler.'

'That's such a shame.'

'Yeah.' He scratched his chin.

Chrissie thought back to the television talent show where she'd first seen Drew as a long-haired, heart-throb teenage star in the making. 'Hang on; was he on that show with you?'

'You saw it?' His eyes widened.

'I have a vague recollection, yes.' And a not-so-vague recollection of racking up a decent sum on her mother's phone bill by voting for him a zillion times. Oh, and crying with joy along with a friend when Drew won the show.

'Barry and two other mates auditioned with me, we called ourselves The Bay Boys, can you believe it?' Drew poked a finger into his mouth to feign puking, then laughed. 'The judges said we were good, but they would only put me through to the next round as a solo artist. They liked the boys, but thought I'd do better on my own. So they got me to sing solo, and that sealed the deal. It was either stick with my mates and leave the show, or leave my mates and go through on my own.'

Chrissie shook her head. 'I can't imagine how hard a decision that must have been. But it was totally understandable you went for it. I mean, they would have done the same thing I'm sure.'

'Well at first I decided not to go through. The judges gave me to the end of the day to decide, and I thought nope, I can't do that to them. I told the boys, but they said "Look, Drew, you shouldn't have to pass up this opportunity because of us. You'll regret it." Barry kept quiet though. I knew I'd regret something either way, and when my mates encouraged me to go for it, I did. Not realising at the time how Barry really felt.'

'So now he feels like you abandoned him for something bigger and better.'

'That's pretty much it. His career never extended beyond casual gigs, and I think he resents me for that.'

'And your other band mates?'

Drew rested his hands loosely on his hips. 'They were happy for me. Adam went on to become a high school music teacher and Craig now owns his own real estate agency — go figure.'

'So you never wish you'd pursued a career out of the spotlight?'

'There've been a few times I wished I could turn back time and be anonymous, do what I want without having an audience, but once I get on that stage and share my passion, there's nothing like it.' Drew's eyes shone, a satisfied smile gracing his face.

'Some people are just born for it, I think.'

'True.' He tapped her arm. 'And you, you're born for teaching yoga.'

Chrissie turned her head to the side and bit on her smile. 'I used to think I was born for journalism.'

'You were a journalist?' Drew crossed his arms over his chest, and a furrow formed between his eyebrows.

'Yes. Though that part of my life is long gone. I don't keep up with media now, there could be a cure for cancer making news headlines and I wouldn't hear about it.' It occurred to Chrissie that Drew was probably uncomfortable around media people. She'd worked with genuine professionals who cared about covering the truth, but there were a few who liked to stretch it, twist and mould a story to attract an audience. Celebrities were often the victims of such ploys, and no doubt Drew had been exposed to that at some point.

He dropped his arms to his side and his face relaxed. 'Oh, right. So what made you leave the industry?'

Chrissie rubbed the back of her neck. 'Ah, got a bit stressful I guess. Lost the passion for it. I had my time, but needed to move on to something different.' It was the truth, but not the whole truth. She didn't exactly want to get into a discussion about the tragic story she'd covered which led to the resurgence of her panic attacks. Despite that awful time in her life, in a way it had been a good thing. It led her to yoga. First as therapy, then as a career. Once she became accustomed to the peace and control it brought, she couldn't go back. If she could bring peace and strength to others, she'd live a happy life.

Drew held his arms out to the side and glanced around. 'And different it is. Do you think you'll always teach yoga?'

'Yes, I think so. I mean, who knows what the future will bring, but I feel like I've found my true passion. And I'd love to eventually run a yoga retreat, work more intensively with a smaller group of people.' Visions of doing yoga outside in the fresh air at dawn floated through her mind. Celebrating a new day and preparing the mind and body for the activities ahead. *One day. One day...*

'That's a great idea.' Drew tapped his chin. 'I know a fair few music industry people who would jump at the chance to have a calming retreat away from their busy lives. You could even tailor it to,' he made quotes with his fingers, '"celebrities".'

Wow, she'd never thought of that. They'd certainly have the money to pay for an exclusive high-end retreat, but who was she to be responsible for their wellbeing? Then again, she *was* getting a bit of V.I.P. experience working with Drew. Maybe he would put in a good word for her with others.

'I could spread the word, put in a good word for you,' he said.

Was he a mind reader? Chrissie held back a smile.

'It's a wonderful idea, I don't know if it's possible to sustain it, but time will tell.'

'Think big, I always say. You never know what might happen. Sometimes you've got to take a leap of faith.'

Drew could practically pass as an inspirational speaker. Did he even need yoga and meditation, or time away? He seemed so together and balanced.

'I'll be sure to remember that. Thanks.' She smiled. 'First, though, I need to get my aunt's house in order so I can sell it.'

'Oh yeah, how's it going?'

'Slow. I'm just making plans at the moment, I'll do a few small things when I can and start more significant renovations next school holidays.'

'Do you have any family close by to help?'

There it was, the inevitable family question that always seeped into conversation at some point between new friends. Friends?

'No, I don't.'

'Bummer. Scattered around the country are they? Or overseas even?'

'No, no, I just don't have any.'

'At all?'

'Nope. It's just me and Kai left.'

Drew ran a hand over his head and shook it. 'Geez, I'm sorry Chrissie. Foot in mouth disease and all that.'

'It's okay, don't worry.'

'So your aunt was the last, er...'

'Remaining relative, yes. My mum died quite a few years ago, before Kai was born. She had ovarian cancer.' Chrissie's head dropped a little toward her chest.

'Oh man, that's tough.'

Chrissie nodded.

'And your dad? If you don't mind my asking.'

'He died when I was a baby. Train accident at Granville.'

Drew's eyes went wide. 'I remember hearing about that. Holy crap.' He shook his head again.

'Yeah. It was one of those wrong place wrong time situations. If he'd sat in a different carriage, he may still be here.' She gulped down a lump of sadness. 'But you can't dwell on the past. What happened, happened, and you've just got to move forward.' Which is what she'd been trying to do all her life, even though she felt like she was attached to her past with a strong length of industrial rope that wouldn't break, trapping her in its hold forever.

'I really am sorry, Chrissie. You've been through such a lot.'

No need to bring up the issue of her sister's death, the poor guy would probably need intravenous Prozac afterwards.

Chrissie shrugged and raised her hands. 'Thanks. That's life I guess. You never know what it has in store for you.'

'No you don't,' he said. 'But you *can* create the life you want. You've done that, by following your heart to a yoga career, and working towards your goal of owning a retreat. You'll get there, Chrissie, I know you will.'

He placed his hand against her arm and gave it a slight but definite rub, sending tingles across her skin, not only at his touch, but also at the conviction in his words. He really believed in her.

He had faith in her. His belief straightened her spine and raised her chin.

'That means a lot, thank you.' She offered a grateful smile. 'Well I better practise what I preach and teach my stuff.' She gestured to the yoga mat and Drew stepped onto it. 'Let's forget about the past for now and think only about the immediate future. By the end of this class I want you to be a pro at *Ardha Chandrasana*.' She placed her hands on her hips in a show of authority.

'As long as I don't have to spell it,' Drew replied with a cheeky grin.

CHAPTER THIRTEEN

'And when you're ready, slowly open your eyes.' Chrissie opened her own and eased herself up off the floor, a calm sense of peace enveloping her as it always did after a yoga session and lying down in *Shavasana*. She rotated her ankles and stretched her arms above her head to wake up her body, then glanced at Drew, still in *Shavasana*. Well, she *had* said 'when you're ready'. She stepped a little closer and repeated, 'Whenever you're ready, open your eyes.' Nothing. She leaned over him, deep rhythmic breathing making his chest slowly rise and fall. The guy was asleep. Chrissie held back a chuckle and turned away for a moment, then back again.

What should I do? Do I wake him up or let him sleep?

She nibbled on her bottom lip and glanced around the room. She'd had students fall asleep before, but they'd always wake up when other members of the class shuffled out. This was different, it was just her and him. She thought if she moved towards the corner table to get her things, the movement and sounds might rouse him, but her legs wouldn't budge. She stood over him, watching the hypnotic movement of his chest, taking in the contours of his gorgeous face. Her fingers wanted to trace them, slide across his skin, curve around his jawline. They tingled at the possibility. *Oh for God's sake, wake the man up and put an end to the awkward situation!*

She bent over and reached out her hand, preparing to touch his shoulder and give it a gentle shake, when his eyes blinked open. Chrissie lurched backwards. 'Sorry, I was just...' *watching you in a completely unprofessional way.* 'Just about to wake you up.' Heat crept across her face.

Drew rubbed his eyes. 'Did I really fall asleep? The last thing I remember is you telling me to breathe deeply and relax my muscles.'

'You were out of it.' She grinned.

'Sorry!' He laughed, easing up into a seated position with his hands supporting his weight behind him. 'How rude of me.' He rubbed his fingers across his forehead and shook his head, still smiling.

'You must still be jet-lagged. It's no problem.'

'How long was I out?'

'Not long. I only finished the meditation a couple of minutes ago. I didn't know whether to wake you or not.'

'It's better if I don't nap, otherwise I won't sleep at night. Nothing worse than insomnia.'

Didn't she know it. She'd suffered for years as a teenager.

'A few minutes of napping shouldn't affect your sleep tonight. Lucky I didn't fall asleep too or we'd both be in trouble.'

He caught her eye and his smile widened.

'Yeah, can't have you sleeping with me on the job.'

Did he just say what I think he said? Chrissie's mouth dropped open a tad and after a moment, so did Drew's.

'Oh my God, that sounded better in my head!' His cheeks grew pink and Chrissie tried to contain her laughter. 'I'm sorry, I didn't mean... what I meant was...'

'Sleeping, *as well as you*, on the job, right?' she suggested.

'Exactly. Geez, I must be *really* jet-lagged, it's messing with my head!'

'Forget about it, God knows I've had more than a few faux pas in my life.' But his took the cake, especially as it was actually true in the literal sense. Sleeping with guests or students was, of course, forbidden. It was even listed in her job agreement: staff members will refrain from any relationships of a romantic or sexual nature with Serendipity guests, clients, or students. Not that it would happen with Drew anyway; he was her student, she was his teacher. Strictly professional. Yes, they'd grown comfortable around each other in only a short time and shared fun and enlightening conversation, but in a few short weeks it would all be over. No sense even going to the place in her mind that wanted to chuck the rules out the window and grab him with both hands. It was obviously just infatuation enhanced by being around him every day. There'd never be any hope of a romance between them, even if he wasn't a guest or her student, she had her life and he had his; completely opposite lives that would in no way fit together.

Why am I thinking all this? Chrissie tried to put the brakes on her rapid-fire thoughts and return to the moment at hand. He'd simply said something that didn't come out right, it just happened to allude to a physical relationship, and now it was time to move on.

'Well, I better let you get some lunch. I don't know about you, but my stomach is grumbling,' Chrissie said.

'My stomach is always grumbling. I'm a man.' Drew rubbed his belly, and Chrissie nodded.

'True,' she said. 'I know Kai will probably eat me out of house and home when he's a teenager. But maybe I'll get lucky and he won't be like other guys.'

'Yeah, good luck with that.' Drew's expression suggested he was being sarcastic, as if the constant desire for food was as common to men as facial hair. Then his expression changed to one of anticipation. 'Chrissie, do you want to join me for lunch in the dining room?'

'In *the* dining room?' She furrowed her brows.

'No, the V.I.P. dining room downstairs.'

'Oh, of course, sorry.' As if he'd share a plate of vegetarian lasagne with a bunch of guests if he was so careful to avoid being seen here. She turned her wrist and glanced at the time. It was either eat lunch with other staff as usual, or share a private meal with her favourite singer. Tough choice. 'Sure, that'd be nice.' She nodded.

'Great, I'll call up a double serving of everything, hang on a tick.' He headed towards the studio door then turned back. 'Meet you downstairs in a few minutes?'

'Sounds good.' Chrissie nodded and watched him disappear around the corner into his room. She took a can of deodorant from her bag and sprayed it under her arms, then slid a lip balm across her lips and plumped them together, before hooking the bag over her shoulder, blowing out the candles, and making her way downstairs.

Drew arrived after one of the kitchen staff set the meals on the table, along with a fresh vase of flowers, a carafe of water, and even a floating candle in a bowl. Every detail was taken care of for V.I.P. guests, and even though she was just a staff member, for the next hour she'd get to see how the other half lived. Sort of.

'Mmm, looks good.' Drew rubbed his hands together as he entered the dining room that opened up into the garden. Chrissie had opened the French doors, letting sunlight and fresh air into the room.

'It sure does. And I think someone else thinks so too.' She

pointed to the butterfly who had decided to pay a visit and was flapping its wings towards the table.

Drew approached the delicate creature. 'C'mon, sweetie, not much for you to see in here. Out you go.' He tried to coax the butterfly from the room, but it evaded his encouraging hands.

'Maybe you offended it,' Chrissie said.

'How do you figure that?'

'You called it sweetie. It might be male.'

'Hmm, you could be right. Although how does one tell?' He tilted his head and tried to peer underneath the flying creature.

'I have no idea,' Chrissie giggled. 'But I think by doing that you're offending it more!'

Drew laughed. 'Poor thing, calling it sweetie then examining it for genitalia. I've probably scarred him or her for life.'

'Maybe not,' Chrissie said, pointing as the butterfly landed on Drew's head.

'It's on my head?' he asked. 'I hope it doesn't poop on me. Quick, take a picture, this'll be a good one to show Sam.' He pulled his phone from his pocket and handed it to Chrissie.

Before swiping the screen she noticed his screensaver, a painting of a sunset. It looked familiar. She snapped a picture and at the sound of the camera, the butterfly flew away.

'Did you get it?' He sidled up to her and glanced at the screen, displaying a goofy image of him with eyes looking upwards and the multicoloured creature atop his head. 'Cool, thanks.' Chrissie handed the phone back to Drew, and as the butterfly approached her, she held out her hand. It rested on her fingertip and she smiled softly at its beauty.

Click! Drew took a photo, and the butterfly took flight again. 'Oh, I wasn't ready!'

'Exactly. Those "not ready" moments make the best photos. See?' He directed the screen towards her.

Her eyes weren't looking towards the camera, they were fixed on the butterfly, and a rare moment of peace had been captured. 'True. If you'd said, "smile", I probably would have tensed up and looked all weird and unnatural.'

'I don't know about weird, but I know what you mean. I've been to so many photo shoots that I've become sick of them. I just tell photographers to follow me around and snap pictures whenever the moment strikes, otherwise they never look like the real me.'

'So what about the one on your latest album?'

'Okay, that was a little bit staged, but I really was singing during the shoot. And it was outdoors, none of that fake background and artificial lighting bizzo.'

Chrissie doubted that Drew could ever take a bad photo. She was sure he looked just as gorgeous first thing in the morning. And guys with short hair had it easy, they didn't get that morning hair mayhem when one's hair looks like it's been caught in a tornado.

Drew walked to the French doors where the butterfly flitted about as if it didn't know where was inside and where was outside. 'Out you go, swee — er — *buddy*,' he slid a glance in Chrissie's direction as if to seek approval for his word choice, 'this way.' His hand hovered next to the butterfly, until it flitted beyond the patio and into the blazing sunlight reflecting off the shrubs. 'See? I have the magic touch.' He brushed his palms over each other as though dusting off sand.

'It appears you do.' She smiled, impressed by the gentle way he handled the butterfly.

'So, I think it's time to dig in.' He eyed the plates of chicken salad, crusty sourdough rolls still steaming from the oven, and a dainty jug of salad dressing on the side. 'Here.' Drew pulled out a chair and motioned for Chrissie to sit.

The gesture took her by surprise. Victor had never pulled a chair out for her; not that it mattered, she was perfectly capable of pulling out her own chair, and for that matter could even lift said chair and hurl it across the room if a situation required it. She'd sure been tempted a number of times when Victor had been ignorant and disrespectful towards her. He wasn't a bad bloke, just a bit of an arse sometimes. He loved Kai to bits, but wasn't cut out for day-to-day care of a child's needs. Alternate weekends worked out much better for him, and although Kai missed his dad, she knew Kai was probably better off with only short periods of time spent with his father.

Chrissie took her seat and flashed an impressed smile in Drew's direction. 'Why, thank you, Mr Williams,' she coated her words with sweetness.

'It is my pleasure, Miss Burns.' He sat on his chair and lifted the carafe. 'Would the lady care for a refreshing drink?' He embellished his words with an English accent.

'The lady would be most appreciative.' She competed with her own best version of an English accent.

'Then I shall oblige.' He poured the water into her glass.

Chrissie chuckled. 'What is this, *Downton Abbey*?'

Drew laughed. 'You know, I've never watched that show.'

'You haven't? Oh, you're missing out.'

'So I've heard. I never got around to watching it. My schedule doesn't always allow for regular TV viewing.'

'You'll have to watch it sometime. Be warned, though, it's addictive.'

'If a show isn't addictive it's not worth watching. Life's too short to waste time with substandard entertainment.'

Didn't she know it.

They delved into their gourmet salads, Chrissie pushing the olives to one side.

'I'll have your olives if you don't want them,' Drew said, pointing his fork in the direction of her plate.

'Go ahead.' She moved her plate closer to him. 'I don't mind them, but I'm not their biggest fan.' *Although I am yours...*

'Can't let a perfectly good olive go to waste.' He poked his fork into the dusky green flesh and popped it into his mouth. He scooped up the remaining olives and rolled them onto his plate.

'Hmm, I don't think they'd do that in *Downton Abbey*.'

'Not ones for sharing, eh?'

'I think it would be considered bad manners. But I agree, can't let good food go to waste. Would you like some extra avocado as well?' She pointed her fork towards the smooth green slices and raised her eyebrows.

Drew smiled. 'Don't tempt me. What did I say before about men and food?' He winked, and Chrissie brought another mouthful of salad to her lips, her gaze not leaving Drew's. 'I've gotta say, this really is delicious. And it looks pretty healthy too.'

Chrissie wanted to speak but her mouthful of food prevented it. She rotated her fork in the air, signalling she was about to speak, when Drew beat her to it.

'It's healthious!' He grinned.

Chrissie swallowed. 'Took the words right out of my mouth.'

'Your son's a smart kid. I really must get onto those Oxford people.' He smiled.

Both the water and conversation flowed, and Chrissie almost forgot she was at work, almost forgot she was in Tarrin's Bay, and for all she knew she could have been having lunch on Mars and would be none the wiser. Drew was so *normal*, so easy to get along with, like he was a friend she'd known all her life. If this lunch ended four hours from now it would still be too early.

When Drew had finished he leaned back in his chair, stretching his arms up in a satisfied way. 'Ah, that hit the spot. Now all I need is a little nap, and—'

'No,' Chrissie said sternly. 'No sleeping for you, Williams. Remember?'

'Was hoping you'd forget. Maybe I could have just a teeny tiny power nap.' He inched two fingers close together.

'Nope. You'll have to wait till night-time.' She put on her authoritative motherly voice.

'Okay. I think I'll go for a walk instead, maybe take a dip in the ocean. Ah, yes, that would be perfect. Nothing like that salty water washing over your skin and the sun sparkling on the waves.' He threaded his hands behind his head.

Chrissie glanced at her plate.

'You like swimming?' Drew asked. 'What about Kai, I bet he's a little water baby now, living in a town that has beautiful beaches?'

Chrissie fiddled with her knife and fork, even though she'd finished eating. 'Oh, um, not really.'

'Not really? Who doesn't like the water? Nothin' like it.'

Exactly. Nothing like it. And no need to have anything to do with it.

'I bet Kai likes splashing in the waves on the shore, though, right?'

Please stop. A lump formed in Chrissie's throat and she pushed it down with a hard swallow, but it only resurfaced. 'Um, he's not too keen on it, he's a bit scared, actually, he's—' Chrissie reached for the water to deflect from the uncomfortable conversation, but her hand shot out too hard and the glass toppled over. 'Oh, damn.' She stood, the chair screeching underneath her. She grabbed a napkin and prodded the spill on the table, then noticing some had dripped onto the floor she bent down. 'I'm so sorry.'

Drew came around to her side of the table. 'It's nothing, don't worry about it.' He bent down too and took the napkin from her hand, pausing to look her in the eye. 'Here, I've got this.' He dabbed at the water puddle, then returned to the table and mopped up what was left. 'It's only water.'

Heat prickled Chrissie's spine and her breath was short and sharp. *Please, not here. Not here.* She turned away and placed a hand on her chest.

'Chrissie? Are you okay?'

She raised her chin and turned back. 'Yes, I'm fine. Just embarrassed by my klutziness is all.' She faked a light-hearted smile, but by the look on Drew's face he didn't buy it.

He dropped the napkin on the table and came closer. 'I've said something that upset you, haven't I?'

'No, no. Nothing. I'm fine.' She edged past him and walked to the daybed out on the patio, taking a seat. 'Gee, the garden's looking nice isn't it?'

In a flash Drew was next to her, the side of his thigh touching hers. Although she was focused on the array of plants, she could feel his gaze on her. It tingled and tickled and urged her to look.

'Talk to me. What's going on inside that mind of yours?'

She flicked a dismissive hand at his probing.

'Oh man, I'm sorry if I brought up the past the other day, when I asked about your parents. Should have kept my big mouth shut.' He lowered his head.

'No, it's not that. You haven't done anything wrong, it's just...'

'Just what?'

'It's just me.' She lowered her chin towards her chest. 'It's silly, I shouldn't be so...' She struggled to find the words, then turned to face him. 'So scared.'

'What are you scared of, Chrissie?' His eyes held curiosity and concern, and part of her wanted to bare her heart and soul while the other part wanted to run and hide.

She swallowed that persistent lump in her throat. 'Water,' she whispered.

'Water?' Drew leaned closer, as though unsure he'd heard correctly.

She nodded. 'See, it's silly. I should just snap out of it and—'

The warm touch of his hand on top of hers took her words away. 'Tell me about it,' he said softly.

She released a slow breath. 'I haven't been swimming in... in years. And I've never taken Kai to swimming lessons. I'm such a bad mother.' She buried her forehead in her free hand.

'Hey, don't say that,' Drew replied.

'If it wasn't for that...' She pointed her thumb over her shoulder in the direction of the beach, '...That ocean out there that everyone loves and adores so much, my sister would still be alive.'

Drew's hand pressed down firmly on hers.

'Danielle drowned, right out there on that beach. She was only eleven years old.' The last three words faltered and she cleared her throat.

Drew's grip tightened, his fingers threaded between hers. He didn't speak, didn't have to. The simple touch of his hand told her he was here for here, he was listening, and he wanted her to continue.

'I was out there with her, having fun. It was late afternoon, the sun was low, blazing like it is today, barely allowing us to see in front of ourselves.' Chrissie's mind replayed each moment, each precious last moment she had with her sister. 'I told her I was going inside for a while, into Aunt Felicia's house, and said she should come out of the water with me.'

'It's getting late, Dani, c'mon, let's go inside,' she'd said. 'And I'm busting to go to the bathroom.'

'Just go in here, Chrissie, no one will know,' Danielle had replied.

'Ew, gross! No way, that's disgusting.'

'Don't be such a princess. Princess Christina,' she'd said in a posh voice.

Chrissie had laughed it off, knowing her sister was teasing, and when Dani said she'd come in after a few more minutes, Chrissie had left her there in the water, alone.

'When I came back outside, I couldn't see her. I thought maybe she was inside already and had gone upstairs or something, but there was no answer when I called out. Felicia came downstairs on hearing me call Danielle's name. We both went outside, but the sun was so bright on the horizon it was hard to see. Felicia called out along the beach while I went into the water, keeping an eye out for her head bobbing in the waves.' Heat filled Chrissie's eyes and the sting of unshed tears pinched at her eyelids. 'I just couldn't find her. It was so frustrating, I'd been with her only moments before, and then she was gone.' She tipped her head back and rubbed at her eyes, desperate to keep the tears contained. Drew's thumb rubbed along her hand, and although it comforted her, it also exacerbated the well of emotion rising up inside. 'Anyway, we called for help, and the surf lifesavers were onto the scene in seconds. All of a sudden, a heap of people were looking for her, in a boat, and then a helicopter. By the time the sun had lost its last rays that day, I'd learned I'd lost my sister. They found her. It was over. They said she may have got caught in a rip and panicked. I couldn't move from that shore. If I moved away, it would become real, and I wasn't ready for the truth.' Chrissie gulped and took a deep breath. 'After that, I couldn't go back to the shore. Couldn't go near the water. It reminded me of her, of her death. It became easier to avoid it all together.'

'Oh, Chrissie.' Drew's hand moved from hers and his arm curved around her back. He squeezed her opposite shoulder, and she allowed herself to lean into him. 'I'm so sorry. It's so unfair, everything you've been through. I wish there was something I could do to... to... make it easier.' He rubbed her shoulder up and down.

'It's okay, I'll be okay. It's just that being here again after all these years has brought back a few memories.'

'No wonder,' he said.

'I just wish I hadn't gone inside without her. I was her big sister; I should have looked after her. Should have insisted she come inside too. If only I'd—'

Drew grasped her chin with his other hand and turned her head to face his. 'None of this "if only" business. It wasn't your fault, you mustn't blame yourself, Chrissie.'

His oceanic eyes peered deep inside her heart, unnerving her. She was vulnerable, exposed. She couldn't bear losing it in front of him. Her toes clenched and she had to move, had to get out of there. She stood, his arm falling away. 'I'm sorry, this has been so unprofessional of me. I really should go now.' She pushed back a few loose strands of hair and forced her emotions back into the near-overflowing well. *Don't let him see you like this, Chrissie. Just keep going, don't stop. Don't let it all come out.*

'Wait,' he said. 'You don't have to go. You can stay as long as you like.' His touch on her arm made her flinch. 'I'm here for you. I want to be here for you.'

'You've been very kind, Drew, really. But I need... I need to go.' She dashed into the dining room and grabbed her bag, Drew following. She walked to the hallway and turned back. 'I'll see you tomorrow, and we'll get back to business, okay?' She faked a smile and turned away before the sight of his comforting eyes could draw her back into his arms, back into the emotional well she was quite literally drowning in, and back to a time and place she had no desire to return to.

'No, Kai, you can't have tomorrow off school,' Chrissie said, taking a seat at the kitchen table and opening her laptop later that afternoon.

'But—'

'Uh,' she raised a finger in warning, 'no buts.'

Kai slumped on the couch with crossed arms and a scrunched up face that looked like a pug dog, and Chrissie searched for more reward options to entice her son to school. By the looks of things, the only event on in town in the near future was the Valentine's Day Love Festival that ran from this Friday night to Sunday. *Pft!* Love-struck couples wandering hand in hand, watching starry-eyed as fireworks lit up the sky, before heading home together to make love a zillion times. Forget that. Real life didn't have happy ever afters. It had work and school and difficult children and stretch marks and housework and bills to pay. Real life had tragedy and loss and grief, and although spending time with Drew had brightened her days, opening up to him like that had been a mistake. She shouldn't have accepted his offer to have lunch in the first place. From now on she'd act in a strictly professional manner. She was his yoga teacher. That was it. The chitchat would have to stop.

Chrissie opened her email inbox and clicked on 'compose'. Kai would be at his father's this weekend, so maybe *he* could think up a reward to give his son if Kai didn't complain for the next two days. Why should all the responsibility rest on her shoulders?

Victor,

Your son is being very difficult and it's hard to get him to go to school. I know you check your emails as often as you check your (she wanted to say 'reflection') *stocks, so please reply tonight with an idea of a reward I can mention to Kai tomorrow morning to make him want to go to school. I came up with one for last week, now it's your turn.*

Chrissie.

She wasn't normally this blunt with him, she wanted things to be as cordial as possible so as to not cause any undue conflict around Kai, but today she was simply over the whole motherhood thing. This weekend alone would be good, for both her and Kai to spend time apart. She could keep her mind occupied by getting stuck into things around the house, and she sure as hell wouldn't be going to the Love Festival. The more she stayed away from things like that, from any idea or hope that she could have true love, the less chance she had of getting hurt. Or worse, hurting someone else. Those close to her didn't hang around long, and if they didn't succumb to an untimely death they'd probably up and leave. Maybe she was meant to be alone, devote her life to raising Kai and helping others find peace. Or maybe her mind was over-thinking, over-analysing everything, and she just needed a nice soak in a hot bath and an early night. Why was she so grumpy? Chrissie checked her calendar. 'Ha!' she said to herself. 'PM bloody S.' When everything was going wrong, one could always resort to blaming hormones.

CHAPTER FOURTEEN

Drew opened his eyes and got up slowly from the floor. He could normally relax easily in *Shavasana* at the end of a yoga session, especially with Chrissie's calming voice, but for the last two days after her revelation, he'd struggled. Instead of quietening his mind, he'd busied it with thoughts of how to reach her again. How to get through to her and help her open up so she could deal with her situation. Chrissie had been distant since their lunch on Wednesday, and despite her obvious regret at having told him about her past, he wished they could go back to the way things were.

'Good work. I'll see you next week,' Chrissie said curtly, then blew out the candle and gathered her things.

'Wait,' Drew said, not sure what words would come out of his mouth next but not wanting her to leave.

Her eyebrows rose in waiting for him to continue, her lips sealed tight in a straight line, as though desperate to keep it together.

'I ah...' What should he say? Normally he just blurted out whatever was on his mind without time for thinking. The whole 'speak now, think later' mantra. But he needed to choose his words carefully this time. If he hit a nerve, pushed her, it might have the opposite effect he desired, and there could be a chance she wouldn't want to continue as his instructor. But the woman needed to let out whatever she had bottled up inside. They couldn't go on with classes when she was like this. He got that she was trying to pull back and be professional, but after two weeks of being together every day except the weekends, it had become more than that. He didn't know what it was exactly, but they'd bonded. The thought of not seeing her next month sent an uncomfortable wave rolling through his body, but he'd deal with that when the time came. For now, he needed to help her. Somehow.

'I, ah,' he scratched his head, 'was wondering if you could help me with something?'

'Sure. One of the poses? Do you want some extra help with the ones you found challenging today?'

'No, it's not about yoga,' he replied. 'Help with a song.'

Her eyes widened in apparent surprise. 'You want my help... with a song?'

'Well yes, just a bit of feedback. I've finished writing it but it can be hard to know how it sounds until someone else listens to it. Objective feedback and all that?'

She shifted on the spot. 'So you want me to listen to your song and let you know what I think?'

'Yeah, if you don't mind. I could always record it and send it to a friend if you'd prefer, I don't want you to feel obligated or—'

'Sure. I'll do it,' she said.

Step one, done. Step two — sing the song and hope it softened her resolve, helped her to get in touch with her emotions as music often did. It could make things ten times worse, he knew that, but he had to try. Music was a great icebreaker, a way to open people up and get them talking. Sure, some feedback on the lyrics and melody would be welcome, but that wasn't why he was doing it.

'Great. Thanks.' Drew headed for the door. 'I'll grab my guitar and be back in a tick.'

When he returned, Chrissie stood at the window with her back to him.

'Right then, here we go,' he said, and when Chrissie turned around he gestured for her to sit on her mat that she appeared to have forgotten to put away. 'I'm a little nervous.'

'Nervous? Why? You've been doing this for years.'

'But not like this, here, with one person.' He sat cross-legged on her mat too, opposite her, and she inched back slightly, but they were still close.

'I'm sure you'll be fine,' she said. 'Go ahead.'

'It's called *Breathe*.' Drew closed his eyes for a moment, centring himself into the feeling of the song. Words were one thing, but if they didn't have emotion behind them, the song would sound flat. Emotions first, song second.

He placed his hands and fingers in position on the strings, and took a deep breath, his chest expanding against the solid African mahogany of his Taylor guitar. Breathing life into it, preparing it to respond to his touch with perfectly tuned sound.

His thumb ran down the row of strings, and taking one more deep breath, he opened his mouth...

'Sometimes life gets away from you,
Sometimes life takes the joy from you,
But when things around you come crashing down,
And the past you'd rather forget keeps spinning you around,
There are three little things that you must do, to bring you back *to you...*
Don't forget to breathe,
Don't forget to cry,

Don't forget to take the time to do what's right, and bring your soul to life,

Don't forget to breathe...'

The words rolled easily off his tongue, each mention of the word *breathe* long and slow like an exhalation in itself. The melody and lyrics flowed and resonated with where he was at in his life right now, and ironically, with Chrissie's too, he was sure.

He continued singing, and on reaching the next chorus, Chrissie's eyes became glossy, and her body softened in front of him. Gently, subtly, unconsciously, she leaned slightly forward, as though her soul was seeking out the words and needed to make them her own.

By the end of the final verse, Drew was overcome with an intense rush, a high coursing through his body. His body, his voice and his guitar were one. And so was Chrissie. She was part of this, she inspired this, and her presence took the music to a whole new dimension.

'Don't forget to breathe,

Don't forget to cry,

Don't forget to take the time to do what's right, and bring your soul to life,

Don't forget to... breathe...'

He strung out the final word slowly and deeply, lowering to a whisper, his own breath extending out in front of him and merging with Chrissie's, her eyes red-rimmed and on the verge of tears.

He placed the guitar aside and got to his knees to get closer to her, still cross-legged in front of him. His hand reached out, caressed the side of her face. His thumb, still tingling from the vibration of the guitar strings, wiped away a tear that had finally escaped. Chrissie's hand covered his, gripped it, held it to her cheek, and like two magnetic charges drawn to each other, her body connected with his and he wrapped his arms around her.

One hand held the back of her head as she buried her face in his chest, his fingers entwining in her soft hair, while the other held onto her back as it trembled with her tears. He didn't need to speak; he'd spoken through his song, and the words had gone right to her heart.

Chrissie's hands gripped his back, spreading warmth through his body. He stroked and twirled her hair, rocking gently side to side as though the music still coursed through his body and manifested in physical form.

This was why he lived and breathed music. This was what it was all about. Expression, realisation, connection. His body melded into hers and he could have stayed like this all day. Holding her, breathing with her, as one.

Chrissie manoeuvred to her knees as well, nestling her face into the crook of his neck and radiating heat that warmed him from the outside in.

'It's beautiful. Simply beautiful,' she whispered against his ear as her soft breath tickled his cheek.

He grasped the sides of her delicate, tear-stained face and locked his gaze on hers. 'So are you.'

Drew couldn't get Chrissie out of his mind. Not when she'd left the yoga studio and they'd held each other's hands until they reluctantly stretched apart and went their separate ways, not during dinner when he longed for her company, and not now, as he stepped out on the balcony on hearing the explosions of fireworks. Her sweet scent filled his lungs every time he breathed, and he hoped she was doing okay. Maybe he should call her? Or maybe...

He went downstairs and snuck out the back door, hurrying down to the beach. The only light showing the way was from moonlight and occasional bursts of fireworks. He slowed as he arrived at the sandy shore, eyeing a group of people further south whose heads were tipped back, admiring the flashes of light in the sky. He glanced left, towards the rocky hill, and moved his feet in that direction. He would have a great view from up there and could snap some photos. Of course, it was near Chrissie's house and she might be nearby, but if they should happen to meet by chance then so be it. Drew convinced himself he was only heading that way for a better vantage point for the fireworks display.

He climbed up the rocks, this time wearing shoes, and forced himself not to look over at Chrissie's house. He didn't want her to think he was stalking her or something. He whipped his phone out of his pocket and snapped a few pictures of colourful, radiating bursts of light, decorating the sky and casting a glimmery light onto the ocean surface.

Tarrin's Bay didn't do things by halves when it came to festivals. The Valentine's weekend Love Festival was a perfect excuse for fireworks. They also had them at Christmas and New Year's Eve, and Australia Day. Drew imagined all the love-struck couples lying on picnic rugs in Miracle Park or beside the harbour, taking in the view and declaring their love for each other. *Smug buggers,* he thought.

The sound of a screen door snapping shut reminded him of where he was and his head flipped to the source of the sound, Chrissie's veranda.

As the door closed shut behind her, Chrissie stepped off the veranda and onto the grass. She turned her head towards the sight of a man on the hill to the right of her property. For a split second she considered going back inside, concerned he might be some weirdo, but when he turned to face her she recognised something about him.

She walked across the grass and over to the sand to get a closer look. A bright flash lit up the sky and his face for a second. *Drew?* She offered a curious wave at the same time he waved to her. She made her way up the sand dunes that sat beside the rocky hill, the tiny particles giving way under her bare feet with each step.

'Hello, stranger.' Drew gestured for her to join him on the top of the hill.

'Fancy seeing you here,' she replied, and he approached her with a hand outstretched, helping her up onto the rocks.

If she'd known she was going to be doing a spot of rock climbing at 9pm, she would have worn shoes. She only meant to wander outside to get a better look at the fireworks of the Love Festival. At least it was dark, apart from the bursts of light. She'd already washed her make-up off and was in track-pants and a singlet. They were her makeshift pyjamas, but as they looked like regular clothes she was sure Drew wouldn't realise.

'I wanted to get some photos of the fireworks, thought this looked like a good place to get a view. Hope I didn't disturb you.'

'Not at all. I wanted to get a better view too.' Chrissie gestured back to the house. 'So this is the house I was telling you about. It's a work-in-progress.' Much like her life.

Drew cast an extended gaze over the property. 'It's in a beaut spot. You're very lucky.' He smiled.

Yes, she was the lucky one. The lucky one who'd survived the rest of her family, but sometimes, dealing with all the turbulent emotions that went with that, she didn't feel so lucky. Kai was all the family she had now. The future of her family tree was in her hands and his.

Chrissie nodded without speaking.

'Oh, I'm sorry if I touched a nerve. I just mean that... the location is... you've got a great—'

She touched his arm. 'It's okay. I know what you mean. It is a great spot, and I'm sure the right buyer, when they come along, will love the place. I hope it goes to someone who will create many happy memories here.'

'I'm sure it will. The work you're doing on the house, I think it will be good. It'll give it a new lease of life, a fresh start.'

And once that occurred, she could have her own fresh start, somewhere she could really settle into, set down roots, and finally give Kai a stable home.

A loud bang exploded and colours filled the sky.

'Whoa, that was a good one.' Drew looked up.

'Pretty.' Chrissie smiled. 'Oh, what a shame Kai's not here. He would have loved this.'

'Here, I'll film some of it and send it to you. It won't be quite the same as the real deal, but better than nothing.' Drew held up his phone and pressed the red button, recording the display in front of them. Flashes of green and red and blue sprinkled over the horizon, embers of colour falling into the ocean like snowflakes as Drew captured the moment.

'He'll love that, thank you.'

'My pleasure. What did we ever do without these things, huh?' He pressed stop and jiggled his phone.

'Had to rely on our memory I guess.' And unfortunately it was often the memories best forgotten that stuck in the mind like glue.

The faint hum of a happy crowd could be heard in the distance, along with muffled music from the festival. If only the locals knew that one of the best sources of music was right here, not being heard. With a voice like Drew's, every moment he wasn't using it seemed a waste.

'Thanks again, for today.' Chrissie touched the side of Drew's arm. 'I'm feeling much better now.'

He stepped a little closer. 'I'm glad.' He reached a hand behind her back and gave it a few rubs. 'So you didn't feel like joining the crowd over there tonight?' He pointed.

'Not really. I had to drive Kai to his father's so I've only been back an hour. Something about long drives makes you want to have an easy night at home.'

'Same goes for long flights. You'd think after sitting for so many hours you'd want to keep moving, but travel is tiring for some reason.'

'Yeah, it's nice to just stay put for a while.'

'It sure is. I'm learning that this month.' He slid a smile her way. 'Can't believe I've been here two weeks, and only another two to go. Come the end of February I might not want to leave.'

Then don't.

'But I know once I get back on the road I'll get into it. Have to do rehearsals for my next lot of shows, so that'll keep me busy.'

'Must be exciting.'

'Yeah, most of the time.' A hint of weariness crept into his voice, like he meant it but was also a bit over it. The poor guy probably needed more than a month off, but he was too in demand. He couldn't disappoint his fans.

'Oh, nice.' Chrissie said, eyes fixed on the sky as blues and silvers exploded into the air in star-like shapes.

Drew held his camera up and snapped a couple more pictures.

Every few seconds the waves rolled into shore along with a tumbling, whooshing, rhythmic sound, in contrast to the sudden loud noises from the fireworks. Along with the waves came a fresh breeze, lifting wisps of Chrissie's hair off her face and neck, and ruffling the sleeves of Drew's white T-shirt. 'Brr, it's getting a bit nippy out here.' She crossed her arms over her chest and rubbed her hands against the skin on her arms.

'Yeah, it is a bit crisp.'

Chrissie looked at his body. 'Though men don't feel the cold as much as women.'

'So I hear. Something about internal body heat?'

'Yeah, from having a higher muscle mass.' And boy did Drew have a higher muscle mass. More than many men she taught in classes.

'I think you give me a run for my money though, look.' He poked her arm and her bicep muscle automatically tensed. 'There's some decent muscle mass in there.' He poked again.

She laughed. 'Oh c'mon, not that much. Not as much as in there.' She poked him back, the firm roundness of his bicep pressing against her finger. She imagined his abs would be even harder. She'd felt the ones on his back while doing her yoga-ly duties, and they didn't disappoint. If he had any fat on his body it was hiding out somewhere, never to be found.

'Hey, that tickles,' he said, flinching.

'Tickles?' She turned to him, a cheeky smirk on her face. 'What are you, a wimp?' she joked.

He laughed. 'I can't help it if I'm ticklish. Don't you remember in class the other day when you were helping me do that twisting thing? It's a curse, I tell you.'

She poked him again. 'Wimpy Williams,' she teased.

He captured her finger before she could poke him again and he held it to her lips. 'Shush, Burns,' he said. 'Or I'll...'

'You'll what?' she tested.

'I'll... tickle you back. Okay, so you might not have the curse I have, but everyone has a threshold. I'll find your ticklish spot.' His eyes sparkled as another flash brightened the sky.

She edged away from him. 'Oh no you won't. Anyway, I'm not ticklish like you. I can take it.'

'Can you? Then why are you moving away?' He leaned closer and jabbed at her side.

'Hey!' She giggled.

'See? Everyone has a threshold.' He jabbed her again and a laugh shot from her like a firework of its own.

'Stop it you!' She jabbed him back. 'Or I'll chuck you over *this* threshold.' Chrissie gestured over the edge of the rocky hill.

'Not if I chuck you first.' He moved to pick her up but she bent at the waist, turning in on herself so he couldn't take hold. As colour burst through the sky laughter burst from them both, and he held into her wrists to stop any further tickling ambushes. 'Let's call a truce now!'

'Truce. No more tickling, I promise!'

They separated from each other's hold and looked towards the sky again. A stronger breeze rose in the air and Chrissie shivered. 'I should have brought a cardi.'

'Me too. I mean, not a cardi, a masculine version of such an item, a...'

Chrissie raised her eyebrows. 'Lost for words?'

'I've gone blank! What's that thing, you know, that covers your arms and keeps you warm?'

'I'm not helping you out, I want to watch you struggle.' She placed her hands on her hips in amusement.

'Oh man, this jet lag must have frozen my brain.' He twirled his finger in the air as though trying to summon the correct word. 'Jacket! A jacket! Geez, it must be past my bedtime.'

Chrissie laughed.

Drew glanced at her arms as she rubbed them. 'If I had a jacket, I'd do the gentlemanly thing and wrap it around you.' His voice was softer now, more genuine.

'Like they do in the movies, huh?'

He nodded.

'Oh well, what a shame. I'll survive.' Chrissie held her arms close to her body and continued watching the fireworks, when a pair of arms slid around her from behind, superimposing themselves on top of hers and spreading warmth across her skin.

'Will these do instead?' Drew asked gently. 'I'll be a human jacket.'

A soft smile floated onto Chrissie's lips. 'Even better,' she whispered. 'I mean, body heat and all that.'

His arms covered hers, pushing more warmth into her skin and sending fireworks of her own off in her belly. The way he held her from behind was so natural, so effortless, so... perfect. They fit together, like a lock and a key, like a piece of timber slotting into the groove in another piece of timber, forming a strong supportive structure. They stood like that, gazing at the explosions that had nothing on the ones going off inside, until a smoky grey blackness hung in the sky.

The display might be over, but whatever was happening between them was not. Drew didn't budge, and his breath gently washed across her skin where his chin sat nestled between her shoulder and her neck. Slowly, Chrissie turned her head to the side a little, her breath seeking out his, and both increasing in rate. In, out, in, out, their breath swirled together in the air in front of their mouths, as the gap between them lessened. All conscious thought had left her mind, there was only need. Deep, magnetic need, moving her head to face his, until his breath was so close, she could taste its enticing sweetness. Her eyes trailed up from his lips to his eyes and in the moment their gaze locked on each other, a loud bang jolted Chrissie's body and she flipped her head back to the front. A huge circle of red sparkles in the sky radiated outwards, growing and dissipating into tiny twinkles that faded along with the moment that had just passed.

'I wasn't expecting that,' Drew said.

Was he talking about the fireworks finale or the fact that they'd almost kissed? 'I guess the show wasn't quite over.'

'Took me by surprise, that's for sure.' She didn't know whether *she* was talking about the fireworks or what had just happened between them.

And whatever *had* happened, the intensity of the moment had now fizzled out, leaving behind a raw awkwardness. Drew's arms fell away from her and she scratched her arm, now cold again from the absence of his touch.

'Well, they were nice,' she said.

'Yeah, they were.' Drew slipped his hands into his pockets, sharing in her awkwardness.

Chrissie's head hung low, and she muttered, 'I guess I better head back inside now.'

'Guess so.'

'Thanks for um, for... thanks,' was all she could manage.

'Sure. Thank you for the, ah, the company.' He nodded a smile.

Chrissie turned away and back again, as though her body was disoriented and unsure which direction was home.

Drew seemed equally as uncertain. He ran his hand over his head. 'So, um, what's on your agenda this weekend?'

'Just some things around the house, sorting through boxes, planning the renovations, that sort of thing.' She'd need to keep busy after what just happened, otherwise she might crack and call Melinda and blurt everything out.

'You'll have to make time for lunch though, won't you?'

She had no desire for food whatsoever right now, it was hard to imagine needing any in the foreseeable future. Her nerves were fuelled to the max with emotions and hormones. 'I'll have to at some stage.'

'Does one o'clock work for you?'

She eyed him with curiosity.

'Chrissie, would you like to join me for lunch tomorrow?' He stopped shifting around and stood strong in one spot, emphasising his invitation.

'You mean, at Serendipity?'

'No, somewhere else.'

'But don't you have to be careful about being seen?'

'Where I'm going won't be a problem.'

'Where are you talking about?'

'My parents' place.'

Chrissie gulped. 'You're asking me to lunch with your parents?'

'Yeah. Why not? They'd love to meet the fantastic yoga instructor I've been raving about. My mum would probably have you show her a few poses in the living room, and my dad would probably try to arm wrestle you to make sure he's still got it, but apart from that, they're friendly and down to earth people.' He grinned.

'I'm sure they are. Though it's a bit short notice, they might not want an unexpected visitor turning up for a meal.'

'I'll text Mum tonight. Besides, Dad always makes enough to feed an army. He used to be a chef; if you come you'll be in for a real treat.'

'Are you trying to tempt me with food, Williams?' Chrissie's self-consciousness from before vanished as they returned to their usual banter.

'Is it working?'

Chrissie tapped her chin.

Drew edged closer to her. 'Roast chicken with balsamic glaze and rosemary potatoes, honeyed baby carrots, crusty bread dipped in extra virgin olive oil, homemade vanilla custard with—'

'Okay, okay, you've won me over!' *In more ways than one.* 'Is that what he's really making?'

'Dunno.' Drew shrugged. 'Just said the first things that popped into my head.'

'Tease!' She slapped him playfully on the arm.

'Payback for all that tickling.'

'If I remember correctly, you were giving as good as you got.'

'You ain't seen nothin' yet, Burns.' He wriggled his fingers in front of her and she smiled. 'So, I'll tell them you're coming? Deal?'

'How can I refuse?' She held out her hand and he shook it. 'Deal.'

What on earth was she getting herself into?

CHAPTER FIFTEEN

After treating herself to a sleep-in, hanging out a load of washing, and sorting through Felicia's old books — some to give away and some to keep — Chrissie sat ready and waiting on her veranda chair for Drew to arrive. Her fingers entangled themselves in each other, her foot tapped against the weathered timber decking, and she nibbled at the inside of her mouth. For some reason she was more nervous about meeting Drew's parents than she had been to meet Drew himself.

She picked up the bouquet of flowers she'd snipped from the garden to give to his parents, as even though Drew had told her not to bring anything, she couldn't come empty-handed. With his father being an ex-chef she didn't want to step on his toes by bringing something edible, in case it didn't go with what he had planned, and as for wine, he would probably have one to match the food. So flowers it was. Simple, easy, and no one had to eat them in order to be polite.

Chrissie stood and, right at that moment, Drew appeared from behind the rocky hill. He walked around it this time, instead of climbing over it, and he smiled as he approached her house. His casual buttoned shirt was open slightly at the top, exposing a light layer of hair, and he must have been wearing aftershave or cologne because the scent greeted her before he did. It was no budget cologne, something exotic and expensive, she could tell. Much nicer than Victor's cheapo one he'd get from the pharmacy.

'Good morning,' she said. 'I mean, good afternoon.' She was so used to seeing him before midday.

'Good morning and afternoon yourself.' He smiled. 'You look nice.' His gaze ran down her body, not in a sleazy way, but in a way that told her he appreciated her style. She wore light beige linen trousers that draped loosely down her legs; thin, gold sandals that accentuated her tanned feet; and like Drew, a white cotton top, only hers had delicate patterning around the sleeves and scoop neck collar. She'd finished off the look with a pair of simple, gold hoop earrings, and her hair was twisted into a relaxed chignon. It was nice he could see her wearing clothing other than Lycra yoga gear, or daggy pyjamas like last night.

'You look nice too. A bit of a change from the yoga gear, hey?'

'Yeah, I don't think we'll be doing any today, unless my mum pesters you into a private lesson.'

'Well apparently Helena is going to be introducing some open classes from next month, so you don't have to be a guest of the retreat to take part. Your mum might like to come along.'

'I'll let her know.' He eyed the flowers. 'And she'll appreciate those, thank you.'

'It's the least I can do, and thank you for inviting me. I should have got an extra bunch for you.' She smiled.

'No need,' he replied. 'And the staff always replace the flowers in my room every couple of days. I'm all good for flowers.' He smiled.

Chrissie turned to walk around the house. 'Shall we get going?'

He held out his arm. 'Lead the way.'

They walked around to the front of the house and she unlocked her small Hyundai with a high-pitched beep. 'After you.' She opened the door for Drew.

'Aren't you the gentleman,' he joked, and she eyed him with a feigned warning look.

As she got into the driver's seat, she said, 'If it gets cold later I'll even put a jacket around you.'

He chuckled. 'Yes, quite the gentleman.'

Chrissie started the engine and wished she'd taken a moment to turn the volume down on the CD player beforehand. Drew's singing voice blared through the car, smack bang in the middle of his upbeat song, *Fired Up*. Her hand lunged for the volume knob, turning it off completely in a flash.

'Sorry about that, didn't realise the CD was in there.' Only five minutes into their lunch date and she was already blushing like a beetroot. She switched on the radio to detract from the fan girl moment.

'That's okay, I'd rather my music be played at full volume than not at all.' He grinned. 'Though it is kind of weird listening to myself, so yes, radio is the way to go.'

Nice one, Chrissie. Mental note — turn volume right down after each trip, just in case hot celebrity who created the music being played at full bore happens to enter the car. A few weeks ago she'd have thought there'd be more chance of being struck by lightning.

Chrissie cleared her throat as she backed out of the driveway. 'So, where do your parents live?'

Several minutes later Chrissie had to force her mouth not to gape as they arrived in Tarrin's Bay Hills and she pulled into the 'long driveway of Honeydew House.

They live here? No way!

The house she'd admired while driving past on her way to the country fair last weekend stood proudly in front of her. Serendipity wasn't just her place of work, it was at work in her life, too.

'You okay?' Drew asked, as she turned off the engine and didn't move.

'Yes, fine, I'm just taking in the beautiful property.'

'It's a great place. Wait till you see inside, and out the back.'

They stepped out of the car, and although she probably didn't need to in such a secluded spot, she locked the car.

The multicoloured loose pebble driveway crunched underfoot as she walked alongside Drew towards the grand front entrance, a glossy burgundy double door with gold door-knocker. The warmth of the door was enhanced by the rich tones of the brick house; deep earthy browns and mottled reds, giving the place an inviting, homely feel you could imagine coming home to on a winter's night and curling up on the sofa in front of the fireplace. Only it wasn't winter, it was the tail end of summer and the sun streamed down through the tall trees, searing the bare skin on her arms.

She followed Drew and stepped onto the porch, where a potted plant she didn't know the name of sat shaded in the corner, a small hand painted sign above it on the wall saying, *Life is a journey, but home is a destination.*

'Cute,' Chrissie said, gesturing towards it.

'And we have reached our destination,' he replied.

'You sound like my car's GPS. Though less female.'

'Is this better?' He cleared his throat, 'You have reached your destination,' he said in a female version of his *Downton Abbey* accent.

Chrissie covered her mouth as she giggled, then whacked him lightly on the arm.

Drew tapped the door-knocker and the sound of footsteps

scurrying to the door came from the inside. The double doors opened, framing a petite woman with white-grey hair that sat in curly tendrils around her face. Her mouth went wide in a welcoming smile, and Chrissie recognised Drew's smile in hers.

'Well, hello!' She stood on tiptoes and leaned towards her son, kissing him on the cheek, before turning to Chrissie. 'Chrissie, how lovely to meet you.' The woman grasped her hand gently. It was soft and silky, like a baby's, and she leaned towards Chrissie too and pecked her on the cheek.

Wasn't expecting that!

'I'm Susan. Come on in.' She stepped aside and they entered the house.

'It's lovely to meet you too. And thank you for having me here for lunch today. You have a beautiful home,' Chrissie said.

'I was thrilled when Drew said he wanted to bring a guest. I love having visitors over, gives me an excuse to do a spot of decorating.' She smiled, and Chrissie admired the well-designed and decorated room.

'Here, these are for you.' Chrissie held out the flowers that, although nice, seemed oddly small and humble for such a grand house.

'How gorgeous, thank you.' Susan hurried over to the open plan kitchen where a man stood, busying himself with food preparation. In a flash she'd filled a vase with water and placed the flowers inside, putting them on display on the coffee table in the lounge area.

The man turned around. 'G'day there,' he said with a small, kind smile. 'Geoff Williams.' He rinsed his hands under the tap, dried them off with a tea towel, and approached Chrissie. 'Nice to meet you.' He shook her hand.

'Likewise. I hear you're a fantastic chef, I'm looking forward to sampling your cooking.' She hoped she didn't sound too keen, like she was just here for a good feed or something.

'I'm glad to have the opportunity to cook for someone new again,' he said. 'I love cooking for the family, but having a new guest here brings back the old days of bringing people together with the simple pleasure of a well cooked meal.'

A flood of relief washed through Chrissie. These people were as lovely as Drew. He was so lucky to have both his parents still around, and a sister, and a niece and nephew.

Chrissie smiled and her attention turned to the large table out on the patio. Susan gestured towards it. 'Since it's such a beautiful day, I thought we'd eat outside. I've got the citronella candles burning so hopefully they'll keep the mozzies and flies at bay.

'It looks beautiful.' Chrissie stepped closer to the screen door that separated them from the outdoors. Susan slid it back and they stepped outside.

The table was covered in a white tablecloth, and silver cutlery sparkled on top, along with polished white plates, and a large tall vase holding several bird of paradise flowers, creating an elegant yet simple display. She peered closer to find her name written in beautiful handwriting on a card, next to Drew's.

'Wow, this is lovely. You've gone to so much trouble.'

'Ah, it's no trouble, I love doing things like this.'

'The name cards are a nice touch, thank you. You're very organised.'

'If I'm having guests I want them to feel welcome and appreciated,' said Susan.

'And you're right about being organised,' added Geoff, stepping outside to join them. 'Susan's the queen of organisation, aren't you?' He nudged his wife and she shrugged. 'She's so organised, she's even pre-written my eulogy.'

Drew shook his head and Chrissie tried not to look shocked. Her raised eyebrows must have conveyed concern because Geoff touched her lightly on the arm.

'Don't worry,' he said, 'I'm not dying or anything, she just likes to be prepared.'

'Oh.' Relief lowered her eyebrows.

'Well, it pays to do things in advance. You never know what's around the corner,' Susan explained. 'And anyway, it's not pre-written, it's just a draft at the moment. I'll have to add a few more details and polish it up when the dreadful day arrives of course, but at least I have a basic outline to guide me.'

'And what if — heaven forbid — you die before me?' Geoff asked.

'Then you can use it as a template to write mine,' Susan said matter-of-factly.

Chrissie turned her lips inward, not sure what the appropriate response to something like that was.

'Anyway, Mum, no need to start talking eulogies and funerals just yet,' Drew said, hooking his arm under his mum's elbow. 'Let's get some drinks organised.' He looked at Chrissie. 'What can I get you? Wine, juice, water?'

'She'll have a nice glass of my best red, won't you?' said Geoff. 'It's been hibernating in my wine cellar for years, now's as good a time as any to open it.'

'Oh, well, don't feel you have to. You might like to save it for a special occasion.'

'This is a special occasion, Drew hasn't brought over a guest since he was, well, about eighteen, have you, buddy?' Geoff patted his son on the back, and Drew's cheeks turned a light pink.

Chrissie smiled. 'In that case, I'd love one.' She caught Drew's eye before he went back inside with Susan, and she realised that when it came down to it, he was just a regular guy, and she was a regular girl. Behind all the glamour and glitz of celebrity life, Drew Williams was your run-of-the-mill average guy with parents who embarrassed him.

'I hear you're fairly new to Tarrin's Bay, Chrissie?' Susan said after lunch had been placed on the table; an entrée of cucumber soup and fresh bread with dipping oil and dukkah, followed by barramundi in a coconut lime broth with vegetables.

'Yes, although I used to come here as a child.'

'A lot of people who move here say that. It usually holds such great memories for them they can't help but return.' Susan smiled.

Drew cleared his throat. 'Mmm, this is good, Dad.'

Chrissie shot him a 'thank you' glance. The last thing she wanted was to have to discuss her childhood again. 'It sure is. I think my fish-phobic son would even like this. The broth is delicious.'

'Thank you,' Geoff replied. 'Maybe I'll get around to writing that recipe book one day, hey Drew?'

'Yeah, you should go for it.'

'Oh absolutely. I'd buy it,' Chrissie remarked.

'Maybe once we've finally sold up and moved house.'

'Oh,' Chrissie raised her eyebrows. 'You're selling Honeydew House?'

He nodded. 'It's time. We love it of course, but it's getting too much for the two of us to maintain, and we want to be closer to town as we, ah...'

'Get older and need home care and Meals on Wheels,' Susan added.

'Home care maybe, but Meals on Wheels? No chance in hell,' he said defiantly. 'I'll be cooking till the day I die. No processed garbage for me.'

Susan glanced at Chrissie. 'Basically we want to downsize, and it'll be good to be in walking distance to everything. Not just for convenience but for my arthritis, and Geoff's—'

'High blood pressure.' He patted his heart. 'You'd think I'd get exercise around this place, but apparently not enough.'

'Well you can walk to the shops every day for your fresh ingredients,' Susan said.

'So have you found somewhere else yet?'

'No, not yet. We won't be selling till the end of this year, so we'll start looking in a few months time. Still got to sort out years of household belongings, including those belonging to someone in particular.' She must have kicked Drew under the table because he flinched a little and said, 'Mum!'

Drew took a sip from his glass. 'I'll try to do as much as I can tomorrow. Surely it couldn't take more than a day?'

'It could,' his mother replied. 'But I know you, you'll keep going without stopping until you've reached your goal. He always goes after what he wants, this one.' Susan said.

Chrissie gulped, even though she'd already swallowed a morsel of food. 'I'll be doing the same thing tomorrow. Sorting through boxes. Things that belonged to my aunt.'

'Oh yes, I'm sorry to hear about that.'

How much has Drew told his parents about me?

'Thank you.'

'And will you stay in the house or sell?'

'Sell. It's too big for just myself and Kai.'

'Oh, I see. Maybe we'll both be selling up at the same time,' Susan mused.

'I hope the town has some good real estate agents,' Chrissie said. Not only to sell Felicia's beach house, but to help her find the right property for the future. God, she'd love to be able to buy Honeydew House, but even with the sale from the house it'd no doubt go for a *lot* more. And so much for saying she wanted a smaller place. That might have been a little lie. She just wanted somewhere not so close to the ocean.

'We know of a couple of good agents. William, at Matson and Moore, he's the son of friends of ours. I know we can trust him.

There's also Colin from Craythornes, been selling houses since he was in nappies, just about.'

'Oh good, I'll have to remember those names.' She made a mental note, then the sign of Honeydew House popped in her mind and she dreamed of walking up to it and getting out her own key to the place. *Stop dreaming Chrissie!* 'So, ah, how did Honeydew House get its name? Are there... melons growing here?' She hoped that wasn't a stupid question. Did honeydew melons even grow in this part of Australia? She had no idea.

'No melons here, unfortunately. The previous owners christened it — honey was their business, and maybe they added the 'dew' bit to make it sound nice, or to represent the morning dew that appears here on frosty mornings. They used to be beekeepers. We could have taken the job on when we bought the place, but alas, I'm allergic to bee stings.' She shrugged. 'I was so glad when they cleared it all out. And anyway, not my thing. At that stage I was running my own interior design business. Ran it out of there.' Susan pointed to a separate building, a granny flat, that stood on the far side of the property, hidden partly from view by tall trees.

'Your talent shows. Your house is beautifully decorated,' Chrissie said.

'Well, thank you. Geoff and I are both retired now, but I loved my job. If you need any help getting your place ready for sale, I'd be happy to help.'

'Really? That's so nice of you.'

'Sure, just drop in and let me know when you're ready.'

Wow, Drew William's mother was giving her an invitation to just 'drop in' anytime? Chrissie hated people dropping in unannounced at her place; she'd much prefer advance warning, ideally twenty-four hours. Or a week. Though she'd probably make an exception for Drew.

'Wow, so Sarah's husband might be helping me build a garage

and extend the deck, Sarah said she'll come house hunting with me, and now you're offering to help me decorate. You're a very generous family!'

'And maybe I can serve free food at the open house and Drew could be the guest of honour to attract a few potential buyers, hey son?' Geoff winked.

Drew laughed. 'Well, maybe I can arrange a special visit to Australia for the occasion,' he joked. *Joked.* Every now and again a reminder of the transient nature of Drew's presence would hit home. Just when she was starting to get used to having him around.

After a dessert of pavlova and fruit, and a game of Trivial Pursuit in which Drew showed his competitive side but lost to Chrissie thanks to one of those science questions about the human body, Chrissie helped the family clear the table.

'C'mon, Chrissie, I'll take you on a tour of the property,' Susan said, hooking her hand under Chrissie's elbow.

'Need a tour guide commentator?' asked Geoff. 'Everything here has some sort of history or significance I'd be happy to tell you about.'

'Go easy on the history lesson, Dad. I'm sure Chrissie would just prefer a casual stroll around,' said Drew.

'I'd be honoured to learn more about the place,' Chrissie replied.

They all walked back outside and over to the granny flat where Susan had based her design business, but was now used as guest accommodation. It had three bedrooms! *Oh, something like this would be perfect for my yoga retreats.* She may not be able to buy this place, but there was no harm in dreaming and getting ideas for the future. They walked around the mature gardens near the guest accommodation, where rosellas fluttered around the red fuzz of a bottlebrush tree. Geoff gave her a botany and horticulture lesson, while Drew seemed off with the fairies as he dawdled behind. Chrissie tested out a hammock hanging between a couple of trees, enjoying the feeling of weightlessness as she shaded her eyes from the sun peeking through the leaves and branches above.

'And here is Drew's hand and foot.' Geoff stopped in front of a paved entertainment area where imprints of childlike hands and feet were ingrained into the concrete. 'Age four, he was.'

Drew sidled up next to his imprint and took off his shoe, placing his bare foot next to the younger version. 'I can barely remember being that small,' he said.

'I can. Couldn't keep you still!' Susan said. 'It's amazing we got you to stand here long enough for the imprint.'

'I'm learning all about keeping still in our yoga sessions, aren't I, Chrissie?'

'Yes, you certainly are.' She smiled.

'And is he a good student? Does he behave himself?' Susan asked, nudging her son in the ribs.

Chrissie eyed Drew and turned the corners of her lips downward. 'Well, sometimes.'

'Hey!' He playfully kicked her leg.

'Okay, he's actually a very good student, and does what he's told. Most of the time.'

'Good to hear. And he tells me that Serendipity might be having open classes. I might just come along one day.'

'I hope to see you there.' Chrissie smiled.

They walked around to the other side of the house, and Chrissie's heart doubled over itself when they approached the swimming pool.

'Oh, should have told you to bring your swimming costume in case you wanted a swim,' Susan said.

'Oh, no that's okay.' Chrissie scratched her head and turned away, pretending to admire some hanging plants on the nearby gazebo.

'Let's show Chrissie the chook pen,' Drew said, gesturing up ahead, away from the water.

'Oh, I wouldn't want her to get her lovely clothes messy. It's just an old wooden structure with a bunch of noisy chooks laying eggs.'

'I don't mind, I'd love to have chooks and a daily supply of fresh eggs.' She walked alongside Drew who led her to the pen. He lightly touched her arm as if to ask if she was okay, and she returned his gesture with a brief smile.

His effort to reduce her discomfort was admirable, though she knew she couldn't go on living with this phobia forever. But for now at least, it was nice to have someone around who understood and knew about her reluctance to get up close and personal with the liquid of life.

Susan gathered up a bundle of eggs for Chrissie to take home, and as they wandered around to the front of the house, Drew and his father strolled slowly behind, deep in discussion about something.

Susan and Chrissie stopped by a birdbath. 'So I hear your son is friends with my grandson?'

'Yes, I'm so glad he's made a good friend. It's been hard for him, moving to a new town and school only a year after starting kindergarten.'

'Poor pet. I'm sure he'll settle in well here after a while. Before you know it he'll be all grown up and you'll wonder what happened.' She glanced back at Drew.

'Yes, I'm sure. Part of me wants him to, and another part wants him to stay little for a bit longer.'

'Oh I remember that feeling all too well. Enjoy this precious time now. It goes so fast.' Susan placed a hand over her heart.

'Tell me about it. I still have Kai's baby picture in my purse and haven't updated it to a more recent photo.'

'Oh, can I have a look? I love babies.'

'Sure.' She followed Susan inside and retrieved her purse from a table in the living room.

'Oh, what a cutie! Even in this, I can see he shares your chin.'

'My chin?'

'Yes, see, the angle of it.' She traced around Kai's photo. 'Drew didn't look like me at all when he was a baby. I'd even wondered if we took home the wrong baby by mistake! Here, let me show you.' Susan led her to the hallway where a collection of family photos graced the wall.

Drew Williams' baby photos? He was still outside and had no idea his mother was about to do the very thing every child dreads.

'That's him?' Chrissie asked, pointing to a photo of a chubby baby with a cranky-looking face.

'It sure is!' Susan laughed. 'He was so cuddly, and don't worry, he wasn't that cranky all the time. I think I took that just before he was due to be fed. You know how men get when they need food.'

'Yes, I do.' She grinned.

'And look at these ones.' She plucked an album from a drawer. 'This is on his first birthday, isn't his outfit just adorable?'

Chrissie grinned at the sailor outfit Drew wore, his finger pointing at his number one-shaped birthday cake. There were also photos of him as a toddler with his baby sister, and one on his first day of school. He'd thinned out a lot by then, his lanky legs almost skeletal-looking below his grey school shorts.

'Hey, what's going on here? Secret women's business?' Drew walked in with Geoff.

Susan tucked the album back in the drawer. 'Oh nothing.'

'You weren't showing old photos were you, Mum?'

'Me?' She flashed an innocent expression.

'Oh you didn't.' He shook his head. 'I'll just die of embarrassment right here shall I?' He gestured to the floor.

Chrissie curled her lips into a cheeky smile. 'Now c'mon, Drew. No need to put on such a cranky face.'

A burst of laughter escaped Susan's mouth at Chrissie's comment, and Drew's lips twisted to the side. 'One of these days I'm going to take that terrible photo down and dispose of it!'

'Oh you wouldn't, darling. It's so adorable.' Susan pinched Drew's cheeks and he closed his eyes in apparent resignation. 'Okay, okay. Enough of the motherly stuff.' She patted him on the back. 'Let's go have some coffee out in the garden.' Susan scurried off to prepare the cups and saucers, while Drew hung behind in the hallway with Chrissie.

'I should have known this would happen,' he said, a rosy glow shining on his cheeks.

'That's parents for you. I'm already keeping a file of future embarrassing photos for Kai. It's just payback for the pain of childbirth.'

'I guess that's fair.' He held up his hands in defeat. Then he pinched Chrissie's cheek. 'I bet you don't have any cranky baby photos.'

'I can't remember. But who says only babies can pull those faces off?' She scrunched up her face and pouted and did her best version of Kai's 'I don't want to go to school and you're a mean mother' face.

Drew burst out laughing. 'That is sooo attractive. Such a good look, Burns.'

'Bet you can't do one better.'

'Bet I can.' He squinted and scrunched up his face too, and Chrissie slapped her thigh with laughter.

'Nice one, Williams.'

He grinned and placed his hand on the small of her back. 'C'mon, time for a hot cuppa, cranky pants.'

When they'd farewelled Susan and Geoff and thanked them for their hospitality, Drew and Chrissie got in the car and she drove off.

'I had a great time, thank you,' she said, stealing a quick glance in Drew's direction.

'So did I. Thanks for coming,' he replied. 'So, back to household duties for you when you get home?' He checked his watch, even though the time was displayed on the dashboard. It was just after 5pm.

'I guess so. Although I'm not really in the mood. Maybe I should have the night off.'

'Funny, I was thinking the same thing.'

'You were thinking I should have the night off? How thoughtful of you,' she mocked.

'I was thinking you should have the night off. With me.'

'You've got the whole month off, Williams.' When he didn't reply right away, she glanced at him. His face was serious. Serious, and seriously delicious.

'Fancy dinner on the beach tonight? I'll even bring a jacket this time.' He smiled.

Chrissie's heart rate rose, and she had the urge to wind down the window even though the air con was on. In two weeks Drew would be gone from her life yet here she was spending all this time with him. Surely it was a bad idea and would only lead to disappointment? Although right now, it seemed like the best idea ever, and one should live in the moment, shouldn't one?

'A picnic?' she asked.

'Why not? I could nab some food from the chefs at Serendipity, get a basket or something.'

Chrissie thought back to the wonderful lunch she'd had. 'No, let me. I'll bring the food.'

'So it's a yes, then?'

'It's a yes.' She smiled. 'On the sand dunes outside my place? Next to the rocky hill?'

'Sounds perfect. About eight?'

'Hmm, maybe a bit before. The sun will be going down around then. How about... 7.48pm?' She tilted her head and hitched up one corner of her lips.

'Make it 7.49 and you've got yourself a deal.'

'Deal.' They locked eyes for a moment and Chrissie no longer saw the ocean rippling in his eyes, she saw stars. Their sparkle sent a shiver up her spine, and she hadn't felt this way in a long time.

'So is there anything you'd like me to bring?'

Chrissie thought for a few seconds. 'I'll provide the rug, the food, and the drink.' She slid a glance his way and poked his arm with her finger. 'And you provide the music.'

He turned to face her.

'Yes that's right. Bring your guitar.'

He smiled. 'Okay then, Bossy Burns. What song should I play first?'

'*A Good Start*,' she said. She did love his new one, *Breathe*, but had had enough of tears for a while. *A Good Start* was upbeat, in a relaxed way, and always made her feel good.

'I'll sing it before we eat. That will get the night off to a very good start.' He flashed a cheeky smile.

'If you do a better job with the song than with your puns, then yes.'

He whacked her thigh.

As she dropped Drew at Serendipity and drove to the end of Dune Road, a comforting sense of happiness washed over her. What a great day. She got to enjoy being in the type of house she'd always wanted, be around the family she'd always wanted, and tonight... she'd be with the man she'd always wanted. Reality could go and get stuffed until Monday.

CHAPTER SIXTEEN

*R*ight, picnic rug — check. Bottle of champagne — check. *Tray of food — check. Candle in a jar — check. Oh, what am I forgetting?* Chrissie's gaze darted here, there, and everywhere. *Oh of course!* She grabbed two plastic wine glasses from the cupboard. *What are we supposed to do, drink from the bottle? Oh, and napkins... do we need napkins?* If Kai was there, yes, but it would just be two grown adults sharing a tray of simple food. *But what if there's a spill or an awkward food on face situation? Oh for crying out loud, I can come back into the bloody house!*

Although the dinner date was right outside her house, it was way outside her comfort zone, and she wanted to be as prepared and dignified as possible. She grabbed a couple of plastic plates and popped them on the tray, then carried her collection of items outside. The air wasn't cool like last night, the heat of the day still hung in the air, despite the refreshing breeze rising off the ocean. The moon shone bright too, and with the outdoor lighting around the house, the candle might not be needed, but it wasn't only about need. What's a romantic dinner without a candle? *Romantic?* Oh God, she was probably reading too much into this.

They'd shared a nice family lunch and now they would share a nice friendly dinner between teacher and student. Nothing more. It couldn't be any more.

She placed the tray on the sand and shook out the picnic rug, laying it neatly on the ground. The sand dune sloped slightly, but a flat area at one end of the rug kept the tray of food and drink from toppling over.

She walked up to the edge of the rocky hill and peered over it, but there was no sign of him yet. Her phone buzzed. *What if it's him? What if he's cancelling?* She dug her fingers in her pocket and retrieved the phone. Melinda. Crap, not the best timing.

'Hi Mel,' she answered.

'Hey, Hun, how are you enjoying your Saturday night without Kai? Working through stuff in the house I bet, or watching a movie?

Chrissie bit her lip. 'Um, something like that.' *Nothing remotely like that.*

'So how are things? Kai go to school okay?'

'In the second half of the week, mostly. His dad said he'd take him to the movies as a reward. At first that wasn't enough incentive, so he said he could also go to the video game arcade after and play in the young kids section. I hate those places, they're so noisy and filled with older kids, but it worked.'

'Whatever works, Hun.'

'Yeah. I just hope we don't have to keep doing this forever. I don't want to spoil the kid.'

'Letting him have fun isn't spoiling him, it's showing him that when he tries hard he gets to have fun, and when he doesn't, he might not get to do the things he wants to do.'

'True. And I'm one step ahead for next week. The local Sunday markets are on next weekend, so that'll be his next reward. I'll give him ten dollars to buy something from one of the stalls. Might even see if his new friend would like to come along.'

'Sounds great. Anyway, you're child-free for the weekend, so what else is going on with you lately?'

'Oh, not much, the usual. How about you?'

'Just the usual for me too. Hubby says we should go on a family holiday sometime soon, before the cooler weather sets in. I told him as long as I can come and stay with you for a night or two in the school holidays like I promised. We might even head down your way and stay a while somewhere nearby.'

'Well, you could always stay—'

'And don't even think about offering for all of us to stay with you. You need the time to work on the house; you don't want us to create more work for you. I'll leave the fam at the holiday park and come and help you out for a bit.'

'Oh, you're awesome.'

'I know.'

Chrissie chuckled at her friend's sarcastic honesty. If such a contradiction existed. She was being sarcastic to avoid sounding egotistical, but it was true. She was awesome. So was the person strolling down the beach on the other side of the hill.

'Um, sorry to cut our convo short Mel, but I kinda have to get going.'

'I thought you were just hanging out at home?'

'I am. I just...' Drew caught her eye and waved with his free hand, the other one carrying his guitar. 'I'm, um, baking! I have a cake in the oven and then I'm going to put cookies in right after so I can't really call back, I don't want to start a fire or anything!'

'You're baking?'

'Guess so.'

'Now I'm jealous. Maybe I should leave motherhood for the weekend and drive down to your place right now. I could eat a whole cake. And maybe a cookie or ten.'

'Oh well, one day. Shame it's a bit late. Anyway, great chatting. Love ya, I'll talk to you maybe tomorrow.'

'Righto, you Baking Queen. Talk soon.'

Chrissie ended the call and tucked the phone in her pocket as Drew came around the corner. It killed her to lie to Melinda, but she had no choice. Maybe when this was all over she could fill her in and apologise. *When it was all over.*

Drew strummed his guitar. 'Well, hello...' he sang.

Chrissie laughed. 'Is that the start of a new song?'

'It could be.' He walked up the sand dune barefooted. Chrissie was wearing slip-on sandals but shouldn't have bothered. She kicked them off when he approached. 'But I actually have a new song I started working on only this evening.' He placed the guitar on the side of the rug.

'Another one? You're on a roll!'

'Must have been inspired by our lunch today.'

'So do I get a sneak peek?'

'Nope. Not yet. Nowhere near ready to be heard by anyone else.'

'Oh, I'm curious! What's it called.'

'I'm not telling.' He made a show of zipping his lips.

'Tease,' Chrissie said. 'So,' she gestured around. 'Welcome to the three hat 'Sand Dune' restaurant.'

'I don't see any hat, let alone three of them.'

'Stop it, you.' She gently kicked his leg. 'I'm sure with your glamorous lifestyle and an ex-chef for a father you know all about how restaurants are rated.'

'Of course. But I think it's a silly thing to call it. They should use something else instead of hats.'

'Such as...?'

'Such as... *mmms* or something.'

'*Mmms?*'

'Yeah, the more *mmms* the nicer the food and service. One hat is *mmm*, two hats is *mmm, mmm*, and three hats is *mmm, mmm, mmm* as in delicious.'

Chrissie's mouth practically watered at the way his mouth made the *mmm* sounds. 'And what if the food was even better than *mmm, mmm, mmm*?'

Drew glanced up at the sky in thought. 'Maybe it would be a *yes! yes! yes!* Like in *When Harry Met Sally.* '

Chrissie laughed. 'Well I don't think the food I've brought will be that... *stimulating,* but I hope it'll at least be a one *mmm.*'

'So what's on the menu?' Drew lifted the lids off the plastic containers.

'Sorry, it's not very fancy. Plastic containers and all that.'

'It's a picnic, and you know me, I'd be happy with Vegemite sandwiches.'

'Funny you should say that,' Chrissie said, as Drew eyed the ribbon sandwiches she'd made.

Drew's eyebrows rose.

'Kidding, no Vegemite ones I'm afraid, but I do have chicken and cucumber and ham and coleslaw.'

'Even better.' He rubbed his stomach. 'And you even brought cheese and crackers and antipasto. Thanks for this, you rock!'

'Ha,' she replied, pointing to his guitar. 'And you.'

He smiled, and tipped his head towards the rocky hill next to them. 'And that.'

'Haha, good pun.' Chrissie gestured to the picnic rug. 'Please take a seat, sir.'

Drew sat and shifted around to get comfortable, the guitar on one side of him, Chrissie on the other.

'Can I get you a glass of house wine, sir?'

'Please.' He held up a plastic goblet and she poured in the sparkling liquid. 'So much for being alcohol free this month.'

'I won't tell anyone at Serendipity.'

'Good.'

Chrissie poured one for herself and Drew held his out and

clinked hers, even though it was more of a dull clunk and barely audible. 'Cheers.'

'Cheers.'

Chrissie tipped wine down her throat, the coolness soon replaced by the warm feeling of the alcohol. The waves in the ocean whooshed and hummed, rolled in and sunk back out, forward, backward, like the thoughts and emotions in her mind. Go to Drew, pull away from Drew — repeat. The more she pulled away the more she wanted to return to him, and the more she returned to him, the more she wanted to stay, despite her conflicting thoughts on the issue.

'These are nice, very posh,' Drew said after munching into a ribbon sandwich. 'Good thing there aren't any crusts, I really don't want my hair to go curly.'

Chrissie's hand reached up to his head before she knew what she was doing. She ran it across the prickly softness of his number two cut. 'You don't have enough hair to make any curls.' She grinned.

'Good thing, then. But you,' he ran his hand through her long wavy hair, 'you've got definite curl potential here.' He twirled a few strands between his finger and they coiled and slipped around it.

'My hair can't make up its mind. It's not straight, and not curly.'

'It's strurly.' He grinned.

'You love playing with words, don't you?'

'It's my job. I spend more time writing songs than I do singing them. Performing is only a small percentage of my career. Then there's the publicity, the photo shoots, the interviews, the management discussions and strategic planning. Sheesh, I'm getting a headache just thinking about it all.'

'You sure one month is enough time off for you?' Had she alluded to a double meaning with her question, as though she wanted him to stay longer? She only realised once the words had been spoken.

'I'll let you know once I get back to the States. But yeah, I'm enjoying the time off.' He caught her eye with his gaze. '*Really* enjoying it.'

When the wine was almost gone and only crumbs remained on the plates, Chrissie put them to the side. 'Now, I do have dessert in the kitchen if you want any. Thought I'd wait and see.'

'I'm good for now, but my stomach will let me know soon enough if not.' He rubbed it. 'Hey, I haven't played for you yet.' He lifted his guitar and sat it on his lap. '*A Good Start*, right?'

'One of my favourites.' She manoeuvred back a little to give him room, and rested on her hands behind her for support.

Chrissie watched his hands, the way they delicately cradled the instrument, the way his fingers knew just where to press and move. It was as hypnotic as his music. She wished she was the guitar, being embraced and adored and caressed in all the right places. The rhythmic tones from the guitar filled the air, each note like a little star, rising up to join the others shining their light on the world.

She could listen to his voice all day. All night. She closed her eyes, rocking side to side in time with the music. When the rhythm intensified in anticipation of the faster tempo of the chorus, she opened her eyes and her lips parted in a smile as Drew sang.

'May not be right, may not be wrong,
But I've been waiting far too long.
Who knows whether I've made the right choice,
But I know, I know, it's a good start...'

When he finished singing he placed his guitar to the side as Chrissie clapped. He gave an exaggerated bow and thanked her. 'And the crowd went wild...' He cupped his hands around his mouth and made a noise like a clapping crowd of thousands.

'I feel honoured to get a private show,' Chrissie said, wriggling closer on the rug.

'The honour's all mine.' He smiled.

'Those people at the Love Festival,' Chrissie cocked her head to the right, 'don't know what they're missing out on.'

'Agreed.' Drew said.

He couldn't have been talking about his own music, so did he mean — being with her? *Oh boy.*

Chrissie looked up at the sky. 'Such a beautiful, clear night.'

'It is.' Drew glanced up too, the stars embellishing the sky like twinkling jewels. 'You know, when I was a kid, I used to think stars were like guardian angels or something. Coming out at night to watch over the world. One star for each person on earth.'

'How beautiful. Maybe they are, who knows.'

'I was quite disappointed when my dad informed me that they were simply collections of gas hovering in the sky and the glow is due to simple physics and chemistry.'

'Trust science to spoil something so wondrous.'

'Yeah. I had it in for science since then. Rebelled by becoming a musician.' He glanced at Chrissie and grinned.

'You know, I'm surprised you still have a hundred percent of your Aussie accent. You'd think after so long in the States you would have developed a bit of an accent.'

'Ah, you can take me out of the country but you can't take the country outta me.' He chuckled.

'Good to see.' Chrissie said. 'So, what do you love most about being a singer?'

'Well, the thrill of singing of course, but mostly I love creating something that didn't exist before. Lyrics, a melody, a beat. Bringing emotions and thoughts and ideas to life and sharing them with others. So satisfying.' His words exuded passion, and a calm, content buzz hung in the air around them, like time didn't matter, only this moment. 'And then there's the bonus of meeting people like you.' He nudged her in the side with his elbow.

Chrissie lowered her chin and smiled. 'Well I never thought I'd be teaching yoga to a celebrity whose work I admire so much.'

'Aw, thanks. Life is strange, eh? But as for celebrity, I've never really got used to that word. I don't feel like a celebrity, I just feel like me.'

'How have you managed to stay so down to earth and humble?' Chrissie asked. 'Your life's been in the spotlight since you were barely an adult and yet, talking to you, being with you, you don't have any of the attitude that some others in your position seem to have.'

Drew shrugged. 'I've had some good mentors to keep me grounded. One of them said to me early on, "Don't put on an act. Let your performances be an extension of who you are. If you pretend to be something you're not, you'll spend your life trying to live up to that image and you'll lose yourself in the process."'

'What wise words.'

'Indeed. I'll have to pass them onto Gemma before she gets carried away with the allure of bright lights and applause.'

'Good idea.' Chrissie thought about her own career, and how much more *herself* she'd felt when she switched from journalism to yoga teaching. 'That's what I love about yoga. It allows people, no matter who they are or what they've done, to just be themselves for a while. Get back to basics and nourish their mind and body.'

'Exactly why I wanted these classes this month,' Drew replied. 'And so far, they've given me all that and more. I'll definitely be keeping up with daily practise when I get home.' Drew lay on his back, his hands joined together behind his head and bent knees pointing upwards.

'I'm glad.' *Well, glad about the yoga, not about the going home bit.* Chrissie followed his lead and lay back too, hypnotised by the sparkling dots in the sky.

'I think for tonight I'm going to believe that those stars really are guardian angels and not just lumps of gas.' Drew said.

'Me too. I like your hypothesis much more.' Chrissie imagined each star as a caring soul whose purpose was to guide and protect her. 'Isn't it funny how you can actually get a star named after you?'

'Ha! I've got one.'

She turned to face him. 'Really? There's a Drew Williams up there?' Her grin grew along with his.

'Sure is. It was given to me as a gift. Hey, I should get one for you!'

'Oh,' she giggled, 'I don't need one. No need to go to all the trouble.'

'But then you could join me and my mates up there.'

'Mates?'

'Yeah.' He released his hands from behind his head and pointed to the sky. 'See, that one there is Bob, that's Dazza, and that's Pete.'

A laugh bubbled out from Chrissie, and as Drew lowered his arm by his side it brushed against hers, sending tingles of bliss along her skin. His arm flinched ever so slightly, as though he'd felt it too, and for a moment they didn't speak, just gazed at the stars and breathed in the salty air as the waves whooshed onto the nearby shore.

There'd be no need for a jacket or cardi tonight; heat ran along her arm from Drew's skin to hers, spreading throughout her body and heightening her senses. Drew's hand moved a little, and breath caught in Chrissie's throat as his pinky finger hooked onto hers. She would have continued focusing on the stars and enjoying the sensation of his skin against hers, had it not been for the unmistakeable feeling that he had turned his head and was now looking right at her.

Slowly, Chrissie's gaze left the stars above and turned to the one lying next to her. His golden-brown skin had a light sheen from the moonlight, his eyes had a glint in them from the stars, and his lips, oh his lips...

Chrissie pressed her lips together and swallowed. 'What are you thinking about?' she whispered, her words merely a passenger riding on her breath as it floated from her lungs.

Drew's breath warmed her face as it swirled across her cheeks. 'I'm thinking how much I want to kiss you right now.'

Chrissie's lips parted and a small sigh escaped. Her unblinking eyes saw deep into his, sought out his heart, and longed to remain there forever. 'Then do it,' she replied.

He rolled slowly onto his side and propped himself up on his elbow, as Chrissie remained still, her body vulnerable, desperate for his touch.

Drew leaned over her and his hand touched her face, tracing the line of her jaw. His thumb moved lightly across her tingling lips as he looked hungrily at them. The tingles intensified as his face came closer, and a ripple of desire shot through her body as the softness of his lips brushed against hers. She reached up and touched the firm, muscular terrain of his back, pulling him closer as his mouth pressed onto hers; around it, over it, into it. His soft lips enveloped hers from every possible angle as though he couldn't get enough, and she received them eagerly, kissing him back with more passion and need than she'd ever experienced before.

Drew straightened his supporting elbow, slid his arm under her neck, and rolled her body forward to meet his. Chrissie tucked her other arm around his back and her body melded into his as their lips grew hungrier. His hand ran down her back, leaving a trail of shivers in its wake, then ran back up her spine and his fingers delved into her hair, twirling and tangling and grabbing.

She pulled away slightly to take a breath, sucking the air into her mouth sharply, then commanding his lips again as she exhaled.

The sound of the waves rolling into shore faded from Chrissie's mind, the only sounds she heard were Drew's breath, their silken lips dancing together, and her heart telling her not to let him go.

CHAPTER SEVENTEEN

T hin slivers of light seeping through the bamboo venetian blinds opened Drew's eyes on Monday morning. Despite his late night after being at Honeydew House all day sorting through old things, now that he was awake, he couldn't drift back to sleep. Not once he remembered he'd be seeing Chrissie in a few hours.

His mouth stretched into a yawn and he rolled over in the bed, his eyes catching sight of the sunset painting. His mind flitted back to Saturday night on the beach with Chrissie, the fun conversation they'd shared, and the completely natural progression to their passionate kiss. They'd kissed for so long, he'd had no idea how much time had passed until he made his way back to Serendipity and it was after eleven. His body had wanted things to progress even further, but his mind had proven stronger. It would be too much, too soon, and he didn't want to mess her around.

Sunday at his parents' house had proven to be an ideal distraction, since all he wanted was to go back to Chrissie's place and be with her. He had decided not to call her, and she hadn't called him either. He knew he'd see her on Monday, and maybe they needed Sunday apart to process what had happened between them.

Drew stepped out of bed and stretched his arms high. His back ached from being hunched over boxes all day, sifting and sorting through items from his childhood. Since he'd left home quite suddenly after winning *Search for a Star*, there'd never been any time to go through absolutely everything, and his parents had told him they could store it until he had time to come back and do it. It had taken him close to twenty years to find that time. He thought he'd need a few more days, but he'd gone through every single box yesterday and hadn't stopped until 10pm. It was cathartic, but an emotionally draining experience. His whole past, condensed into a ton of objects, and he had to decide which things to keep and which to chuck away. The same went for his life in general. It got him thinking about which habits and beliefs he needed to keep and which no longer served him. The thought that he needed to keep up at the same speed he'd always travelled gnawed at him. He wasn't an up and coming twenty-something anymore, always on the lookout for the next thrill and the high of performing. He'd be forty in a few years, and no longer desired to live life at high speed. How could he slow down and still do what he loved? Music was competitive, new stars were popping up all over the place, and he needed to keep his exposure in the industry to maintain his success. But was it worth the constant workload?

The box of old photos he'd looked through yesterday had taken the longest. It'd been like a movie passing before his eyes. He'd gone out to the living room every now and again with a photo in hand saying, 'Hey, Mum, remember this?' and 'Dad, check out your hair and beard in this one!' They'd chatted about old times and shared memories over coffee and Dad's award-winning scones. There were photos of his young days at athletics, running races and winning medals and ribbons. He'd been quite the runner until he'd discovered he could sing, and took up playing the guitar. As a teenager he'd surf on weekends with his mates, Barry included. He really needed to see him again before he left, try to make an effort to set things right.

But first, there was the Chrissie issue.

If he wasn't leaving in two weeks there'd be no question about it — he'd continue seeing her. *If* she felt the same way, which by the look of things the other night, she did. But he wasn't staying; he couldn't.

He unplugged his phone from the charger and checked his phone for messages. No texts, but a few emails, just the usual ones, nothing that he needed to read right now.

Drew stripped off his trunks and turned on the shower, running his hand under the flow of water until it heated up. He stepped in and revelled in the warm, firm spray of water waking up his body. He squirted the Serendipity shower gel onto his palm and rubbed his hands together, then rubbed the foamy liquid over his face and body. His thoughts turned to Chrissie again. How beautiful and innocent she'd looked lying under the starry sky, the way she'd laughed when he'd pretended the stars were called Bob, Dazza, and Pete. Being around her brought a sense of calm and a sense of excitement at the same time. An innate primal urge wanted to protect her, help her, stand strong by her side, and show her how special she was. He knew she'd been putting on a brave face for too many years, but had recently started to open up and share her heart and soul with him. How was it that he'd only known her for two short weeks but felt like he'd known her much longer? Their connection was so strong, so deep on some unconscious level, and so magnetic.

He closed his eyes as water ran down his body, and Chrissie's face hung in his mind. He could still feel her long, soft hair tangled between his fingers, her strong, sculpted body as he'd ran his hand down her back, and her luscious, inviting lips as they'd kissed with an intense and delicious passion. His chest rose with a sharp intake of breath and heat spread through his body, not only from the water. His eyes snapped open and he forced a slow exhalation, then reached for the faucet and turned the water cold.

When soft footsteps padded along the hallway, Drew headed for the door. He made his way to the yoga studio where Chrissie stood at the corner table fiddling with her bag, her blonde ponytail cascading down her back.

Drew cleared his throat and she spun around. 'Hi. Hi, how are you. Good?' The words catapulted from her throat. It was charming how nervous she got sometimes, and it made the corner of his mouth twitch upwards.

'I'm good. How are you?'

'I'm good too.'

'Good.'

'Good.'

She lowered her head and swung her foot to the side, then glanced up. 'Drew,' she said, taking a few tentative steps towards him.

Oh no, just what he feared. She was about to tell him she'd made a mistake and they needed to forget it ever happened. Not that he ever could.

'Drew, I... I'm sorry about the other night. I've been so unprofessional. You must think I'm some desperate, lonely single mother trying to—'

'No, I don't.' Drew walked forward. 'And there's no need to apologise.' He stopped in front of her, the sun shining on her freshly glossed light pink lips. 'I should apologise. I'm your student, and I'm only here for February. I shouldn't have got carried away, shouldn't have pursued you when I'm supposed to be here taking a break, not getting in the way of someone else's life.'

A light crease tainted her brow. 'You're not getting in the way, please don't think that.'

'I just don't want to... confuse you, confuse myself, start something that...'

He couldn't find the words to end his sentence. Or just didn't want to say them.

'Something that can't be continued,' Chrissie whispered, hitting the nail on the head.

Drew looked her deep in the eyes. 'I'm sorry if I've made things uncomfortable for you, being here, having to teach me.'

'No, it's okay. It'll all be okay. We can still do this; I can still be the teacher you need me to be.'

But I want you to be so much more...

Drew's heart felt like it was in quicksand, falling fast. The more he resisted, the more he slipped under. The hold she had over him was all encompassing and it took a truckload of willpower not to grab her and continue what they'd started on Saturday night. Drew stepped backwards, confused and unsure of how to handle this situation. Chrissie seemed equally unsure; though she had that expression on her face, the one that portrayed being confident and in control, something beneath the facade hinted at a conflicting emotion.

Drew took another step back, and took his mind to the idea of going back to a purely professional relationship with Chrissie. Two more weeks of yoga lessons, and that was it. That's all he'd signed up for, all he'd expected, and all he'd...

No, it wasn't all he'd wanted. Once he'd started getting to know Chrissie he'd wanted more and more to be around her, and not just for yoga. He'd wanted her conversation, her unexpected moments of humour, her laughter, her playfulness, her... her everything.

Drew shook his head then ran his hand over his scalp, each

prickly hair assaulting the skin on is palm and protesting the current scenario.

'Actually,' he piped up, looking her straight in the eyes. 'I'm not sorry. Not at all.' He walked up to her and grasped her arms. 'I don't regret a single second. I don't want to stop this... this... whatever it is. I know it's crazy and illogical and stupid of me to even think you'd want it too, but I can't help it.' His gaze bore into hers, her blue eyes clear and vibrant and sparkling. 'So there you go. I'm not sorry one little bit.' He offered a vulnerable, lopsided smile.

Chrissie's lips turned up slightly at the corners. 'Your non-apology is accepted,' she said. 'And just so that we're even, I'm not sorry either.'

Something went all warm and squishy inside on hearing her words, and his thumbs rubbed across her arms as he held them. 'What are we going to do?' he asked, as though he was really asking himself.

Chrissie shrugged. 'I have no idea. You'll be gone in a couple of weeks, we lead such different lives, and... God, if anyone here found out, I could lose my job.' Her gaze dropped to the side.

Drew lifted her chin with his finger. 'I'm not going to let that happen. And I don't want to hurt you in any way. All I know is, Chrissie, you've captivated me and I can't get enough.' Her skin warmed his finger as he slid it along her cheek. 'There's so much going through my mind right now, my past, my life overseas, my family here, my future... I don't know what my next step should be.'

'Maybe you, maybe *we*, should just put one step in front of the other for now.'

'Like, going with the flow?'

'Going with the flow. It's something I was once told I needed to do. I've always been so busy thinking ahead, sometimes way ahead, and anxious about things that haven't even happened, that

I forget to be in the present, except when I'm doing yoga,' Chrissie explained. 'But you, you've taught me to be in the present at other times too, and somehow you help me relax and enjoy simple pleasures.'

'You've made it easy to show you that. You make me want to share simple pleasures with you.'

Chrissie placed her palms against Drew's chest. 'My head is telling me I'm crazy but my heart is saying give me more.'

A smile tickled Drew's cheeks. 'Then let's do as you say; one step at a time, go with the flow, enjoy the moment.'

'And,' she turned her lips inward and lowered her gaze for a moment, 'no expectations.' It was as though she was trying to convince herself of such a rule.

'No expectations,' Drew echoed.

Chrissie's hands fell to her side and she took a deep breath. 'Well, we better stop talking and start—'

'Yoga-ing?'

She grinned. 'Another word to tell those Oxford people about?'

'I'm onto it.' Drew winked, and went to the shelf to take a yoga mat. Chrissie took one for herself and they placed them on the floor, a little closer than they usually were.

'So, stand with feet shoulder width apart, and take a deep breath, in... and out...'

He locked his eyes on hers as they both breathed. Breathed the same air, at the same time, in the same way, while the same emotions swirled within. Familiar desire spiralled up from his belly to his chest and, as though he was a laser and she was his target, in an instant he was in front of her, on her mat, his hands sliding around her back. Chrissie's breath quickened at his touch and without warning she brought her hands to his face, pulling him close as she pressed her lips urgently against his.

CHAPTER EIGHTEEN

'Why are we stopping, Mum?' Kai asked, peering out the car window on Wednesday morning.

'See those kids with their parents?'

He nodded.

'They're waiting for the school bus. Would you like to join them and catch the bus to school, like the big kids?'

Kai shook his head fiercely. 'No way.'

'Why not? It'll be fun. You'll be up so high; you'll be able to see the whole town like a giant.' Chrissie added a touch of excitement to her voice. 'It'll be just like a ride at the fair.'

'I don't want to.' He slumped in his seat and crossed his arms.

'I'll follow the bus in my car, and if you sit in the back you'll be able to see me the whole time. I'll travel all the way to school with you.'

'That's just silly,' he said.

What was silly was that in her blissful emotional state from Drew's affections she'd thought she could do anything, including get her reluctant school-goer to catch the bus for the first time ever. Chrissie leaned her head against the back of the seat. Maybe it was a bit much to expect. Just like she'd agreed to with Drew, she'd have to try this one step at a time.

'Okay, well I'll tell you what.' She twisted her body to face him in the back seat. 'I'll drive you to school like I normally do, but we'll follow the bus. So you can see where it goes and what happens when it stops at school. After a few days, maybe we'll go up to the bus stop and talk to some of the other kids and parents so you know who they are. Then, we'll still drive to school and follow the bus, and after a while of doing that, you could try getting on the bus and going to school with the other kids and I'll drive behind the bus the whole way and make sure you're okay. How does that sound?'

He twisted his lips in various directions as though chewing on her suggestions, and Chrissie totally expected him to say, 'I don't wanna', but instead he said, 'Maybe we could follow the bus.'

Chrissie smiled. 'That's a boy. Let's do that today.'

Kai sat straighter again and peered outside, as the bus pulled up just beyond the curved part of the road in front of them. Chrissie wound the window down, and petrol fumes filled her nostrils. Melinda had told her that new experiences for kids were often frightening because of the overwhelming sensory stimuli to process. Things that adults took for granted, like smells or sounds, could be unfamiliar and scary for sensitive children. By exposing him to the diesel smell and the jarring halt of the breaks before dealing with actually getting on the bus, she hoped it might make him less wary.

The bus doors folded open and chattering children filed in, while Chrissie pointed and explained what was happening.

'Aren't the parents going to follow the bus too?'

'I don't think so. Their children are used to catching the bus now, so they prefer to go alone. I bet they were scared too when they first caught the bus, though. But now they're not, see?' She gestured to a kid who was laughing along with another.

Kai eyed the scene with narrowed, cautious eyes.

The gravelly sound of the engine rolled towards them and the bus edged back onto the road. Chrissie flicked on her blinker, checked for cars, and pulled onto the road behind the bus. Hopefully the driver didn't think she was stalking him or had him under surveillance for an undercover operation. Parenthood sometimes called for strange and desperate measures. Maybe she should speak to him after the kids got off the bus, tell him about Kai's reluctance. He might be able to encourage him.

'Why is the bus stopping?' Kai asked.

'It has to pick up more children from a different part of town, see?' She pointed to a few kids waiting on the side of the road.

The bus made two more stops then made its way to the school drop off zone.

'See, that wasn't too bad, was it?'

'It was a bit longer than usual.'

'Yes, I know, because it had to pick up the other kids.' Chrissie pulled into a spare spot and quickly helped Kai from the car. 'And now the kids are hopping out of the bus and ready for school, just like you are now. There's not much difference.'

Kai frowned. 'What if I couldn't get off the bus in time and it started moving again? Would I be left on it all day?'

Chrissie bent to her son's level, grasping his arms gently. 'No, sweetie. The bus driver would make sure all children are safely off the bus before driving away. It's his job to take care of his passengers and get them where they need to go.'

'What if I needed to go to the toilet on the way?'

Oh dear. Kai was definitely a worrywart in training. 'Well, they don't have a toilet on school buses because it's such a short trip. That's why you go before school so you don't need to go again until you're at school.'

'I might have to go twice at home beforehand, just to make extrally sure.'

Chrissie smiled at her son's strategic thinking. 'Good idea.' She took his hand and walked to the school gates. The last of the children were getting off the bus, but she'd talk to the driver tomorrow. Kai seemed open to the idea now, so that was enough progress for one day. She walked him into the school grounds, wondering about the day that lay ahead and what sort of progress would be made between her and Drew in their morning yoga session.

Three hours later things were progressing quite well. Chrissie would have been happy with an all day chatting and kissing session, which the yoga classes were now becoming.

'C'mon, you can do better than that, Williams.' Chrissie tilted his pelvis slightly with her hands so that it faced the front as he performed *Parsvakonasana*. 'Turn and open up the left side of your torso.'

'I'm trying,' Drew strained. 'And cut me some slack, Burns, this is the first time I've done the pose without the support block underneath my hand.'

'Even more reason to make sure you get it right, then.' She liked exerting authority over him; it gave her a kind of thrill, and she had a feeling he liked it too. 'Okay, now that your torso is in better alignment, let's work on these spaghetti arms.' She tapped them, then pulled his left hand to extend his arm higher and straighter.

'They are not spaghetti arms,' he replied.

'Are too.'

'Well you had me all focusing on my pelvis and torso, how am I supposed to focus on my arms at the same time?'

'The mind can focus on more than one thing, you just have to practise.'

'Oh, I don't know,' he said through strained breath, 'I think you female kind are better at multi-tasking.'

'I won't argue with that.' She grinned, even though Drew couldn't see her face from where she stood behind him. Motherhood had taught Chrissie to be a great multitasker. She could cook dinner, answer Kai's ridiculously difficult questions about outer space, and do her one hundred bi-weekly calf raises while writing the next day's shopping list. 'Good, that's better,' she said, taking her hands off Drew and letting him sustain the pose. 'I don't want to see any more of those spaghetti arms.'

'You going all *Dirty Dancing* on me?'

'Whatever works.'

Drew's posture loosened slightly as he chuckled. 'Just don't put me in the corner if I do things wrong.'

Chrissie laughed. 'Don't worry, nobody puts Drew in the corner.'

Drew eased out of the pose and turned to face her. 'My puns are rubbing off on you.'

'If only it was your singing ability.'

A smile formed on his lips.

'How do you know *Dirty Dancing* so well, anyway? I thought it was a chick flick.'

'I've seen it. I have a good memory.' He shrugged. 'And anyway, Sarah was obsessed with it as a young teenager, she watched it over and over again on the only television set in the house. The script and songs are ingrained into my subconscious memory.'

Chrissie found herself swaying playfully side to side. 'Are you a good dancer?'

He held his arms out to the side. 'Am I a good dancer?' he asked confidently as though he was Johnny Castle himself. 'I'll let you be the judge of that.' He waltzed over to her in a sexy swagger and grabbed her, tipping her torso backwards.

'Whoa!' Chrissie straightened up. 'Wasn't expecting that.'

'Expect the unexpected,' Drew said dramatically, placing one hand on her waist and the other on her hand, in dance position. He stepped forwards and she moved with him, he turned and changed direction and she followed, trusting his lead, until she stepped on his foot.

'Ouch! Lucky you weren't in heels.'

'If I was in heels I would have fallen over back there.' She pointed to the direction they'd come from. 'How those ballroom dancers do it I have no idea.' She broke away from his grasp. 'Anyway, this isn't exactly yoga now is it? You, Mister, should behave.' She jabbed her finger towards his chest.

'You were the one who asked if I could dance. And besides, what's wrong with mixing up the classes a little?'

'So you want to... *dance* with me?'

'Why not?' He shot her a cheeky grin.

She matched it with one of her own. 'Then there's only one thing that's missing.' She walked over to the corner table and plucked her phone from her bag. She went to scroll through the playlists but opted for YouTube instead. When she found what she was looking for she placed her iPhone in the speaker dock on the table, pressed play, then turned to look at Drew.

His face lit up in recognition when the music began. The unmistakeable song, *The Time of my Life*, filled the room, its slow, breezy start encouraging her to saunter across the room towards him. Drew eyed her with anticipation, curling his finger to entice her closer, then her body was against his, captivated by a playful eagerness in his eyes. He took hold of her waist and she placed her hands around his back. They swayed and moved together slowly, until the part in the song where the tempo hastens, and in the movie Johnny and Baby begin dancing properly. Drew did some fancy footwork that brought an amused smile to Chrissie's face, and as though at a nightclub they boogied and twisted and danced — apart, and together — teasing and playing with each other as the music ran through their bodies. Drew was no expert, but he sure had rhythm.

When the lyrics mentioned taking each other's hand, he took hers, using it to pull her towards him, the heat coming off his body like the sun's radiation on a summer's day. They moved in time together and Chrissie realised how appropriate the lyrics were to their situation. With adrenalin fuelling her confidence she mouthed them to Drew, telling him through the safety of the song that she couldn't get enough of him. He mirrored her lip-syncing as the song continued, getting to the bit that mentioned the 'L' word and looking her directly in the eye as he mouthed it.

Could it really be love? Was that even possible? Or was it just infatuation and lust under the pressure of a time limit? She didn't have time to think it through, because he twirled her around and wrapped her in his arm, then unwrapped her, her body coiling out away from his, then back in again like dancers do. They sang and danced to the chorus, and an ecstatic sensation came over Chrissie, both for the fact that she hadn't danced for ages and it felt fantastic, and for the fact that she was with someone who made her feel safe, excited, hopeful, happy, and herself, all at the same time. Tingles danced through her muscles and nerves, lifting her energy and planting a permanent smile on her face. She was, literally, having the time of her life.

The chorus merged into the next verse and Drew separated from her, moving about in a teasing way that made her want to pull him back. He sang, 'Hey baby', and curled his finger at her again. Chrissie mouthed the lyrics of the verse, the *sexy* verse, telling him how much she wanted him, more than he knew, and the glow on his face intensified. He pulled her close during the bit about it being okay to lose control, and he bent her body backwards at the waist and swung her around in a sensual arc, his hand supporting her lower back.

She returned to his level, tingling at the rush from being

upside down, and resisted the urge to look away at the next part of the lyrics. Her lips recited the words that suggested 'staying with her tonight', and deep inside she wished he could.

He swayed with her as one body, their hot skin separated only by a thin barrier of clothing, and as the song built up to the chorus, Drew gave her a questioning look. She knew he wanted to lift her up, like Johnny did to Baby in *Dirty Dancing*. Well, not *exactly.* A feat like that would take some practise, but he wanted to lift her nonetheless.

He gripped under her arms and she nodded, and as the chorus built up to that iconic moment, he bent a little and lifted her off the floor, like a parent lifts a toddler to hold them high in the air. His strength was amazing, making her feel as light as the breeze wafting through the open windows, and she looked down at him, his gaze pinned to hers. He held her there for a few moments, then lowered her back down, sharing smiles between each other. They moved as one, the music a part of their intimate dance, joining their hearts and bodies together.

When the song slowed near the end, he serenaded her, his own voice overtaking the singers. Chrissie felt like she was the star of a movie, a leading lady, adored and cherished and desired. She didn't want this moment to end, but as the music faded so did their energy; their bodies softening and relaxing onto the floor. They spread out flat on their backs, chests rising and falling, hands joined together side by side.

'That was the most unconventional class I've ever taught,' Chrissie panted.

'I'm all for unconventional,' he replied. 'But I'm spent!'

'Me too! Yoga isn't as full on as dancing. It's still strenuous, but in a calming way. But that — I haven't done anything like that in a long time.'

'I haven't done anything like that, ever.'

Neither had she. She'd danced and let loose, yes, but relive a moment from one of the best romantic movies ever? It was like a dream, a beautiful, surreal dream she didn't want to wake from.

Her body buzzed even though she was still, the adrenalin still coursing through her body. 'To satisfy my need for consistency and because I'm pooped and need to lie down, I think we should do *Shavasana* as usual,' she said, removing her hand from his and arranging herself into a more structured position instead of one resembling a person who'd passed out after one too many vodkas.

'Good plan. I need a few minutes to catch my breath anyway.' He turned his head and gave her a brief smile before looking up at the ceiling.

'Close your eyes now, breathe deeply, and relax your whole body starting from your toes...' She ran through her usual spiel, shortening it somewhat as right now she didn't feel at all like his teacher and didn't want to sound like one. Soon there was silence as they both relaxed and breathed in complete stillness. Her body gave her that familiar floating sensation, not being able to feel the floor beneath her, like she was lying on a bed of clouds, and the post-exercise bliss engulfed her.

Chrissie didn't know how many minutes had passed, but she guessed it was time to return to the land of the living when the faint sound of a car in the distance pulling out of the parking lot brought her attention back to reality.

'Ahh, that was nice,' she said. 'Time to get up now.' She rolled to the side and pushed herself up with her hand, looking at Drew's idle body beside her. His chest slowly rose and fell, his breathing was smooth and even, and his face relaxed, shiny, and oh so beautiful. His eyes were still closed. She held back a chuckle. *Asleep again?* She watched him for a moment, her finger wanting to desperately trace the curves on his face, but she settled for tracing them with her gaze instead. She lowered herself onto her elbow next to him, watching him sleep. Everyone said that sleeping children were gorgeous, but no one ever mentioned sleeping celebrities. Only he wasn't a celebrity to her any more. He was a man. A talented and creative man, and a damn good dancer.

Watching him was like a meditation in itself, centring her mind and calming her breathing. She was about to snuggle up next to him when his eyes snapped open.

'Gotcha!' he said, a cheeky grin on his face.

Chrissie sat up. 'You weren't asleep?'

He shook his head.

She whacked him lightly on the chest with the back of her hand. 'You trickster.'

'You were watching me, weren't you? I could feel it.' A smug look graced his face.

'No I wasn't,' she said. 'I was just... waiting for you to wake up.' She tightened the elastic on her ponytail and looked away.

'Come here.' Drew pulled her on top of him and whispered, 'I would have watched you too.'

Chrissie confessed the truth with an honest smile, and her finger finally traced around the side of his face as she took in every perfect detail.

'Your eyes,' Drew said. 'You've got *Hungry Eyes*.'

Chrissie smiled, remembering the song of the same name from *Dirty Dancing*.

'Well then, you better feed them,' she said, lowering her face to his and taking his lips in hers.

CHAPTER NINETEEN

A one hour strenuous jog along the scenic walking track did nothing to quash Drew's desire or distract him from thoughts of Chrissie. Neither did a cold shower. Nor the organic gluten-free steak sandwich he'd had the kitchen staff make him for lunch. It was just past one o'clock on Saturday, only twenty-four hours since he'd last seen her and he was already having Chrissie withdrawals.

His head told him he shouldn't be getting involved with anyone, especially considering the fact he'd be out of here in just over a week's time, but he couldn't stop thinking about her, wanting to be with her. She was such a contrast from the women he often met in L.A. She was honest, charming, funny, and stronger than she knew. His attraction to her was beyond physical. Sure, desire had flickered within the first time he'd seen her, only intensifying the more time he spent with her; but she was a beautiful woman, he wouldn't be a red-blooded man if he hadn't felt at least some attraction initially. But something else about her had taken hold, something deeper, something that affected him emotionally, mentally, and spiritually, as well as physically. It was surreal he'd only known her for three weeks.

He reached for his guitar to keep his hands occupied, but placed it back down and grabbed his phone instead.

He pressed contacts and then Chrissie, and his finger hovered over the screen. Kai would be with her this weekend; he didn't want to interrupt their mother and son time. But he ached for some contact with her, even if only via text. He typed in a message:

> Hope your weekend is off to A Good Start (hehe). Last week was the best.

He hesitated for a moment then added:

> Thinking about you - D.

He hit send and took a deep breath, then opened his email and scrolled through the messages, deleting some along the way. He was in the middle of replying to a message from his manager when Chrissie's text came in:

> Yes it's off to A Good Start (that pun's getting really old btw). Kai & I are Fired Up (hehe) for an afternoon of sorting stuff and painting the rooms upstairs.

> Thinking about you too - C. xx

The addition of two kisses brought a smile to his face. He loved how women often did things like that. Sarah was always adding smiley faces to her texts and emails, and Gemma used plenty of LOLs and exclamation marks to make everything look super exciting.

He typed back:

> Maybe I'm all out of pun ideas. I might have
> passed the skill onto you. Good luck painting. :)

He smiled as he added the smiley face, hit send, then had a thought. Should he? No, probably not a good idea. But...

Before he could stop himself, he typed:

> Do you need an extra set of hands?

Sent. Too late now.

A few minutes passed without a reply. Crap. Maybe he crossed a line. What was he doing, offering to help her paint? And with her son around too. He should have just—

His phone beeped:

> I thought you didn't want to risk your visit being
> public knowledge. My son's not the town gossip
> or anything, but you know kids, they can be
> unpredictable.

Damn. He should have thought more about it before hitting send. Now he's put her on the spot.

Beep. Another message:

> But if you're okay with it, I'd love nothing more
> than to have your extra set of hands. ;)

Drew grinned. What a relief. And was the mention of his hands a subtle attempt at flirtation? He liked it. The wise thing to do would be to stay put and continue with his relaxing time off, but he needed to keep busy, and Chrissie had a lot on her plate. If he could help her in any way, it would make him feel good. Plus, he loved hanging out with kids, and he wanted to meet the famous Kai.

> My hands can be there in ten. Can the rest of
> me come too? Looking forward to meeting Kai.

Chrissie replied:

> Please bring all of you. I won't tell Kai exactly
> who you are, just in case. I'll say you're a friend
> helping out with the painting.

He typed back:

> Fine with me. I'm on my way :)

She replied with a simple smiley face, and Drew assessed his clothing for painting suitability. Nup. He pulled his white top over his head and zipped off his jeans, exchanging them for a casual pair of cargo shorts and a dark grey T-shirt. He gave his underarms a quick spray of deodorant and grabbed his phone and room key. There was one week left in Tarrin's Bay, and he didn't want to waste a single minute.

———

Chrissie checked her reflection in the hallway mirror, smoothing her hair and tightening the ponytail that had come loose. She glanced down at her painting outfit. Denim capris with a couple of frayed holes in them, and an oversized lemon-coloured T-shirt with a picture of palm tree on it. Oh dear. She shrugged. *Oh well, who cares. He's seen me at my worst.* She picked up the two storage boxes she'd bought and approached Kai in the living room.

'Kai, here are the boxes. I've laid everything out upstairs, and I want you to put all the things made of paper in one box, and everything else in the other, okay?' He nodded. 'Good man.'

Kai laughed. 'You called me man.'

'That's because you're being very helpful and acting like one.' She leant forward and kissed him on the forehead.

'I'll carry them upstairs, Mum.' He took the boxes from her — almost the size of his body — and heaved them over to the stairs.

'Oh, Kai? A friend of mine will be arriving soon to help with the painting. His name is Drew.'

'Oh,' he said. 'Then there'll be two men in the house.' He smiled and turned to walk up the stairs.

Chrissie chuckled and walked to the back door that opened onto the veranda facing the ocean. She was used to the sound of the waves again now and had become immune to the salty smell, but not once had she set foot within metres of the water's edge. *One thing at a time,* she reminded herself.

She ducked inside to fill a jug of water then returned to the veranda, pouring the water into a couple of potted plants near the doorway. The wind chimes she'd hung from the beam on the veranda roof clinked and twanged as a breeze floated over, and a nice feeling rose within knowing who would be walking towards her any minute now.

She placed the jug back in the kitchen and through the window saw Drew walking around the rocky hill, sunglasses covering his eyes and golden skin glowing in the sun.

She sucked in an anticipatory breath and pressed her lips together in a smile as she walked outside.

'Well, here they are.' He held up his hands. 'Where do you want them?'

Chrissie turned to check Kai was out of sight and whispered, 'Right here.' She placed them on the sides of her waist, then lifted his sunglasses onto his forehead.

Drew smiled and leaned forward, giving her a brief but tender kiss on the lips.

Chrissie tugged on his hand and led him inside. 'Welcome to the beach house.'

'What a nice place. I already feel at home.'

'It does have that effect. I think it's all the knick-knacks. And maybe the toys and clutter I have lying around!'

'It's nice. I love being in people's homes. Hotels get so formal after a while.'

'Can I get you anything to drink?'

'Nope, I'm good, thanks.' He glanced around. 'Where is the young man of the house?'

'Upstairs.' She gestured to the staircase. 'Shall we?'

Drew walked in front of her and she watched the way his calf muscles bulged with each step. She may have looked a little further north too.

They reached the top of the stairs and the large open area that served as a multipurpose room. Bookcases framed the walls, a desk sat under the front window, armchairs in the corner, and an old radio sat on a side table. It had become an extra playroom for Kai, and he often set up his train tracks along the worn-out carpeted floor. This time, he was placing items in the boxes as she'd instructed. He looked up with curious eyes at Drew.

'Oh. You're the painting friend.'

'I sure am. I'm Drew. And you must be Kai, the man of the house?'

Kai grinned. 'Yep.' Although he was obviously impressed at being called a man twice in one day, his eyes still held a touch of caution at this stranger in the house.

'Looks like you're doing a good job there, mate.'

'I am.' He picked up a couple of old magazines and placed them in a box.

Drew glanced at Chrissie and smiled.

'Well, over here is one of the spare bedrooms.' She walked Drew to the room, the sparse furniture already covered with protective sheets. 'I thought we'd start in here. It's already had a base coat, so we'll be putting the top coat on now.'

Drew checked the tins of paint on the floor. 'Golden Dawn,' he said. 'I wonder who has the job of coming up with names for paint colours?'

'And I wonder what job title they'd have... Paint Colour Namer? Name Designer?' Chrissie mused.

'Or, Executive Creator of Paint Colour Names,' Drew suggested.

'That sounds more distinguished, we'll go with that one.' She handed him a paint tray and roller. 'How about you start at that corner, I'll start over here, and we'll meet in the middle?'

Drew frowned. 'I thought you said nobody puts Drew in a corner.'

Chrissie gave him a light whack with her paint roller.

'If that had paint on it, you'd be in big trouble, Burns.' He smiled.

'Then we'll both have to behave ourselves and make sure the paint goes where it's meant to go.'

'I'll do my best.'

When they were halfway through the painting of the room, the sound of something falling or colliding broke their rhythm. It was followed by Kai saying, 'It's not fair!'

Chrissie exchanged curious glances with Drew then got off the stepladder. 'Wonderful. I'll go see what that's about.'

Kai stood in the open area with arms crossed and his trademark cranky face that outdid Drew's version as a child.

'What's wrong, Kai?'

'My stupid yo-yo doesn't work properly.'

Chrissie glanced at the plastic round shape on the floor, string spilling out of it. She picked it up. 'Well that's no reason to throw it.'

'It made me so angry. Why can't it just work, why?'

Chrissie glanced around, noticing the items she'd laid out were no longer in piles on the floor. 'You finished putting things away in the boxes?'

'Yes. That's why I started playing with my yo-yo, but the string's all tangled and I still can't do the tricks that Dad taught me. They're too hard.'

'Okay, well first of all, good work with the boxes. Secondly, if you're angry about something I want you to come and tell me, not throw things, okay?'

His cranky face remained.

'Okay?'

'Okaaay.' He sighed.

'Now, why don't you go play with something else for a while so Drew and I can get this painting done? I can help you with the yo-yo later.' Though she didn't know if she could. She'd have to Google yo-yo tricks to get some tips.

'But I really want to play with it now.'

'Yo-yo, huh? I used to have one of those when I was a kid.' Drew appeared behind them. 'Here, let me take a look.'

Chrissie handed the toy to Drew and he studied it and pulled all of the string out. 'Just a few knots. I'll try to get rid of them.' He fiddled with the clumps, pulled and threaded and untangled them one at a time, then rolled the string back around the yo-yo. 'There, all fixed.' He smiled. Kai's face softened a little but he didn't take the yo-yo from Drew's outstretched hand. 'You want me to show you a couple of tricks?'

'Yes, but not hard ones.'

'Okay, give me a minute.' Drew hooked the string over his finger and flicked his wrist, rolling the yo-yo down and back up again. 'Ah, I haven't done that in years. Brings back memories.'

'I don't recall ever mastering the yo-yo,' Chrissie said.

'Let's see if I can still do this.' He rolled the yo-yo then grabbed the string with his other hand, then again with the other hand, forming a triangle. The yo-yo rocked back and forth between the shape. 'Ooh yeah, I've still got it. This one's called Rock the Baby.'

A smile flashed onto Kai's face, and in response, onto Chrissie's. Kai stepped closer to Drew, who let go of the string and snapped the yo-yo back to his hand.

'Did you see that, Mum?' Kai asked. 'It was like magic.'

Drew beamed. 'Just takes patience and practise, that's all. Here, let me do something else.' He spun the yo-yo and did a fancy circular throwing thing. 'You know,' he said when he finished the trick, 'that one was one of the first tricks I learned, apart from Walking the Dog. If you like I could teach it to you.'

'Can he, Mum, can he?' Kai looked up at Chrissie as he tugged on her hand, and Drew mouthed, 'If that's okay?'

'He sure can. I'll get back to the painting while you boys — oh I mean, *men* — play with the yo-yo.'

Kai grinned. 'Yes!'

Chrissie went back to the bedroom and picked up her paint roller, smiling to herself as she listened to Drew teaching Kai the trick. Something fluttered inside, a cosy sensation that threatened to bring a tear to her eye. She loved being able to teach her son new things, but sometimes it was nice to have someone else take over. Victor had tried teaching him some yo-yo tricks, but he wasn't the most patient person. He said Kai just ended up frustrated so he took him to the oval to play soccer. Drew's voice as he spoke to Kai was so calm and gentle, so caring and encouraging, that she wanted to lock the doors and never let him leave. If only she could have someone like him in her life all the time.

A while later, when Chrissie had made a start on the next room, Kai called out, 'Mum! Come and look.'

She put down her paint roller and went into the other room.

Kai stood next to Drew, the yo-yo in his hand. 'Watch this!'

He spun the yo-yo and swung it like Drew had done earlier, then he let it spin down to the floor where it rolled smoothly along the carpet as he walked forward. He then flung it back up, and although he missed catching it, he tried again and managed to get the string rolled back into the yo-yo. The sense of achievement in his smile and rosy cheeks warmed her heart. Such a simple thing, yet something so important for Kai's self-confidence.

Chrissie clapped. 'That was brilliant, Kai! Well done. I have no idea how you did that, but it was impressive.'

'I know,' he replied, not one for modesty. 'But I can't tell you how I did it, it's mine and Drew's secret.' He looked at Drew and gave him an exaggerated wink, and Drew returned it with one of his own.

'Put one here, buddy.' Drew held up his hand for a high-five, and Kai hit it with a victorious slap.

'Can I give you a high-five too?' Chrissie held up her palm in front of Kai.

'Okay then.' Kai slapped it, then Chrissie held it up for Drew too. He high-fived her then gripped her fingers for a brief moment.

'Thank you,' she whispered to Drew, as Kai wandered off to practise.

'It was my pleasure. I had fun.'

'Really, it means a lot,' she said. 'I'm glad you're here.' She held his gaze and knew that whatever was going on between them, Drew was feeling it too. They'd have to say goodbye eventually, but neither of them wanted to admit that yet.

'I'm glad to be here. And Kai's a great kid. Smart. I can tell there's so much going on in that mind of his, he thinks carefully about everything.'

'He does. Sometimes too carefully!'

'It'll serve him well in life, I think.'

'Thanks.' She smiled.

'Well, I better help you with the rest of the painting.' He placed his hand on the small of her back and walked with her to the room.

Half an hour later a knock sounded at the door. Drew turned his head to face Chrissie, his eyebrows raised.

She shrugged. 'I'm not expecting anyone.' She got off the ladder and walked out of the room and over to the window. The veranda roof hid her visitor, until they moved out from underneath and over to a plant, leaning forward to smell its flowers. Her brown wavy hair tumbled over her shoulders. Melinda!

She turned around to Drew who had come out of the room. 'My friend from Sydney is here! I had no idea she was coming, she didn't say anything.'

'It's okay, I'll head back to Serendipity.'

'But she might see you. You still want to keep your presence a secret, right?'

'Well, yes, I would like to.' He scratched his head.

'Melinda is trustworthy, but I don't want to cause any problems for you.'

'I'm sure it'd be fine if we crossed paths. Unless she happens to be a journalist!' He chuckled.

'Actually...'

Drew's eyes widened. 'She *is* a journalist?'

Chrissie nodded. 'But she wouldn't say anything, I'm sure.' Chrissie hovered at the edge of the stairs. 'Oh, I know what to do. Stay here, I'll be back in a minute.'

She left Drew there with his palms turned up as if to say 'what's the plan?' and scurried down to the door.

'Mel! What are you doing here?' She hugged her friend, keeping her on the doorstep.

'I'm child-free for the afternoon and evening and thought I'd go for a nice, long Saturday drive and surprise you! I've obviously succeeded.' She flashed a smile. 'I'm here to give a helping hand in any way I can. Though I'd have to leave by about eight tonight. And who knows, maybe I can manage a glass or two of wine a little later?' She nudged her in the ribs, then glanced inside. 'Hi there, Kai!' Kai waved then returned to his yo-yo practise.

'That's lovely of you! It's so good to see you!' Chrissie slapped her forehead. 'But, oh damn it, I'm all out of milk, and I know you love your coffee.'

'Well then, I'll go pick some up,' Melinda replied, her thumb pointed behind her shoulder.

Exactly what Chrissie hoped she'd say.

'Oh, could you? That would be great. It's just I'm halfway through painting a wall and I don't want it to dry before I've blended it all together and reached the corner.'

'No worries at all. I'll go do it now and then we can have a coffee and a chat before getting stuck into more painting or whatever you need help with.'

'Thanks, Hun, you're the best.' She gave her a hug and told her where the nearest store was.

When her car had driven out of the driveway Chrissie dashed to the kitchen and opened the fridge. She grabbed the carton of milk and took it to the sink, then poured it down the drain.

'Mum, what are you doing?' Kai asked, as she turned on the tap to help the milk disappear.

'Oh, um, just... the milk was a bit old and yucky, so I had to get rid of it.'

'But I just drank from that.' He pointed to the now empty milk carton. 'Does that mean I'm going to get sick? Oh no!' He brought his hands to his face in typical worrywart fashion.

'No, not at all!' Chrissie chucked the carton in the recycling bin and grasped her son's arms. 'You'll be fine. I think it only went off in the last couple of minutes. Sometimes milk, um, does that.' Oh dear. Lying to her son? All in the name of keeping Drew's visit private. *Drew!*

She dashed upstairs. 'Sorry! My friend, Melinda has gone to pick up some milk. So...'

'So I better skedaddle before she comes back?'

Chrissie bit the corner of her lip. 'I'm sorry, I mean, you *can* stay, I just didn't know if you wanted anyone else to know you're here.'

'It's totally fine. I'll head back and leave you girls to have a catch up. I'd love to meet your friend, but I really need to lay low right now.'

'Of course, I understand. And sorry to cut short our time together.'

Drew wrapped her in his arms. 'No more apologies. No expectations. Go with the flow, remember? And I'll...' he pulled back from the embrace, '*flow* on outta here.' He made a flowing movement with his hand and offered a small smile.

'Thanks again for your help. Especially with Kai.' She placed her hand on his cheek and he took hold of it, kissing her palm.

'It was nice to do something else with you, apart from yoga.'

'It was.' She wished she could do more things with him this month. Go for walks and out to dinner, visit art galleries and have picnic lunches in Miracle Park. But those things weren't allowed. Everything had to stay behind closed doors, or in a secluded part of the outdoors. Her sadness at their limited time was overtaken by a thrill at the fact that she, reliable and honest Chrissie Burns, actually had a secret lover. It was kind of exciting, having to keep secrets and pretend and make up excuses. Not that he was *completely* her lover; their affections hadn't gone beyond delicious kisses and tender touches, and maybe it wouldn't. That would probably be a bad idea and make their inevitable separation even harder. Not to mention the fact that her job could be in jeopardy by breaking the rules. *Oh God. What am I doing?*

Before she had time to agonise over the situation, Drew spoke again. 'So you're off to the markets tomorrow with my sister and Sam, I hear?'

'Yes, I'm looking forward to it.'

'Maybe I'll give you a call afterwards.' He took her hands in his.

'That would be nice. Only if you want to, of course.'

He leaned close to her. 'I want to.' He kissed her softly on the lips. 'I *really* want to.' He kissed her again, firmer this time, with the urgency of an unfulfilled need. Was he talking about calling, or something else? Whatever it was, she *really* wanted it too.

CHAPTER TWENTY

Kai ran his hand through the water of the Wishing Fountain in Miracle Park as they walked around it, ripples spreading outwards.

'Kai, don't put your hand in there, please,' Chrissie said.

'It feels nice,' he replied. 'When am I allowed to do swimming lessons?'

Familiar guilt and fear simmered inside her belly. 'I thought you didn't want to do them?'

'But Sam does them and he can do a roly-poly under the water. I want to do a roly-poly under the water too.'

Chrissie swallowed. 'When I'm not so busy I'll have a look at the lessons and see what we can do, okay? Maybe in the school holidays.'

'When are the holidays?'

'Um, about five- or six-weeks' time, I think.'

'And how long till Christmas?'

'Christmas? Kai, that's a long way off. We only just had one!'

'But I love it. And maybe you and Dad and me will have Christmas dinner together like we used to.'

Chrissie sighed, stopped, and turned to Kai. 'Honey, I know

you miss your dad, and I know things are different now, but we both love you very much. And I promise, our next Christmas is going to be the best one ever.' She rubbed his back.

'Can we have turkey *and* ham?'

'Yes, we can have both. I might even get a gingerbread house, what do you think of that?'

'A gingerbread house to actually eat?' His eyes bulged.

'Yep. You can start with the front door, and I'll have one of the windows.'

'Can I eat the whole roof off?' He laughed and snorted. 'Imagine living in a house with no roof!' He laughed some more. She'd have to teach him about homelessness and Third World countries sometime and how lucky they were here in Australia. There was a lot she had to teach him. Sometimes the responsibility of what lay ahead for years to come overwhelmed her. Parents not only had to be caretakers, but teachers as well.

'Actually,' Kai said. 'I think I'll let Dad eat half the roof and I'll eat the other half.'

'That's kind of you.' They walked towards the assortment of market stalls scattered throughout the park and spilling over onto the stretch of grass alongside the harbour.

'I can't wait to show Sam my yo-yo tricks,' Kai said, pulling the yo-yo from his pocket and turning it around in his hand.

'He'll be very impressed, like I was.'

'Mum, is the painting man coming over again? I want to learn more tricks.'

The painting man. Chrissie chuckled, then realised she should have thought things through when she'd agreed for him to visit yesterday. She needed to be more careful who she allowed into their lives. She didn't want Kai to get hurt by someone leaving again.

'Um, I'm not sure sweetie. He might not be staying in town

much longer. But I'll do my best to learn some tricks and help you with them.'

'Oh, but I like the painting man. He's awesomely cool.'

Chrissie smiled. 'Yes, he is definitely awesomely cool,' she said softly.

Chrissie kept an eye out for Sarah's jewellery stall; she'd said it was near the bottom of the park where it merged with the side of the harbour. She passed an enticing-looking stall called Homemade for You, with various gourmet relishes, sauces, and spices, packed into cute little jars. Nearby was a stall with pictures of the human body, various health books, and an iridology camera. She'd seen one at Serendipity, in the naturopathic section. The man behind the table peered into it, then a moment later a close-up image of someone's eyes appeared on a monitor. Fascinating. She'd have to give it a go sometime. A few people were lining up for their turn. *Mark Bastian, naturopath and acupuncturist, Tarrin's Bay Medical Clinic* was written on a sign attached to the stall. It was good to see doctor's surgeries embracing complementary therapies. She'd have to remember his name. Maybe she could take Kai to him to make sure he was getting all the nutrition he needed. Sure, she could make use of the practitioners at Serendipity, but would prefer someone outside of her work environment.

She was about to walk past when she noticed his business cards on the side of the table. She leaned in and took one, and he looked over at her and smiled appreciatively. He certainly looked healthy; his skin was clear and smooth, and he had no bags whatsoever under his eyes.

'Oh look, here we are.' Chrissie pointed to the jewellery stall where Sarah was finishing up early so she could spend time with her and their kids. Her daughter, Gemma, had agreed to watch over the stall along with the help of a friend.

'Chrissie, you found me,' Sarah smiled. 'Hi, Kai.'

Kai waved and immediately joined Sam at the side of the stall, showing him his yo-yo.

'Wow, you've got some beautiful things.' Chrissie scanned the array of bracelets, earrings, necklaces, rings, and accessories, shining and glittering in the sunlight. A girl came up to the table from behind the stall, her wavy dark hair parted down the middle and earrings swinging below her ears.

'You must be Gemma?' Chrissie asked.

'Hi. Nice to meet you.' She held out her hand and Chrissie shook it. 'You have beautiful hair, such a gorgeous shade of blonde.'

Chrissie patted her hair. 'Oh, thank you. That's nice to say. I was just admiring yours!'

Gemma smiled. 'So you're a yoga teacher?'

Chrissie nodded.

'That's so cool. I'll have to try it.'

'I highly recommend it.' Chrissie eyed the jewellery again, and a unique ring caught her eye. It had three different coloured stones in an asymmetrical abstract arrangement. She picked it up. 'This is nice.'

'Only ten bucks too.'

'Gemma, don't do the hard sell on Chrissie, I don't want her to feel obligated to buy something,' Sarah said.

'But I'm just saying it's a bargain, Mum.'

'I'll take it,' Chrissie said, taking ten dollars from her purse and handing it to Gemma.

'Cool, thanks. My first sale.' She held the note up in her hands and did a happy dance.

'Now, any problems, you call me, okay?' Sarah glanced at Gemma first and then her teenage friend, who was sitting on a chair to the side.

'We'll be fine. Might even sell more than you did in the morning.'

'I'll see you back here at three o'clock.'

Chrissie walked away from the stall with Sarah, Sam, and Kai, Kai with a smug look on his face having showed Sam his yo-yo trick.

'Mum, can I buy a yo-yo?' Sam asked.

'If we find one.'

Chrissie smiled at Sarah. 'It's good he's asking for a good old-fashioned toy. I've heard when boys get older it's all expensive video games.'

'Yeah, I'm trying to delay that as much as possible. He plays Liam's Xbox sometimes, but most games are violent so he's not allowed near it when Daddy's playing.'

'Yeah, so much violence. Why can't they all just hug and smile and be happy in games?'

'Now there's an idea. Instead of seeing how many baddies you can shoot, see how many people you can hug. Much better.' Sarah smiled, then rubbed her shoulders like they were sore or she was fatigued.

They walked down to the harbour, and Chrissie veered to the grassy side of the stalls instead of the water side. Crowds of people weaved around them, the pace was slow and breezy, the smell of sausages sizzling hung in the air, and seagulls squawked and swooped down at people throwing bread crumbs on the grass.

'Can we buy something, Mum?' Kai asked, peering at the stalls as they passed by each one.

'Depends what we find.' She glanced around. 'Oh look, there's a bookstall, why don't you go and choose a book?'

'Okay, Sam you help me choose.' He tugged his friend's sleeve and they busied themselves amongst the display of children's books.

'How's the house coming along?' Sarah asked. 'Managed to do any renovations yet?'

'A few small things. Got some painting done yesterday, which was good.' She almost said 'with Drew', but thought better of it. No need to suggest there was anything going on between them, she didn't want to affect her growing friendship with Sarah by saying, 'Oh and by the way, I'm totally hot for your brother and we can't keep our hands off each other.'

'It all takes time, doesn't it?'

'Yes, slowly but surely I'll get things finished. If I didn't have a full-time job I'd get a lot more done.'

'I bet. How is work going? Is my brother becoming a yoga expert?' She smiled.

'He's quite good, actually. Bit of a chatterbox though.' She chuckled.

'Oh yes, Drew's always up for a conversation.'

And other stuff, but I won't tell you about that.

'Found one, Mum.' Kai held up a book and Chrissie inspected it.

'Looks good to me. How about you, Sam, would you like a book?'

'This one looks good.' He held up a small chapter book.

'Two books coming up.' Chrissie got out her purse.

'Oh, you don't have to do that, Chrissie. I'll pay for it.' Sarah got out her purse.

'No, seriously, I'd like to. They don't cost much.' She paid the stall-holder who put each book in a paper bag, which the kids tucked under their arms.

Wandering along, Chrissie's stomach grumbled at the array of food stalls and tempting smells wafting nearby. 'I might grab a bite to eat, you want anything?' Chrissie asked Sarah. 'Corn on the cob?' She eyed the golden yellow corn being barbequed, brown flecks searing the edges of the kernels.

'Looks good,' she said. 'Want some, kids?'

They nodded and each bought a couple of cobs on sticks. The buttery flavour satisfied Chrissie's stomach, and they had to stand still to eat as Kai kept dropping his book. When they finished, the boys stood near a magician showing some tricks, wonder and smiles on their faces. Sarah covered her mouth, and her face went pale.

'Are you okay?' Chrissie placed her hand on Sarah's arm.

'Just a bit light-headed. Been on my feet all day.' She sat on the concrete wall separating the footpath from the harbour. It was a little too close to the water for Chrissie's liking, but she couldn't do anything about that right now.

Sarah's stomach heaved forward and she covered her mouth again.

'Oh no, was it the corn? Not agreeing with you?'

'Something like that.' She took a sip of water from the bottle in her bag.

'Is there anything I can do, or get for you?'

'No, not to worry. I'll be fine in a minute.' She clamped her lips together in a brave smile, then looked at Sam and Kai enjoying the magic show, and her eyes welled up.

'What is it, Sarah?'

Sarah turned to face Chrissie. 'I'm pregnant.' She held up her hands in resignation.

The thought had crossed Chrissie's mind but she hadn't wanted to ask about it. 'Oh my God, that's fantastic. Congratulations!' She placed a hand on Sarah's back.

Sarah leaned closer to Chrissie. 'Shh, no one knows yet.'

'What about Liam?'

She shook her head.

'Why not?'

'I only found out this morning. He rushed off to the gym just after I got out of bed, and I had to get things ready for my jewellery stall. I wasn't even going to do the test yet, but I had it in my drawer and had a few minutes alone so I thought, "What the heck".'

'Wow, well, how do you feel about it?'

'I don't know, to be honest. It wasn't planned. I don't know how it happened. We hadn't talked about having another child, with Gemma and Sam I sorta felt I was done.' She gestured to her belly. 'But apparently not!'

The magician made long lengths of ribbons appear from his hat and the kids clapped, picking them up and running them through their fingers. Thank goodness they were occupied right now. It could be hard to have serious conversations around kids.

'Well you're a great mum. I think you'll be fine.'

'Thank you. It's just such a shock.' She ran her hand through her hair. 'And I sure know how to have large age gaps between kids. An eighteen-year-old, six-year-old, and now a soon-to-be newborn. So much for the family holiday I thought we could take next year.'

'Do you think Liam will be okay with it?' Chrissie asked.

'He'll have to be, I guess. It's half his fault.' She laughed, then her eyes teared up again.

Chrissie handed her a tissue.

'Thanks, Chrissie. Sorry to blurt it out like that. I had to tell someone. I guess I better tell someone in particular when I get home later on.'

'I think so.' Chrissie smiled. 'But I'm here anytime you want to talk. I've only been through it all once, but it's not something I'll forget in a hurry!'

'I just might do that,' Sarah replied. 'You and I should get out together someday. Go to the movies for a chick flick or something, leave the boys at home with Liam.'

'I'd love that.'

'Consider it on my To Do List.'

'I'll put it on mine too.' Chrissie helped her friend up. 'Will you be okay?'

'Yeah. If I need to throw up I'll just do it in the water.' She gestured to the harbour.

They were about to get the children when Sarah's phone rang. 'I hope Gemma's okay at the stall.' She picked up her phone. 'Oh, it's Mum.' She put the phone to her ear. 'Hi Mum, how's things?' Sarah's face turned even paler. 'What?' She sat back down on the wall. 'Is he okay? What happened? Where are they taking him?'

Dread pooled in Chrissie's veins and her heart rate rose. Was she talking about Drew? Or Liam? Or her father? Not more bad news she had to witness... please.

'I'll be there as soon as I can. I'll call Drew and pick him up on the way.'

Sarah hung up and Chrissie asked, 'What's happened?'

Fear creased Sarah's face. 'My dad. He's had a heart attack.'

They dashed to the stall to tell Gemma. 'We have to go, but I need to pack things away, we can't leave them here.' Sarah's voice shook with worry.

'I'll help. I can handle this if you just want to go,' Chrissie said.

'No, it won't take too long if we all do it. Gem, you grab the stands and fold them up. Put all the day's takings in your bag and bring it with you.' She picked up containers to store the jewellery. 'Pack everything in these. It doesn't matter if they get tangled, I'll fix them later.'

Chrissie packed things away, and the boys grabbed all the price tags and signs and put them in a pile. A fellow stall-holder came over to ask what was wrong and on telling him, he pitched in to help. In minutes the stall was packed away, and Chrissie helped carry the folded table and chairs back to Sarah's car. Once everything was packed in, Sarah looked at Sam and bit her lip.

'Do you want me to look after Sam while you're at the hospital?' Chrissie asked.

'Could you?'

'I'd be happy to. I can drop him home later or you can pick him up whenever you're ready. No rush.'

'Oh, thanks Chrissie, you're a life saver.' She hugged her.

'Will Grandpa be okay?' Sam asked.

Sarah bent down to her son and kissed him on the forehead. 'Yes, sweetie, I'm sure he'll be fine. The doctors are taking care of him.' She gave him a reassuring smile but it disappeared as soon as she straightened up and broke eye contact with Sam.

Chrissie rubbed the boy's back. 'You can come and play at our house. We might even watch a movie, what do you say?'

Sam nodded and grasped hold of her hand gently. Chrissie's heart doubled over at his needy gesture. The poor boy was scared. But he'd be even more scared if he went to the hospital. Sarah and Drew needed to be there with their mother. Chrissie would have to keep it together and take care of both boys, and hope like hell that Drew and Sarah's dad survived. She couldn't let fear of another tragedy shake her emotions and affect her ability to take care of the kids.

She texted her home address to Sarah's phone and waited until she'd driven off with Gemma, her young friend having walked to her nearby home herself, then crouched to face the boys. 'Right, let's all have a group hug and send our good wishes to Sam's grandpa.' She stretched her arms around Sam and Kai. 'I want you to close your eyes and imagine all the best feelings in the world, and see them flying in the air to the hospital. Can you do that?'

They nodded.

'Good. Now close your eyes and let all those good feelings enter your mind. Have you got them?' They nodded, their faces strained in effort touching to witness. 'Now imagine them flying, like superheroes, towards Sam's grandpa at the hospital and surrounding him with good feelings.'

'My good feelings are wearing capes,' Kai said, and tears built up behind Chrissie's eyes.

'That's wonderful, Kai. Now let them fly where they need to go.' She gave them a moment. 'Are they all there?'

Both children nodded.

'Good. Now I want you to put a big smile on your face, knowing that the good feelings are taking care of Sam's grandpa. The bigger the smile the better.'

Sam and Kai stretched their mouths wide, teeth gritted and gums showing.

'Now open your eyes.'

Their eyes blinked open and Sam said, 'My good feelings flew so fast, even faster than an ambulance.'

'Fantastic, Sam. Your grandpa would be proud.'

He nodded and smiled, and Chrissie realised that, sometimes, the best way to be strong was to help someone else be strong. 'Now, let's go get some movie snacks!'

'Yes!' Kai said, and Sam's face lit up.

Chrissie hoped that while the movie and junk food did their thing keeping the boys minds off the situation, the express delivery of good feelings would do their thing and keep Geoff Williams alive.

CHAPTER TWENTY-ONE

'I'll come back first thing tomorrow,' Drew said to his mother, after a long afternoon and evening of worry and uncertainty. 'Will you be okay?'

'Yes, I'll be better off here than at home. You go get some sleep and I'll see you in the morning.' She pulled Drew in close to her. 'I'm so glad you're here.'

Drew clamped his lips together as the emotions of the day overwhelmed him, and held his mother in a comforting embrace.

'C'mon, let's go get Sam,' he said, turning to Sarah when he pulled away.

Gemma had gone home with Liam an hour ago, and Sarah was anxious not to keep Sam up too late at Chrissie's. Sarah hugged her mum then walked alongside Drew to the hospital exit. A couple of women stared at him and whispered to each other.

So much for laying low.

His dad was now considered stable, but needed to be watched closely over the next twenty-four hours or so. The doctors said that's when another heart attack was most likely to occur, but at least this time, if it happened again, he could get immediate treatment, instead of waiting in pain for the ambulance like when he'd collapsed in the kitchen at home.

Drew's nerves were on high alert; he couldn't believe this had happened. Not to his dad. Things like that happened to other people, not the strong and resilient Geoff Williams.

They got in Sarah's car and began the thirty minute drive from Welston to Tarrin's Bay, when a ballad came on the radio and Sarah sniffled, her eyes becoming shiny.

'I'm sure he'll be okay,' Drew said, placing his hand on her arm as it held onto the steering wheel.

'I know. At least I hope, it's just...' She pulled over to the side of the road and tears spilled down her face.

'Hey, it's okay.' He wrapped his arms around his sister.

'I'm sorry, it's just my damn hormones,' she said, wiping her face with her hands.

'Oh, in that case. Say no more,' Drew replied. He'd learned not to question anything when it came to women and their hormones. 'Just let me be sad and comfort me!' an ex-girlfriend had told him once. 'You can't fix it!'

'It's not those types of hormones, it's... I'm pregnant again.'

Drew's mouth opened wide. 'You are?'

She nodded. 'So much for having days to myself with Sam at school. I'll be back to full-time motherhood in another seven months time.'

'You didn't plan this?'

'Nope. And Liam doesn't know yet, only you and Chrissie.'

'Chrissie knows? How is it that the father of your child is yet to find out? Sarah, you need to tell him as soon as you get home.'

'I will, I will. It all happened so fast this morning, and then there were the markets, and then Dad, and there just wasn't time. I'll tell him tonight. I guess with everything that's going on we won't get much sleep.'

'If there's anything you need me to do, let me know. I can take care of Sam any night this week if you need me to.'

'Thanks. We'll see how Dad goes and take each day as it comes,' Sarah sniffled. 'I wish you could hang around town a little longer.'

One week from now he'd be spending his last night at Serendipity, and leaving early the following Monday morning. 'You right to drive?' he asked as Sarah grasped the steering wheel again and took the handbrake off.

'Yep. We need to get Sam. Poor Chrissie's had him for hours. She was a godsend today, helping pack up the stall, and offering to mind Sam and give him dinner. I owe her big time.'

'I'm sure she was just happy to help.'

'So, her address is on Dune Road, not far past Serendipity.'

'Yep, I know where it is, no need to look for the number.'

'You do?'

Oops. 'Yeah, I was walking on the beach one day and saw her out the back. I remember her house from years ago, the nice one right on the beach.'

'Ah, she's in a great spot. I really admire her, raising Kai on her own, working full-time, and doing up the place.'

'Yeah, she's pretty special.' After the stress of the day, Drew ached to have Chrissie's arms around him, feel her soft, comforting skin against his.

Sarah glanced at Drew. 'Do you have a bit of a crush?'

'A crush? What, are we still in high school or something?' He shifted on the seat.

'C'mon, you know what I mean. She's an attractive woman and you've been spending a lot of time together.' A faint smile replaced Sarah's sad expression.

'So? Yeah, she's attractive. I meet a lot of attractive women. But I'll be gone in a week so there's no point discussing this, is there?'

'No need to get all defensive, I was just asking.'

Silence sat between them for a few minutes.

Drew opened the window and let the refreshing night air wash over his face as it whooshed past. Who was he kidding? He was head over heels for the blonde beauty who called him Williams and danced with him and inspired him every day. And he had absolutely no idea what to do about it. His responsibilities lay in America. His career. His life. He'd worked hard to get to where he was. He had commitments, a busy schedule, and it was not compatible with a long distance relationship. And it wouldn't be fair on her. She needed someone she could rely on, to be there for her, and a role model for Kai. His life didn't fit those requirements. 'Keep an eye on Chrissie when I'm gone,' he said. 'She needs a good friend around.'

Sarah eyed him curiously. 'Of course. I will.'

They pulled into Chrissie's driveway and got out of the car. Chrissie had opened the door at the side of the house before they got to it. 'How is he?' she asked, her face creased with concern.

'He's stable, finally.' Sarah blew out a long exhalation.

Chrissie put her hand over her chest. 'Oh, I'm so glad. You must have been so worried. Come in, Sam's been an angel.'

'He has? I'm so sorry to leave him with you for so long, but—'

Chrissie held up her hand. 'Don't apologise. Nothing to it. And I'm here to help again if you need to be with your father during the week.'

Sarah kissed her cheek and thanked her again. Chrissie's gaze caught onto Drew's, and he wanted to kiss her too, pull her close and relax in her arms for hours.

'How are you?' she asked softly.

'I'm okay,' he replied. 'Long day.'

'I bet. Can I get you both anything?'

'No, but thanks. I really should get Sam home and ready for

bed.' Sarah walked through to the living room where Sam and Kai were huddled on the couch in front of a cartoon on television.

Sam turned around. 'Mum! Is Grandpa all better? I sent him my good feelings as fast as I could.'

Sarah embraced her child. 'He's better than before, but still very sick. The doctors and nurses are taking care of him, and, I'm sure your good feelings are too.' She ruffled his hair.

'Poor Grandpa. Mrs Chrissie said I should close my eyes and think good thoughts and send them over to him with superhero capes on.'

Sarah laughed, and a ripple of happiness rolled through Drew's body. Yes, Chrissie certainly was something special. He stole a glance in her direction and she shrugged. She looked tired. Beautiful, but tired.

'Kai, say hello to our visitors,' Chrissie said.

Kai peeled himself away from the television. 'Hey, you're the painting man.'

'Kai, his name is Drew.'

'Drew, the painting man,' he said.

'He's not the painting man, he's my uncle,' corrected Sam.

'Oh,' Kai said. 'Does he do painting at your house too?'

Sam shook his head, confusion scrunching his face.

'Painting man?' Sarah asked, her gaze alternating between Chrissie and Drew.

Drew rubbed the back of his neck. 'Um, yeah. I helped Chrissie out with some painting yesterday.'

Sarah's lips twitched a little. 'Is that right?'

'Yeah, he's been, um, very helpful,' Chrissie said. 'Well, Sam, it's been a pleasure having you here. Thanks for keeping Kai entertained.' She shook the boy's hand, but he wrapped his arms around her waist. 'Ohh, that's lovely.' She patted him on the back.

'Say thanks, Sam,' Sarah said.

'I think he just did,' Chrissie replied, Sam still attached to her lower half.

After walking them out to the car, Drew hovered at the door.

'You coming?' asked Sarah.

'Actually, I might walk back. It's not far, I could do with the fresh air.'

'Okay then. I'll pick you up tomorrow morning after school drop off,' she said, starting the engine and waving goodbye.

When the car was out of the driveway, Drew said, 'I'll have to cancel tomorrow's class, hope that's okay.' He needed to be with his family right now, do whatever was needed and support his mum and sister.

'It's more than okay. Take as much time as you need,' she replied, then turned to Kai. 'C'mon Mister, time for bed.'

On cue, he yawned, and headed inside.

'You sure I can't get you something before you walk back?' Chrissie raised her eyebrows. 'I made chocolate chip cookies while the boys watched a movie today.' She smiled.

'You know just how to get my attention, don't you?' He grinned, and hung an arm loosely around her back as they walked inside together.

CHAPTER TWENTY-TWO

'What will it be today?' Jonah, the barista, asked as Chrissie walked up to the counter at Café Lagoon on Wednesday afternoon with Kai by her side.

'One vanilla milkshake, and a...' she eyed the blackboard menu, 'what's a dandelion chai?'

'It's a mixture of dandelion — a herb — with chai spices. So it's like chai tea but without the tea. Has a warmer, more robust flavour. And apparently it's good for you, according to our resident naturopath in town.'

Chrissie's eyes widened and she nodded, impressed. 'That's not Mark, by any chance, is it?'

'Yes, Mark Bastian, you know him?'

'No, I just picked up his business card recently.'

'Nice bloke.'

'I think I'll take his advice and have a dandelion chai, then.' Chrissie smiled.

'Coming right up. Having here or take away?'

'We'll have it here, I think.' She glanced at Kai who was eyeing the array of cakes in the display cabinet. 'And some banana bread too, please.' She could share it with Kai.

'Sure.' He took her payment. 'Haven't seen you in here for our music nights yet.'

'Oh, haven't had a chance. Soon hopefully.'

'What about this Saturday? Barry Reynolds, a local guy, will be kicking back with a few tunes for the crowd.'

Barry... Drew's old friend and Gemma's dad? Kai would be at Victor's this weekend, so she could make it if she wanted to. Kind of sad, going out alone, but she probably couldn't ask Sarah to come and watch her ex perform.

'I just might do that,' she replied.

'Well I hope to see you there.' Jonah smiled.

'Do you ever *not* work?' Chrissie asked.

'Ha, not much. It's my parents' café so I'm here most of the time. Except when I backpacked around Europe for a while.'

'Well, you do a great job.'

'Why thank you.' He bowed. 'Here's your number and I'll bring it out to you.' He handed her a silver stand with the number four on it, and she sat at a table against the wall with Kai, who took a book from his schoolbag and started reading, his little legs swinging back and forth underneath the table. He'd come close to catching the bus today, but chickened out at the last minute. It didn't matter. He was making progress and that's all she could ask for.

As for progress with her and Drew, it had come to a standstill. She'd gone two days without seeing him after their Sunday evening chat on the couch while Kai was in bed. Had his father not been ill who knows what might have happened, but his mind was preoccupied and she could tell he was worn out emotionally, so they just chatted and drank and ate, and then he walked back to Serendipity. It was good that Drew was here to be with his family. Geoff had undergone some kind of procedure to unblock an artery, and was now on medication and strict instructions to take it easy, and was due to be discharged tomorrow morning. Drew had told her all this today, when he'd returned to yoga, after taking Monday and Tuesday off.

'Here you go,' Jonah said, placing their drinks on the table, then returning with a plate of banana bread, butter melting on top and steaming upwards in thin, smoky ripples.

'Yum,' Kai said, grabbing a piece and putting almost the whole thing in his mouth.

'Thanks, Jonah.' She smiled and sipped at her chai, while Jonah remained standing near their table.

'So?' he asked, gesturing to the drink.

'I like it. Quite nice. Thank you.'

He bowed again and returned to the counter, while Chrissie's thoughts returned to Drew. It had been nice to get back to yoga with him today, he needed the peace of it. They hadn't been flirty and chatty like they usually were; something heavy had hung in the air between them, emphasising that their time was nearly up. Maybe what happened to Geoff had shocked Drew back to reality, made him realise there was no point continuing their secret affair. And maybe Chrissie's fear of potentially losing her job had knocked some sense back into her. She hated to admit it, but it seemed their time had passed.

Despite Drew's change in his demeanour, he did mention he was almost finished writing his new song. When she'd asked if she'd get to listen to it before he left, he seemed unsure. 'I don't know if I should,' he'd said, and then changed the subject. He wouldn't even tell her the title, and she didn't want to pry. Maybe she'd just hear it on the radio one day, like every other fan of his.

When Kai had finished and she'd had enough of dwelling on her own thoughts, she left the café and walked down the street with Kai. She didn't have to be anywhere else, it was nice to dawdle and browse the shop windows, take in the atmosphere of the friendly town. She walked past the newsagent then did a double take. A news headline caught her eye. Normally she'd ignore them and look away, not wanting to get caught up in the media world that had caused her panic attacks to return, but there was no looking away from this news headline: *Is Drew Williams hiding out in Tarrin's Bay?*

A photo of him looking evasive accompanied the headline.

'Hey, is that painting man?' Kai asked, pointing.

'Ah, it might be.' She edged closer to the paper. Who could have let it slip? Did someone at Serendipity sell him out for a few decent bucks?

She glanced around, as though someone might come up to her and say, 'why are you buying a newspaper after all this time?' then picked one up off the stand and paid for it at the counter.

'C'mon, Kai, let's go to the park. You can have a play for a while.'

'I can? Yes!' He pumped his fist and they crossed the road hand in hand, the newspaper tucked under Chrissie's arm.

He ran to the playground equipment and Chrissie nabbed a seat nearby. She tried to look casual as she read the paper, but her hands wanted to grip it tightly and her mouth wanted to gape. Someone must have recognised him at the hospital when he went to see his dad, that was the most obvious explanation. The article said that people on social media had posted about seeing him, and the news had spread to fans and journalists who obviously jumped on the opportunity for a scoop. His poor parents. Susan, after everything she was going through, had been contacted by journos trying to get her to tell them if he was staying with them. 'Drew's mother was uncooperative', the article said. Uncooperative? Her husband was in hospital. *Geez.* They'd also tried calling all the local hotels, B&B's, even the caravan park, to see if anyone was prepared to give him up. Serendipity, of course, had been contacted, but offered no comment. What shook Chrissie about the article was not all of that, but the reason why he apparently needed to hide out in the first place. If she'd kept an eye on the media she would have known, but she'd been oblivious to it this whole time... Drew's ex-girlfriend had accused him of being abusive.

A dead weight sank in Chrissie's gut. *No way. She must be lying.* She read the article, scanning repeatedly left to right as fast as she could, and then she turned the page and the photo brought her hand to her mouth in a gasp. Bruises. Cuts. A black eye. On a woman close to her age, probably several years younger. She had blonde hair like hers, long and wavy, and the words the woman used sent a sour feeling winding its way around Chrissie's body...

'He treated me like I was so special, I really thought he was the right man for me, but just when things got serious, he turned on me. Something snapped, and he got violent at the tiniest little things. I couldn't do anything right. It's taken a lot of courage for me to speak out about this, because I know everyone loves him, but I had to. For my sake, for the sake of others he may have hurt as well, and for his sake. He needs help.'

The paper trembled under Chrissie's grasp, and her heart wanted her to look away, throw the paper in the bin and forget it, but she couldn't drag her gaze from the page.

'He sang for me, even wrote a song he said was inspired by me, and I couldn't believe how lucky I was to have Drew Williams interested in me — an unknown aspiring actress from Oklahoma.'

An actress. Well, surely she was acting, then. Wasn't she? But the bruises, they didn't look photoshopped, and police reports proved that she did report the assault and they had taken photographic evidence. Although they couldn't prove it was Drew, the media was hounding him. No wonder he'd had to get away. But what if he got away because he did do something? Maybe he just got a little angry and hurt her by accident and she fabricated the rest? Thoughts and conflicting ideas swirled in Chrissie's mind, and she gripped the edge of the seat as dizziness overtook her. She Googled the woman's name, Jolene Burrows, and found more articles and interviews and even a statement by another woman who said she'd left Drew when he'd showed signs of aggression.

What was she thinking, risking the stability she was striving for by getting involved with a celebrity? They led crazy lives, so far removed from normal life. He was from a different world, a world that was all about appearance and money and ego and competition, a world she didn't fit into — would never fit into. She shouldn't have broken the rules and let it develop as far as it did, and she knew it couldn't last, so why did she have to go and set herself up for heartbreak?

Chrissie put her phone in her bag and looked up at the sky, the afternoon sun sending rays of sharp orange through her skull, a headache festering underneath. Whether he was guilty or not, she couldn't get involved in all this. Stability for herself and Kai was top priority. She didn't need the stress and drama of this sort of stuff impacting on her life. She was here to do one thing — fix up the beach house, sell it, and move on. That was it. It was time to put her silly emotions and hormones aside and get back to doing her job, and doing what was best for Kai and their future.

CHAPTER TWENTY-THREE

On Friday morning when Kai was finishing up his breakfast, Chrissie stared at the text message she'd received from Drew the day before, when she'd chucked a sickie from work. She just couldn't face him. And the day off had been good for her. She'd shopped for new blinds and curtains and replaced the old ones around the house. It had given the place a new lease of life, and had kept her busy. But of course, when Helena had to tell Drew that she wouldn't be in for his yoga session, he'd wondered why.

> Chrissie, you okay? Helena said you couldn't come in today. ~ D.

She hadn't replied at first, until his third text that came last night:

> I'm worried. Are you sick? Is Kai okay?

She'd replied:

> I'm okay, thanks for checking.

And that was it.

He hadn't replied after that, and Chrissie knew he was probably upset, but if she got into a discussion with him it might go on and on and she wouldn't be able to regain her focus. She popped the phone into her bag, asked Kai to carry his plate to the dishwasher, then got him to clean his teeth. Today was the day. She hoped. The day that Kai would finally catch the bus.

She drove him to the bus stop where a few children and parents were waiting, as they'd done every day for a while now, followed by tailgating the bus all the way to school. Kai had met the bus driver yesterday and he'd said he'd save him a spot in the back seat so he'd be able to see Chrissie in the car behind. All was set.

'Okay, sweetie, time to wait at the bus stop.' She got out of the car and he did too.

'Mum, you don't have to call me sweetie. It's babyish.'

'Oh, I'm sorry. I'm just used to it.' She led him towards the bus stop and nodded hello to the other parents. Yesterday he'd tried to get on the bus but changed his mind half way along the aisle and turned around.

A young mother approached her. 'Would he like to sit with my son in the back seat of the bus? This is Jake, he's in kindergarten.'

Chrissie eyed Kai, and whether it was the fact that he'd have a friend to sit with or the fact that the kid was in the year younger than him and he felt silly for being so nervous, he nodded with enthusiasm.

'Thanks,' Chrissie said, and the woman smiled.

The screech of the bus's breaks approached, and the loud puff of air as the bus stopped had Chrissie nervous herself. The doors flapped open and the bus driver stood and hung out the door. 'Today's V.I.P. passenger is Kai, where's Kai?' He scanned the children's faces. 'Ah, there you are. Come on up. The back seat is waiting for you.'

Kai's eyes widened, and Chrissie's did too, not expecting this sort of special treatment. What a lovely gesture. Kai looked at the other boy, Jake, then pointed. 'Can he be a V.I.P. passenger too?'

The driver nodded, holding out his arm to show the way, and Chrissie half expected him to say 'All aboard!' and blow a whistle.

Kai and Jake stepped onto the bus, only a few other children from the outskirts of Tarrin's Bay already on it. Kai turned briefly and looked at Chrissie. She waved, then he continued down the aisle and... sat on the seat in the back! Relief washed over her. Before he could change his mind, she walked to the back of the bus where her car was, and waved again at Kai, then got into the driver's seat. She sat there until all the children had boarded, and when the engine grew louder, Kai sat up tall in his seat with his gaze directed towards the front. When the bus pulled onto the road and Chrissie followed, he looked back at her, then at Jake who said something to him. He alternated between checking she was still behind him and talking to Jake for the whole trip, and soon they arrived at the primary school. Chrissie parked nearby and jumped out, a smile permanently engraved on her face at his achievement. She hung back, not wanting to make a big deal of it in front of everyone, and waited for the children to filter out.

Jake stepped out, then stopped and waited. The skinny legs of Kai Cavanaugh hopped off the bus, his backpack bouncing behind him, and he took a few steps forward then glanced back, his face lighting up on seeing Chrissie. She smiled widely and was about to wave when his two little thumbs pointed to the heavens in a show of victory. Chrissie's bottom lip quivered and she gave him a thumbs up sign too. It may not have been a big thing for anyone else, but for her, it was the highlight of her week.

She wiped the corners of her eyes as she got in the car and readied her mind for work. It was Friday, the twenty-sixth day of February, and what was supposed to be her last day of teaching Drew. But with all that had happened, she thought it best if someone else took over, and she could write the past few weeks off as a casual fling.

She arrived at work and told Helena of her preference, leaving out the bit about the casual fling, and mentioned how much Damon would be honoured to take her place in Drew's yoga studio today.

'You sure you can't just do the last day? What's caused your reluctance? He hasn't been making advances and making you uncomfortable, has he?' Her eyes narrowed.

Chrissie decided to answer only one of her questions. 'I read something in the paper and online about him, and it's made me feel a bit uncomfortable, that's all.'

'You mean the media scandal about his ex-girlfriend?'

'You knew about it, before now?'

'I knew before he even got here.' Helena tided some papers on her desk.

'Why didn't you mention it when you asked me to take on the role?'

'Because it's our job to be professional and discreet. Our V.I.P. guests are the lifeline of this retreat; they add a large sum of profit to the yearly takings.' She pushed her glasses high on the bridge of her nose. 'You don't believe the hype, do you?'

'About him hitting his girlfriend? I don't know what to believe. She seemed so genuine. Anyway, it's just unnerved me. I'm sorry to be a hassle.'

'Give me a minute,' she sighed. 'I'll call him and tell him Damon will take over.'

Chrissie glanced towards Helena's window where the V.I.P. garden could be seen through the slats in the blinds. He wasn't out there. She remembered the first day she'd seen him, sitting on the swing seat with his guitar, every bit the Aussie superstar. But now, how things had changed.

Helena told Drew that Chrissie wouldn't be available today, then paused. 'Are you sure?' she asked him. 'Damon would be more than happy to teach you today.' Another pause. 'Well alright then. Please let me know if there's anything else we can do for you today.' She hung up and glanced at Chrissie. 'He only wants a yoga class if you're the one teaching it.'

Crap.

'He said if you're unavailable he'll just skip the class.'

Guilt trip time. Chrissie bet he'd text her any minute, asking why. She should at least let him know, but didn't know quite how to put it, and knew that if she saw him again, she might change her mind and want to forget the media scandal ever happened, and beg him to leave his awesome life behind and stay with her. But that would be stupid. It was easier to leave things now, before they got out of control. She'd always remember the fun they had, but it would have to remain a memory. She was only just keeping it together now, if she rocked the boat, she may fall apart, and couldn't risk it.

'Well, I better get ready for my morning class. Again, I'm sorry about all this.'

'You sure he didn't make any advances to you?' Helena stepped towards her. 'Has anything happened I should know about?'

Chrissie's heart skipped a beat. *More than you should know.* 'Nothing. He's been a great student.' She smiled and walked out, leaving Helena not looking too convinced.

When her afternoon class had finished, Chrissie sat by herself in the staff lounge, staring at the message on her phone.

> What's going on Chrissie? Today was supposed
> to be our last yoga class. Please talk to me. D.

He'd sent the text earlier, but she hadn't replied. She leaned back into the comfortable sofa, her elbow resting on the armrest. Then she checked her watch. Not long till she had to pick up Kai from school, as catching the bus to school was one thing, catching it home was another. She pressed her finger to the screen and typed:

> I heard about your ex-girlfriend. It's all a bit
> much, I needed some time apart.

He replied:

> You don't believe her do you? Chrissie, you
> know me! I'd never do that.

Just what she'd expected him to say.

> Either way, it was a mistake to get carried away,
> my boss is suspicious, and I just don't need this
> kind of drama in my life.

There was longer a pause before his reply:

> I don't need this drama either, but that's life.
> Chrissie, I can't leave without saying goodbye.
> Can we meet later?

She'd said one too many goodbyes in her life and wasn't about to put herself through another one. She typed in her response:

> I don't think that's a good idea.

She switched her phone to silent and opened her web browser;

it was still open at one of the interviews with Jolene. She scanned it again, as if to cement her resolve, then something made her type a new search into Google.

The short life of Stephanie Shaw.

It was the title of an article she'd written years ago for the newspaper she'd worked for. Stephanie was a nine-year-old girl, a talented young actress, whose tragic drowning had broken the hearts of many. Chrissie's boss had sent her to report at the scene where she was last seen, despite asking him if someone else could do it. She didn't want to upset her boss, so she'd done it. She thought she'd just be talking to police and witnesses to find out what happened, but hadn't expected Search and Rescue to find the girl's body while she was there. She'd never seen Danielle's body, hadn't wanted to, but had seen Stephanie's, and knowing that the same fate claimed her sister had haunted her from that moment on. After Stephanie's funeral, Chrissie had been assigned to interview the family and write about the young star's short life as a sort of tribute, and she'd done it, but not without consequences. The nightmares started soon after, then the headaches, then the panic attacks. Two months later she quit her job, commenced yoga on the advice of her therapist, and went on unemployment benefits. Victor had come along at just the right time, when she needed someone, and they'd married quickly after a short period of dating.

Chrissie read her article, and flashes of Stephanie's bloated face flashed through her mind. Then it was Danielle's face, quick, sharp flashes, searing through her skull. She sucked in a breath, her heart pounding, and the phone slipped from her grasp. She shot up, panting, and dashed over to the sink, leaning over it to try catching her breath. Sweat clung to her chest and that familiar fear rose up like a surge of lava ready to explode from a volcano.

'No, no more, please!' she said to herself, her hand on her heart. *Techniques, Chrissie, do the techniques.*

She breathed in and raised her palm upwards, drawing in oxygen, then pushed out a slow breath as she pushed her hand downwards. She repeated the movements, forcing herself to be calm. If anyone at work saw her like this she'd feel like a total fraud and they might deem her unfit for her teaching duties. She had to get it together. She'd done so before, she could do it again, and never, ever would she look at that article again.

The heat died down, her breath slowing, and her mind stabilising. This was crazy. She couldn't keep going on like this. The attacks weren't occurring that often, but there was obviously some residual fear and grief simmering away inside.

First thing Monday morning, after Drew would be leaving, she'd call a therapist and book an appointment. It was time to take back control and leave the past where it belonged.

CHAPTER TWENTY-FOUR

The first thing Kai said to his father that night when Chrissie dropped him off for the weekend was, 'I caught the bus today!'

Victor's reply? 'Oh, I thought you already had before.'

Did he not pay any attention to her emails? Anyway, she'd told Kai after school how proud she was of him, and that she loved him very much. Then she'd asked him to show her one of his scary faces and they'd collapsed in laughter at trying to outdo each other's faces. It was moments like that that made all the hard times bearable.

Chrissie got back in her car after kissing him goodbye, and rummaged in her bag for her phone to check for any messages. It hadn't beeped all afternoon. She removed her purse and water bottle, but the phone wasn't there. Panic almost set in; it was a strange and uncomfortable feeling to be without one's phone in this day and age. She frowned, leaned her head on the headrest and thought back to the day that had been and gone behind the clouds and darkening sky. *The staff lounge!* She hadn't put it back in her bag after her 'episode', dashing out to go and pick up Kai from school.

Chrissie started the car with a view to picking it up on the way home. The night staff would be there, though there wouldn't be many at this time.

Just over ninety minutes later she pulled into the staff parking area of Serendipity and quietly slipped in through the private entrance. The hall was dimly lit, and conflicting emotions swirled inside; comfort at the beautiful atmosphere that resided in the retreat, and caution knowing that Drew was probably not far away. She ducked into the staff lounge and looked on the sofa, but it wasn't there. Maybe someone found it and kept it for her. She moved the cushions and the shiny plastic of her phone cover caught her eye, stuck in the crevice between the edges of the armrest and the seat cushion. *Phew.* She picked it up and checked it as she walked out of the room. No messages.

As Chrissie walked past Helena's office, movement caught her eye. She backtracked and peered through the glass windows of the dark office, towards the window that had a partial view of the V.I.P. garden. Movement again. She narrowed her eyes and looked closer. Two figures were in the distance. Who was out there with Drew? As her eyes tried hard to focus she got a better picture. One of the figures was outside the fence of Serendipity, in a dense area of shrubbery that wasn't really made for pedestrian access and ensured privacy for the V.I.P. guests.

What was going on? Curiosity prickled the back of her neck, and when Drew flung his arms about she sucked in a sharp breath. He was arguing with someone. Maybe she should check if everything was okay, since she was a staff member and he was their guest. It was partly her responsibility to make sure guests were taken care of. Or maybe the ex-journalist inside her just wanted to find out what was going on.

She grabbed her key card, checked no one was looking, and walked down the corridor to the V.I.P. entrance. She unlocked the door and edged along the hallway, towards the dining room doors that were open. The closer she got, the louder the music got. She peeked through the doors. A bluetooth speaker was on the side table, playing music she didn't recognise. The good thing was it would help hide the sound of her footsteps, because, yes, she was walking through those doors and had left all rational thought behind.

Her feet stepped lightly into the room. The doors leading out to the patio and garden were wide open, and a cool breeze rushed in. Darkness filled the room, apart from a lamp in the corner and a tea light candle in a holder on the dining table, where a collection of papers lay along with a pen, a notebook, and Drew's phone. As if sensing her presence, his phone gave off a low volume jingle and the screen lit up. Instinctively she glanced at it, freezing on the spot and wondering if Drew had heard it. Probably not, he was too far outside and the music overtook it.

Chrissie's mouth gaped on looking at the screen, not at the message, a simple reminder saying, '*Remember to email Steven*', but at the screensaver picture. The sunset he'd had on it was no longer there. In its place was a picture of her. The picture he'd taken that day they had lunch in this very room, when the butterfly had landed on her hand. Chrissie didn't know whether to be flattered or creeped out, but some kind of jolt ran down her spine.

She stayed close to the wall and crept along, Drew's voice becoming louder. She couldn't understand exactly what he was saying, but he was angry. Briefly, she thought of turning around and getting out of there. What if what she'd known of Drew was just for show? What if he really did have anger problems and he was about to make them known? No, she *had* to find out what was going on.

Cool air nipped at her face when she slid through the open

French doors. She edged to the right along the patio, in the direction of the voices beyond the wall that shielded her presence from them. When she got to the corner she tilted her head slightly, her view partly filtered by a tall potted fern. Her eyes focused on Drew, barefooted and in track-pants and a T-shirt, and the other person, a woman, with long blonde hair. It was her! The woman from the newspaper. Jolene. What on earth was she doing here, in Australia, in Tarrin's Bay, at the perimeter of private property? The answer became obvious.

'Why won't you come back with me?' she asked. 'I came all this way for you.'

'Because we're over, Jolene. Do you really think I'd want you back after what you did to me?' His voice was firm and strong, he sounded completely different.

Without thinking, Chrissie held up the phone in her hand and pressed the camera button, sliding it onto the video function.

'But I only did it to get your attention. Please, Drewy, come back. Things will be so much better this time.'

'Don't call me Drewy, and don't even think I'm going back with you.'

Jolene's demeanour changed, like she had transformed from a needy, desperate young woman to a vicious, evil witch. Her posture straightened, her face hardened, and she gripped the metal of the fence like she had the strength to rip it to shreds. 'Then I'll make things worse. I'll make your life hell. You'll wish you did what I wanted.'

'Pretty soon the media is going to get sick of you clamouring for attention.'

'Not when I tell them you hurt me again. They believed me the first time, they'll believe me again. I'll tell them I came here to try and help you and you attacked me.' She picked up a stray branch, held out the underside of her forearm, and scratched it fiercely.

Chrissie covered a silent gasp with her free hand. The woman was crazy.

'Jolene, stop it!' Drew tried to take the stick from her through the small holes in the fence, then realising she probably wanted him to touch it for evidence, backed away. 'Look, you need help. You need to go home, and get some help, okay? I can't help you anymore.' His hands flailed to the side in frustration. 'Just go, Jolene.'

Chrissie gulped and stepped out from behind the wall. 'You should do as he says.'

Drew spun around and Jolene's eyes bulged.

'Chrissie, what are you doing here?' Drew held up his hands.

'Chrissie? Is she your new girlfriend?' Jolene's voice had the tone of an overdramatic teenager scorned. 'Look, girly, he'll do the same to you. He'll hurt you like he did to me. He'll act all sweet and perfect, and then — bam!' She slapped her palms together. 'The real Drew Williams will emerge. What do you think about that?' She crossed her arms.

'I think you're talking a load of crap.' Chrissie stepped to the side of Drew in an act of alliance. 'And I have proof.' She held up her phone and clicked play.

Jolene cowered behind the fence, rubbing the sides of her arms. 'No, no, give it to me!' She lunged forward and the fence rattled, her fingers trying to reach through to get the phone.

'You're going to retract all allegations publicly, tell everyone you made it up, or this goes to the press, and the police.' She'd still send it to the police anyway, but wanted to make sure Drew's name could be cleared publicly, and she was sure this aspiring actress would not want her reputation tarnished with a video such as this, showing how messed up and desperate she really was.

'You bitch,' she seethed.

'Leave, Jolene,' Drew said. 'Here, call a cab to the airport.' He shoved some money through the fence and she picked it up.

Jolene narrowed her eyes at Drew, then Chrissie, and said, 'Fine. I'll go. But you'll regret leaving me, Drew.'

'I seriously doubt it.' He crossed his arms. 'If you don't leave right now, you can forget about a cab, I'll have the police come get you instead.'

'I'm going, I'm going,' she said, flinging her hand towards him and turning away to trek through the bushes.

Drew shook his head as she disappeared through the trees, her voice as she booked a cab over her phone sounding like nothing had even happened.

'How did she track you down?' Chrissie asked. 'I can't believe she just turned up here.'

'She's resourceful, and it was leaked all over social media that I was in Tarrin's Bay, which wasn't helped by the local newspaper story. She called up Serendipity asking if the V.I.P. room was available, and when they said it wasn't, she put two and two together that I was probably a guest here.'

Chrissie ran her hand through her hair. 'Oh man.'

'You really filmed all of that?' He pointed to her phone.

'Yep, I'll send it to you.' She pressed the screen and delivered it to Drew. It was probably best if he passed it onto his lawyers, though they might want to speak to her as well, but that was okay.

'Thanks, Chrissie.' He attempted a smile but it faltered. 'What were you doing here anyway?'

'I left my phone in the staff lounge. Came to pick it up and heard some commotion outside. I'm sorry for sneaking in like that, but I don't know, must have been the journalist in me.'

'I thought you said that part of your life was history.'

'It is. It's just... something made me come in here to see what was going on. I was curious.'

Drew put his hands on his hips and turned his head away. 'If you'd just asked me, *trusted* me, you would have found out what was going on.'

'I know, and I'm sorry. I don't know what happened, I read the article and that was the first I'd heard of the drama with your ex. I didn't know what to think.'

'But you did think. You thought the worst. You believed that I was capable of doing something like that. How could you?' Disappointment creased his face.

A pang of guilt pinched Chrissie inside, and she wanted desperately to see his happy demeanour return. What had she done? Once again, people around her were getting hurt. 'Drew, I'm so sorry. I didn't really believe it, not deep down inside, I just got scared. My mind was trying to give me excuses not to see you again, not to risk getting hurt, and since your stay was almost up I thought it was a sign that it was best to leave things as they were.'

'But for a moment at least, you believed it was possible, that I'd hurt this woman, that I might even do it to you. I thought you knew me and trusted me.'

'Well we haven't exactly known each other for long, it's a bit of an ask to expect me to trust you when I barely know you!' The higher volume of her own voice surprised Chrissie.

'What do you think we've been doing these last few weeks, chatting about the weather?' He raised his hands in a questioning way. 'No, we've been getting to know each other! Or did our time together mean nothing? Maybe the journalist in you just wanted the inside scoop on the Tarrin's Bay "golden boy".' He emphasised the nickname with finger quotes. 'Maybe you've been feeding information through to your journo friend, and next week I'll be front page news again!'

'No! It wasn't like that! I would never do that.' Frustration tensed the muscles all over her body.

'But how would I know if I can trust you? I barely know you,' he mocked her statement from before.

Chrissie turned away, heat burning through her veins. 'I'm not like that, and I'm not a journalist anymore,' she said softly.

'Yet you barged in here without asking, camera at the ready.'

'I saved your ass, didn't I? And it was just a one-off situation; you can't blame me for wanting to know what the arguing was about in my place of work.'

'Once a journo...' he muttered, not needing to add the next part of the sentence as it echoed in her mind... *always a journo.*

Chrissie clamped her mouth shut, then it burst open. 'You think all journos are evil people out to make celebrities' lives hell?'

'In my experience, about eighty percent are, yes. They take photos without asking, they write things we never even said,' he struck off each statement on his fingers as though counting, 'and they mix up all the facts and take them out of context!'

'Well I'm sorry you've had such a hard time. What a tough life you've had, if media hype is all you've got to worry about.' She shook her head.

'You don't know what it's like. How would you cope with having your every move documented, photographed, written about for the public to read? Especially when they don't even get it right.'

'I'd stop worrying about what's going on outside my life and start focusing on what's going on *inside* my life,' Chrissie said. 'You let them get to you, Drew. Life's too short to care what people say about you.' Chrissie turned away, tired and fed up with fighting, then turned back. 'And just so you know — not that you'll necessarily believe me — but when I was a journalist, I was one of the twenty percent who had decency and integrity and did things right,' Chrissie blurted, turning on her heel and marching out of the V.I.P. quarters, and quite possibly, out of his life.

Drew stayed in the shower for well over twenty minutes that night, the hot water reddening his skin, not wanting to leave its comfort. How did things go so pear-shaped? This month had been going so well, and as soon as the media found out where he was, all hell broke loose, mostly in the form of Jolene. He would have been happy to stay in his happy bubble at Serendipity a lot longer, away from the prying eyes and gossip. He barely had a chance to get any privacy, and even when he did, this happened.

'You let them get to you,' Chrissie had said. She was right. He had. Too many years of putting up with their lies, and it had all compounded into a big clump of irritation. How did he get to this point? If the yoga classes had taught him one thing, it was that no matter what was going on in the world, you could choose to be in peace any moment you wanted. The bad stuff would still be out there, but what was the point in letting it get to you? It didn't change anything. Jolene was gone. His name wouldn't be tarnished. Why should he let what had been and gone affect him now?

Sure, it had hurt that Chrissie had doubted him, but it sort of made sense that it was her mind's way of giving her an excuse to bail out on their relationship. She was, first and foremost, Kai's mother, and children needed a stable home life. Tonight's goings on were far from stable.

He thought back to what he'd said to her, the way he'd taken his anger and frustration at Jolene's unexpected appearance out on her, bashing her former profession. It wasn't fair, and he hated the way he was with her tonight. If only the day could rewind so he could start over. He thought of Chrissie's beautiful face the first day they'd met, and then her face tonight, creased and annoyed and sad...

Drew thumped his fist on the shower tiles. *He* did that to her. He'd allowed things to get to him and she'd become collateral damage. He buried his face in his hand, squeezing his eyes shut, as regret seeped through his fingers and hot water scorched his back.

CHAPTER TWENTY-FIVE

Chrissie didn't think she'd get a minute of sleep on Friday night, but surprisingly, she slept like someone who'd just run a marathon. In a way she had, an emotional marathon, and she had yet to make it to the finish line, if there even was one.

Without Kai at home to take care of this weekend, breakfast merged into brunch, and Chrissie could barely move from the dining table. As she often did when overwhelmed, she wrote down lists and plans, giving her a sense of control about her life. She knew she had to get help again for the panic attacks and water phobia, and get Kai into swimming lessons; it was unfair for her issues to become his. One thing that no lists or plans could help her deal with, though, was Drew. And she couldn't even talk to anyone about it, that was what made it so hard. When her love life got rocky, she could always turn to a friend like Melinda and talk it through.

Chrissie tapped her pen on the table, then remembered that Drew's presence in town had already been discovered. And anyway, he was leaving in less than forty-eight hours. She'd done her bit, kept quiet, but it wasn't really relevant anymore.

Stuff it! She picked up her phone and did what she'd been dying to do all month.

'Chrissie, how are you, Hun?' Melinda's voice was welcoming as always.

'Do you have a bit of time?'

'I have kids wandering around and being noisy but I can talk. What's up?'

Where to begin?

'Um, there's something I've been wanting to talk to you about all month, but I've been sworn to secrecy. I don't think it matters now, so I'm going to go ahead and tell you.'

Melinda sucked in an anticipatory breath. 'Ooh, do tell! You're not pregnant are you? Or getting back with Victor?'

'No, no, nothing like that,' Chrissie replied. 'Oh, but firstly, I want to apologise for lying to you last Saturday.'

'You lied to me? What about?'

'I didn't really need any milk, when you came to visit. At least, not until I tipped out the milk I had left so you wouldn't get suspicious.'

'Milk? Why would you need to lie about milk? What's that got to do with... hang on, did you have something there that you didn't want me to see and needed to hide? A present perhaps?' Her voice was laced with curious hopefulness. Bless her.

'No, not something...'

Melinda was quiet for a moment then gasped. 'Do you mean, *someone*?'

'Uh-huh.'

'But Kai was there too, surely you couldn't have been having a secret rendezvous with some guy while he was in the house? Ooh, was it the other yoga teacher?'

'Damon? No!'

'Then who?'

'Okay, I better backtrack a little. I just wanted to apologise first about the milk thing, I felt bad.'

'Oh Chrissie, every now and again we need to tell a little white lie, it's no biggie. Forget about it, I'm sure you had a good reason. Now spill, girlfriend.'

Chrissie gulped and cleared her throat. 'At the start of the month I was allocated an important job at work, private yoga instructor to a V.I.P. guest, and all was going great until I blurted out about my sister's death and lost it in front of him, and then we kissed on the beach one night and then again during class and I could have lost my job if anyone found out, and then we even danced together to *Dirty Dancing* music which was wonderful but then his father had a heart attack and everything went downhill after that and I found out a scandal involving him and thought the worst and now he's angry with me and he's leaving on Monday so we can't be together and I don't know what to do because...' She finally inhaled a deep breath, '...Because I think I've fallen in love with him.'

The words she'd spoken shocked her, an uncertain vulnerability shook her from within. She wasn't supposed to say *that*. She was supposed to say she was going to try and move on and focus on her and Kai, not that she loved him. How could she love someone after only four weeks?

'Mel?'

'Holy freaking hell,' she whispered. 'I think I caught most of that, but you've been holding all this in, all month?'

'Yep.'

'Who is he? Who have you fallen in love with? Who did you kiss and dance with and whatever else it was you said?' she asked with urgency.

Chrissie thought of his smiling face, his sculpted body and his soulful voice. The memory of his gentle touch on her face when she'd cried after hearing his new song, *Breathe,* when he'd told her she was beautiful too. The charming, wonderful man who taught her son how to use a yo-yo, and helped her paint the house. How could she have even considered, for the briefest of moments, that he wasn't who he'd shown himself to be? She shook her head at the lapse in judgment and her chin trembled.

'Drew Williams,' she said.

A clunk sounded on the line, then a muffled sound, as though Melinda had dropped the phone.

'Mel?'

'Did you just say *Drew Williams*?'

'Yes.'

'As in, hot singer from Down Under, multiple Grammy award winner Drew Williams?'

'The one and only.'

'Are you having me on?' She laughed.

'No, I swear, Mel. He was here that day and I couldn't let you see him. I signed a legal form to not let his presence in town be known, because he was hiding out from a media scandal involving his ex-girlfriend — which was a bunch of lies by the way — and wanted some peace and quiet for a month.'

'You kissed Drew Williams?' She sounded like a teenage girl.

'Mel! Yes, I kissed him, yes, we danced, and yes... he's the one I've fallen for.'

'I think I'm going to faint.' Mel's voice was quiet. 'I can't believe it. He's, I mean, he's super awesome, I love his music, and oh my God, that body. You... and him?'

'It's all true.'

'If I wasn't your friend I'd be writing up an article right now.' She laughed. 'I'm sorry, you've taken me by surprise. Oh, Hun, what a month! And he's leaving soon? But you love him? How does he feel about you?'

'The last time I spoke to him, last night, we had a huge argument. I won't go into the details but he's pissed that I let myself get sucked into his ex's story and wasn't sure who was telling the truth. Then I got angry because he suggested I was trying to get the inside gossip on him and sell it to my journo friends, and I stormed out.'

'Apart from all that, is he as nice as he seems?'

Chrissie closed her eyes for a moment. 'Mel, he's better than I could have imagined. In every way. Oh my God, what am I going to do?'

'You have to see him, talk to him, before he goes. Don't leave it like this,' she urged. 'Even if it can't continue — because I hate to say it — he lives a whole different life on the other side of the world, Hun, but at least leave things on a good note. Write it off as a secret fling. Cherish the memories.'

'I hate that what you're saying is true.'

'So, um, did you,' she dropped her voice to a whisper, no doubt from kids being in her vicinity, 'sleep with him?'

'Mel!' Chrissie's face burned. 'No, I didn't. It didn't get that far, but... oh man I wanted to. I think he did too.'

'What stopped you?'

'Common sense? Knowing it could make things extremely awkward? I don't know. I didn't want to seem like the fan girl groupie, and I think he didn't want to be seen as the womaniser celebrity. Which he's not. He's really sweet, and caring, and great with Kai. I even met his parents and I'm friends with his sister.'

Melinda laughed. 'All this, in only one month? Your life could be a book, Chrissie.'

'Ha, don't I know it.'

'If he introduced you to his family, that's really saying something. Maybe I jumped the gun. Maybe he's wanting to spend more time back home. I don't know. But what I do know is you need to talk to him.'

'I know.'

'Let me know what happens, okay? And Hun?'

'Yes?'

'I know this is no consolation, but if it doesn't work out, just remember, I'll always love you.' Chrissie could hear the smile in her voice.

She was right, it was no consolation in terms of Drew, but in another way, it was even better. 'I'm so lucky to have a friend like you, have I ever told you that?'

'You just did.'

Chrissie farewelled her friend and clicked on Drew's name in her contacts list. She flinched when a text message appeared on the screen, beating her to it.

> I'm hoping we can talk sometime before I leave.
> I'm dealing with family stuff today, so Sunday?
> Don't want to leave things the way they are.
> Drew.

Chrissie's hand shook when she typed in her reply. She wanted to say so much but though it best to wait till they were face to face.

> I don't want to leave things the way they are either. I'll talk to you on Sunday. Chrissie.

She left out the kiss symbols. Sunday would tell her if she'd be able to use them ever again.

'Thanks, Drew, it's been awesome having you here.' Gemma's jewellery jingled as she leaned forward and hugged her uncle.

'It's been awesome being here. I'm so proud of you, you're getting better and better. But remember what we talked about, yeah?'

'Yeah. Your advice makes a lot of sense. Thanks.'

'My pleasure.' He'd given her a good rundown of the industry. The good, the bad, and the ugly. Hopefully he'd managed to fuel her desire to stay true to her passion, but also give her a realistic view of what could lie ahead too. He'd arranged some assistance for her to get a demo album recorded professionally, telling her to go ahead once she had at least seven songs of her own, since her song writing ability was quite impressive. She could always sing covers at gigs, but the earlier she established her own unique flavour, the better. The industry could easily influence young talent to go a certain way in order to make money, and although there were positive sides to that, he'd learned what was most important was being true to the artist you wanted to be, and being yourself both on stage and off.

Sarah kissed him on the cheek. 'Thank you, bro. Don't stay away too long.'

'I won't. I have to come back and see my new niece or nephew when they're born.'

Sarah patted her stomach. 'Still can't believe it.' She shook her head.

Gemma patted her mother's stomach too. 'I can't believe I was in there once. How bizarre.'

'And now look at you!' Sarah said.

'Crazy huh? I wonder what my brother or sister will be like. Maybe they'll be a singer too, who knows?'

'Time will tell. And time is getting away from Drew, so we better let him get a move on, with only one and a bit days left here.'

'Well, this is probably it.' Drew clapped his hands together. 'I'll call you when I get back to the States. Look after yourselves, and look after Dad for me.'

'We will.'

Drew held his sister's gaze, and she must have known what he was thinking, because she gave him a single nod. She would look out for Chrissie too.

He hugged his sister and Gemma and Sam, gave Liam a handshake and a man-hug, and they waved in the doorway as he walked out. His mum had done the same thing earlier today, but not his dad. He had remained in his armchair and he'd said his goodbyes there. 'I'll be right,' he'd said. 'I have to be. I can't let your mother keep doing all the cooking.' He'd winked and they'd shared a chuckle. Dad taking it easy was new to Drew. But he knew the seriousness of the situation and would do what he was advised to do. Drew knew that his father would be back on track in no time, though, cooking and exercising and putting his health up high on his list of priorities. The shock of the situation had really put life into perspective for Drew, and the big picture of everything had been on his mind for the last week.

Before he got on his bike, he checked his phone. Nothing new, but he glanced at the email from his manager again. He had some decisions to make, and the pros and cons of each swung back and forth in his mind.

He took hold of the handlebar and rode off. There was one more stop he wanted to make before he went back to Serendipity for a quiet Saturday night, so he turned off in the other direction and arrived at Barry's red brick house, sandwiched in a street between the contrast of the retirement home and the fitness centre.

Drew didn't know if Gemma's father would be home, but knocked on the door anyway.

The door opened and Barry's eyes widened. 'Drew. What are you doing here?'

'Just on my way back from Sarah's, thought I'd drop in to say goodbye.'

'When do you leave?'

'Monday.'

'Right.' He rubbed at the back of his neck. 'Want a beer or anything?'

'No, better not drink and ride.' He pointed to his bike and offered a feeble smile. 'Anyway, a lot's happened while I've been here, and ah, I wanted to say that whatever affected our friendship, I'd love it if we could just put it behind us. If not for our sake, then for Gemma's. The past is the past. I know you cared about Sarah back then, but when you left her to raise a baby on her own, well, you know how I felt about that.'

Barry shoved his hands in his pockets. 'I was practically a kid, Drew. I wouldn't have been surprised if you'd done the same thing in my situation.'

'Who knows, but Sarah had no choice. She *had* to be there. It just got to me that you ran for it.'

'But I came back, right? Even though by that stage she didn't want me.'

'Well, yeah...'

'And we're okay, me and Gemma, me and Sarah even. So, the good old Liam may have filled my shoes, but at least I'm around now.' He shifted on the spot, crossing one foot over the other.

'And this whole thing about the TV show,' Drew continued. 'You know I felt bad for splitting up the band. But maybe, as you said in relation to Sarah's situation, you would have done the same thing too.'

If the rift between them was healing over it had just cracked open again, as Barry shook his head. 'No, see that's the difference between you and me. I wouldn't have left the group. I would have stayed and made it in the industry our own way, without the help of a talent show. We could have done it, I reckon we could have.'

Familiar frustration crept across Drew's skin. They never got anywhere when they banged on about what had happened back then. 'Well I believe things happen for a reason, and I think things turned out the way they were meant to.'

'What, you on the world stage and me stuck in a cruddy bank all day, with a few bucks made from local gigs? Of course you'd think that.' He crossed his arms.

'Barry, I didn't come here to argue, I came here to set things right.'

Barry ran his hand through his hair. 'Look, I appreciate the gesture, but maybe we should just go our separate ways. You have your life, I have mine.'

Drew shook his head. 'You know, Barry, if you don't like your job, you should do something about it. It's up to you what happens in your life, not someone else.'

'Easy for you to say.'

'Well actually it's not. I've got some big stuff going on at the moment and I'm torn. All I know is that things are going to be different in some way, and I have to make some changes, take some risks.'

Barry shifted again, clearly uncomfortable at this deep and meaningful debate. 'Well I hope whatever it is works out for you. I'm sure it will.'

'And I hope you find a way to be happier, but it's up to you.'

Barry checked his watch. 'Well, I guess you have to get going.'

'Barry, if we could just—'

'Bye, Drew. Go back to L.A. and live your life, and I'll go back to my small-town café tonight and perform for a huge crowd of twenty people. Unless you want to come? But no, that would be below you, wouldn't it.' It wasn't a question.

Drew sighed. Barry wasn't a bad guy, but he was bitter. Bitter and hurt and probably bored and lonely. Continuing to talk wouldn't do any good, and he didn't want to make things ten times worse by probing any further. Maybe they'd make amends eventually, but right now wasn't the right time.

After an early five o'clock dinner, Drew had sunk into the comfort of his bed at Serendipity, and fatigue from lack of sleep and stress had claimed him. Two hours later he'd woken, groggy, his mind swirling with everything that had unfolded during his time here. His thoughts returned to Barry, and he felt kind of sorry for him. No longer guilty though; what was done was done, and Barry needed to get himself out of his rut and move on with his life. There was no point having further discussions on the issue, it was best left alone. If they kept feeding off each other's resentment they'd get nowhere. They'd have the same conversation over and over again.

A realisation hit Drew between the shoulder blades. He'd been trying to talk Barry around, apologising numerous times for leaving the band, telling him he still wanted to be mates, but Barry didn't need words to realise that Drew still gave a damn about him. Words didn't always convince. He needed to *see* it. Sure, he wished Barry would make the effort to tell him he was forgiven for putting himself first and going after a solo career, but Barry was stubborn and wouldn't take the initiative, even though Drew was sure he'd feel a whole lot better if they could finally put the past to rest. No, it had to be Drew.

He pushed himself up off the bed and grabbed his guitar. It was time to step up.

CHAPTER TWENTY-SIX

Chrissie sipped on her latte and tucked into the chocolate hazelnut cake as she sat at a corner table at Café Lagoon. She needed this. Time out, on her own, with no potential for arguments, disagreements, or rejection. Jonah had introduced her to a couple of the locals and they'd chatted briefly, but now she had only her Kindle eReader for company and the cruisy, husky singing voice of Barry Reynolds. He was good. Not as stand-out as Drew Williams, but good, and easy to listen to over a meal. She decided against introducing herself as Drew's yoga instructor; she didn't know where the pair were at with their longstanding feud.

The dim lighting gave a comfortable balance of visibility and cosiness, and her mind had phased out the chatter and hum of the small crowd gathered around tables. Until something shifted. Someone gasped, someone cheered, followed by a few 'hello's' and 'what are you doing here's'. The music from Barry's guitar and voice stopped. Chrissie peered over a table of people and her breath halted. Guitar in one hand, someone's handshake in another, Drew had entered Café Lagoon.

She gulped and her heart pounded. She hadn't expected to see him tonight, especially not here, in a public place. His presence was certainly no secret now.

A young woman's hands covered her mouth, and her friend sidled up close beside her with a surprised grin on her face. Jonah came out from behind the counter and greeted Drew, and by the looks of things offered him something to eat or drink, but Drew politely waved the offer away. He edged through the crowd that had gathered around him, and Chrissie's gaze darted to the direction he was heading. Barry's expression could only be described as dumbfounded. He sat there, frozen, his hand where he'd left it on the guitar. So they obviously hadn't planned to meet here.

Drew approached Barry and took him aside. Chrissie swiped loose hair from her face, and took an awkward sip of her latte. He hadn't seen her.

The men spoke; Barry's arms were crossed, then they dropped by his side. Drew's hands helped with the talking, he appeared to be explaining something, then he held one out in front. Barry glanced at it first, then at Drew's face, then slid his hand into Drew's grasp and gave it a short, sharp shake. Barry pulled up an extra stool next to the microphone, and they both sat side by side.

Some members of the crowd were saying, 'Oooh', and, 'Ahhh', and Drew smiled at them.

Barry took hold of the microphone. 'Change of plans, folks. This next song is going to be a duet. An old mate of mine, as you can see, has dropped in unexpectedly, begging me for a chance to be in the spotlight.' He slid a grin in Drew's direction and Drew shrugged. 'You probably haven't heard of him so I better introduce him. Ladies and gentleman, please give a warm welcome to Tarrin's Bay born and bred, Mr Drew Williams.'

A wolf whistle sliced through the air, people clapped, and cheers rang out in the crowd. Some people got out their phone cameras, and Jonah leaned eagerly against the counter.

Drew's gaze scanned the crowd and landed on Chrissie's. His eyes widened, and she hoped her presence wouldn't interfere with his impromptu performance. Drew lifted his right hand from in front of his guitar and gave a small wave, and nodded a hello. She waved and nodded back. Friendly, but still holding some tension from their unresolved conflict.

Drew's guitar came to life with his hands, and Barry's joined the party. Barry started singing the first verse of an unknown song. His voice reached a crescendo, and the tempo intensified, then Drew sang the chorus along with Barry...

'This has been the best day, the best day, the best day, the best day,

And it's gonna be the best night, the best night, the best night, the best night,

Don't want it to... end.'

It sounded familiar, and Chrissie wondered if this was the song they'd performed in their audition for *Search for a Star*. From memory they'd had to sing two songs, after which they'd got Drew to sing solo. The lyrics weren't as accomplished as Drew's later songs, but the music gave off a feeling of teenage fun, experimentation, and partying. The beat was good, the chorus catchy, and both men had smiles on their faces as they sang.

Drew sang the second verse, and when the chorus returned, the crowd clapped along and some got up and danced between the tables. The vibe rubbed off on Chrissie and she clapped along too, Drew eyeing her as he sang, his smile widening. Music was such a powerful way to communicate, to reach out, to heal. The enjoyment was palpable, and Jonah was probably wishing he'd known Drew was coming so as to advertise and make a killing from coffee sales.

The final chorus tailed out...

'Don't want it to... end...'

Drew and Barry gave a final strum of their guitar strings,

finishing with a flourish of their hands. The crowd applauded and cheered, and Drew stood and held his free arm out towards Barry. Barry did the same, the men leaning forward and embracing in the manliest way possible. The top of Drew's face, scrunched over Barry's shoulder, revealed shiny eyes. He blinked them shut as he patted Barry on the back. The moment sent a shiver across Chrissie's skin. Two men with a twenty year grudge had just put their differences aside for a few minutes and bonded over a combined love and talent for music. Did anything else really matter but this moment?

Chrissie stood and clapped, a wide smile on her face. If only Gemma had been here to witness it, but by the looks of things it would probably end up on YouTube, and Drew didn't seem the least bit concerned.

The men spoke for a bit, shook hands again, and Drew took the microphone. 'And now I'll let you get back to what you were doing, thanks folks,' he said, stepping away from the makeshift stage area. Barry played an instrumental piece, a smile still on his face, as Drew braved the crowd. People shook his hand, patted him on the back, and some asked for autographs and photos. He obliged, graceful and modest and friendly. He moved like peak hour traffic through the gathering of people, until he was able to break away and turn in her direction. He stopped where he was, his lips clamping together, then he mouthed, 'I'm sorry.'

Chrissie smiled at his apology, then mouthed, 'I'm sorry too.'

He walked over to her. 'Nobody puts Chrissie in the corner.'

She laughed and stepped out from behind the table. 'What are you going to do about it, Williams?'

'I'm going to ask the lady if she would like to get the hell out of here with me.'

'The lady would love to.'

He held out his hand and she took it, slinging her handbag

over her shoulder. She glanced at Barry who had a look of curiosity on his face as he waved goodbye to Drew.

She weaved through the tables with him, and he stopped at the counter, opening his wallet and holding out a credit card to Jonah. 'Everyone's bill is on me tonight, mate.'

Jonah's eyes widened, and he took the card. Café Lagoon had full table service on Saturday evenings, so unlike their daytime process of paying and taking a number, no one had yet paid their bill and it would rack up to quite a lot.

'That's very generous, thank you,' he said.

'And add a ten percent tip for the café.'

'You rock,' Jonah replied. 'In more ways than one!' He laughed. 'Sorry, couldn't help it.'

'Ah, I love a good pun.' He shook Jonah's hand and after payment was made, Drew held onto Chrissie's hand as they walked out of the café.

Just as they left, Jonah called out to the crowd, 'Your bills have all been taken care of, guys, courtesy of our unexpected guest.'

People clapped and cheered yet again, the sound of Barry's voice and his guitar soon took over, and the melody followed them down the road and across into Miracle Park.

'Did you walk here?' Drew asked.

'Yep, no wheels tonight.'

'Mind if I walk you home then?'

'Not at all.'

They walked down to the harbour and followed the footpath until they reached the stretch of beach that led to both Serendipity and Chrissie's house.

'That was great, what you did in there. I think Barry really appreciated it.' The slow whooshing of the sea followed them along the beach.

'I'm so glad I came. Things were awkward between us earlier

today, and I couldn't leave it like that. Just like I couldn't leave us like that, after last night.' He glanced at her briefly, then returned his focus to straight ahead.

'Drew, I hope you'll forgive me, I should have known you wouldn't do anything like that, what happened to Jolene. It was stupid of me to allow myself to consider it.'

'It's okay, I understand where you were coming from now. I forgive you, and I hope you'll forgive me for the terrible way I handled the situation.'

'I do. You must have been pretty worked up with Jolene turning up out of the blue like that. And what I read online about the scandal, I can't even imagine what that must feel like; people accusing you of something you didn't do, tarnishing your reputation. I should have been more sympathetic to what you were going through, especially after what happened to your dad. How is he?'

'He's recovering well, doctors are pleased. Mum's treating him like a king, which I think he's kind of enjoying, though he can't wait to get back to the kitchen.'

'I bet. He is an excellent cook.'

'They really liked you, my parents.' Drew smiled softly.

'They did?'

'Uh-huh.'

'I really like them. And I'm so glad your dad's doing well. I was worried.'

'Thanks. And Sarah was so grateful for you looking after Sam like that. It was a big help,' Drew added.

'Sam's great. He's been like a brother to Kai lately.'

'And how is Kai going?'

'Good, he even caught the bus for the first time yesterday.'

'That's awesome! Tell him the painting man said well done.'

'Ha, I will.' She chuckled.

Relief swept throughout Chrissie's body. Last night may have been terrible, but tonight had showed her there was always hope. Bad situations could always be turned around if both parties were open and understanding. If a twenty year feud could be mended, a one-off argument was nothing. If anything, it had made her appreciate him even more, knowing what he'd been going through and how much it had shaken his sense of ease. Last month he'd been an inaccessible star in her eyes, now, he was just another human being — an equal — with emotions, frustrations, fears, and goals. If she couldn't be with him she'd just want him to be happy, to go on and do what he did best and share his gift with others. Life was what it was, and regardless of the outcome, February had been a gift.

They walked beyond the section of beach alongside Serendipity, and around the rocky hill where they'd watched the fireworks, then past the sand dunes where they'd watched the stars and shared their first kiss. The beach may hold bad memories, but things were starting to even out with some good ones too.

'I'm glad we didn't have to wait till tomorrow to talk,' Drew said.

'Me too.' Chrissie stopped at the edge of her veranda. Maybe this was the right time to say goodbye. There was still Sunday, but wouldn't it only make things a whole lot harder if they saw each other again? Tonight had been a nice ending to his time here; making amends with Barry, then putting aside their argument and forgiving each other. A goodbye, now, she could probably handle, but tomorrow could be a different story. 'So, I guess you'll be packing up tomorrow and getting ready to leave.'

'Yep. Not that I have much to pack, though.'

'You men have it so easy.' She smiled.

Drew smiled too, then looked at her with serious eyes. 'I know everything's been leading up to this moment. To the inevitable,' he said. 'I just want to say that you've given me the best damn holiday I could have asked for.' He touched the side of her arm. 'And look, I can touch my toes easily now with no knees bent.' He placed his guitar against the railing and bent forward, touching his hands to his toes.

'Very good. I'm impressed.' She grinned.

'And I promise to never fall asleep during *Shavasana* again.' He winked.

Chrissie thought back to the time he'd faked it, pulling her on top of him for a kiss, his body under hers firm and supportive.

'And I promise to never use the word *buttocks*,' she added.

He laughed and tipped his head back, his cheeks rippling with the curve of his smile. 'When it comes down to it, the bottom line is...' he grinned, then his lips straightened and his serious expression returned. 'I'll never forget you, Chrissie.' His eyes were unblinking, the graduation of blue hues merging and swirling together in the moonlight.

A lump formed in her throat, and she was reminded of going fishing in Tarrin's Bay as a child when she'd caught such a beautiful fish she'd decided to let it go. She had to do that now. Drew was — pardon the pun — a great catch, but she couldn't stifle his future and career by expecting him to hang around a small town just to be with her.

'And you, Drew. How could I ever forget you?' She touched the side of his face. 'This has been the best February I've ever had.'

'It's a shame it wasn't a leap year.' A smile snuck into the corner of his lips. 'Of all the months, I had to go and pick the shortest one to spend with you.'

She smiled in resignation. 'So I guess this might be the best opportunity to say goodbye?'

'It looks that way.' He glanced sideways into the distance, then he stepped forwards and wrapped her in his arms. 'You're an amazing woman, Chrissie,' he said, his head buried in the crook of her neck. She rubbed his back, revelling in the warmth and comforting firmness, and willed herself not to cry.

When she pulled away, her gaze rested on his guitar sitting lonely by itself. 'Oh, I never got to hear your new song.'

'Oh, that's right. I was going to play it for you on our last day in the yoga studio, but...'

'I went and boycotted the class.' She rolled her eyes.

Drew gently touched the tip of his guitar, tracing its shape with his finger, as though asking the instrument what to do. 'Maybe this is a better time to play it anyway.' He picked it up. 'You sure you want to hear it?'

Chrissie nodded. 'I'd love to.'

'It still needs to be polished and arranged properly, but I've got the basics done.'

She led him to one of the chairs on the veranda, and she took the one next to it, facing him at a forty-five-degree angle. The ocean's low hum filled the silence as he positioned the guitar on his lap and seemed to go within himself, finding his place in the song that was yet to be.

Chrissie leaned back in her chair, crossing one leg over the other, wanting to dwell on this moment and capture it in her memory forever.

Drew's gentle fingers moved easily into position, and the strings vibrated with his touch, producing a slow, hypnotic melody...

'I've been counting down the days
With each sunset's blaze,
They're going faster, what can I do
When all I want is to be with you?

February, or forever,
Should I stay, or should I go?

The past has made us wary,
But what if February
Never ended, oh should I go?

Each memory is a gift I'll take,
Wrap it round my heart so it won't break,
The sun, the moon, the stars will remind me of you,
You're my inspiration, I want the world for you.

February, or forever,
Should I stay, or should I go?
The past has made us wary,
But what if February
Never ended, oh... should I go?'

He closed his eyes as his voice strung out the last line, and ended in a pitch perfect falsetto. Brilliant.

Chrissie's nerves shook, her heart billowed out with each beat, overflowing with emotion. The song was about her, their time together, and his conflict about leaving Tarrin's Bay, February, and *her,* behind.

Drew stood, and Chrissie followed his lead.

'It was amazing. You're amazing,' she whispered, shaking her head.

He smiled. 'Glad you liked it. I wasn't sure whether to play it for you.'

'I'm glad you did. I'll never forget it.' Her eyes burned with hidden tears. She scratched her cheek, turned away, turned back again, and goddamn, if he didn't leave soon she didn't know if she could let him.

'I'll be going then,' he said, his head lowered, their eyes not daring to look at each other. He stepped off the veranda and stood in front of Chrissie. 'Bye, Burns.'

She smiled. 'Bye, Williams.' She kissed him on the forehead and gave him a quick embrace, pulling back before his touch could meld his body to hers and become impossible to part.

He walked backwards for a few steps, his guitar hanging loosely by his side. He gave a singular wave in a small arc in front of his body, then turned away and walked down to the sand.

Chrissie turned to her door and poked the key in the lock, then turned her head around slightly. The moonlight outlined his figure as he walked further away, his back to her. She impressed the image into her memory then turned back, turning the key and pushing open the door, dumping her bag on the floor to the side.

The pain was unbearable. Her heart ached, stung, and burned, and tears threatened behind her eyes. *Just one more look, just one more...*

She turned around slowly, preparing to see his darkened figure getting smaller in the distance as he approached the front of the rocky hill, but it got larger. He was coming back. And fast.

With power in his stride and fierce longing in his eyes he approached, leaning his guitar against the railing and stopping only an inch from her body, his breath panting. 'February's not over yet.' He grabbed her face with his hands and pushed his lips onto hers.

Chrissie flung her arms around him, moved her hands under his shirt, digging her fingers into the firm flesh of his back. His lips commanded hers with authority, hunger, and need, and she let him lead her backwards into the house, kicking the door closed behind them.

She lifted the fabric of his shirt higher and he raised his arms, the shirt coming off in a flash. When his arms lowered, his hands approached the front of her satin shirt, slipping the top button out of its buttonhole, then the others, one at a time, until the fabric hung loosely from her shoulders and the cool night air grazed her chest. Drew's lips moved to her neck as he slid his finger under her shirt's collar and his palm ran over her shoulder, along with a shiver, dislodging the shirt from one side. The other side followed with his assistance, falling into a silky pile on the floor. Breathing hard and fast, he took her lips again, her breasts pressing into his bare chest and spreading heat across her skin.

She took the lead, threading her fingers between his and showing him the way to her bedroom, stealing kisses on the way. They kicked off their shoes and fell together onto the bed, arms tangling and exploring. Drew helped Chrissie manoeuvre up to the head of the bed, cradling her head in his hands and moving a pillow underneath it. He lay half beside her, half on top, taking a moment to look at her.

Though the moonlight seeping through the blinds gave only subtle light to the room, the desire in Drew's expression was illuminated. His gaze ran over her face, then locked with hers, his eyes saying only one thing. He rolled on top of her and she welcomed the warm weight of his body between her legs, and his soul back into her heart.

CHAPTER TWENTY-SEVEN

Chrissie squinted as her eyes inched open and were met by a sharp stream of sunlight. Her body ached, in a good way, as though she'd done three hours at the gym. *Drew...* A satisfied smile eased onto her lips as she rolled over. Her eyes opened wider. The other side of the bed was empty.

Chrissie propped herself up on her elbows, her loose hair tickling her bare back. He was gone. Well, they *had* said their goodbyes last night, several times in fact. If that was the last memory she got to have of him, it was worth it. Heartbreaking, but worth it. She breathed deeply, his inviting masculine scent still hanging in the room. She got up and went to the bathroom and freshened up, threw on the closest outfit she could find, and went out to the kitchen. Nope, as she'd expected, he wasn't there cooking pancakes and making fresh juice. Those kind gestures were reserved for someone who planned on hanging around.

Chrissie filled a glass with water, and turned towards the fruit bowl to grab a lemon, when movement caught her attention outside. She put the glass down and walked to the veranda door, opening it to find Drew walking up to the house, water dripping over his bare chest. He picked up a towel that was hanging over the veranda railing. *He didn't leave...*

'Good morning sleepyhead,' he said. 'Did you get my note?' He pointed to the kitchen.

Chrissie went back inside and picked up the scrap of paper from under the kettle, walking outside with it.

Going to Serendipity to grab my board shorts and towel for a swim. Back soon. :)

She smiled. 'I only just got up. Thought maybe you'd...'

'Gone?'

She shrugged.

'As I said last night, February's not over yet, and I plan on making the most of it.' He wiped the towel over his body and stepped onto the veranda, pulling her in close and planting a kiss on her lips.

How many times would they have to say goodbye? This was like her worst nightmare mixed with her best dream ever.

'And anyway, I was hoping we could do something together.'

'Like what?'

Drew's eyes held caution, and he pointed to the ocean.

'Swim?' Was he serious?

'It's a perfect opportunity. The sun is shining, it's private, and I'm here to help you.'

Dread rolled through her veins. 'No, no, you know I can't do that.' She stepped backwards, into the house, but he followed.

'All you have to do is take that first step. Let me help you, Chrissie.'

She continued to shake her head. Why did he have to spoil a perfectly good morning after a perfectly good night together?

She grabbed the glass of water she'd set down before and sculled it. 'I better make some breakfast, do you like eggs?'

'Chrissie.' He held her forearm as it reached for the frypan.

'Come with me.' He led her towards the bedroom. 'You must have a swimming costume somewhere, right? Show me.'

'I'm not going to show you my private things.' Well, too late for that, but anyway.

'All you have to do is put it on, get used to it. You don't even have to get in the water, just take that first step.'

When she crossed her arms, he sighed, then pulled open her top drawer. 'Do you have one in here?' He rummaged through it, his hands moving her underwear about.

'Drew! I don't want to put on my swimming costume.'

'Ah, so you do have one.' He closed the top drawer and pulled open the next, repeating his search.

'Why are you doing this to me?' she pleaded. 'I'll deal with my issue in my own time!'

'When, Chrissie, when? It's been years and years, and you can't let what happened affect your ability to live your life, or Kai's.' His gaze targeted hers.

That hit her like a punch to the heart. 'He's *my* son; I'll do things my way, thank you very much.' She turned away from him and shook her head.

'Chrissie, I'm not trying to upset you, I'm trying to help you. You'll never get over it if you don't take a step forward, as uncomfortable as it may be.' He opened her third drawer, Chrissie knowing too well he wouldn't find it in there, but realising she had about thirty more seconds before he would.

'I... I need to plan ahead for something like this. Prepare myself.'

'If you did that you would probably work yourself up even more. It's better this way, less time for your body to feel scared.' He opened the fourth and final drawer, and she gulped as he pulled out her simple black one-piece swimming costume, tags still attached. Her therapist had told her to buy one years ago to get the ball rolling, but she'd shoved it away as soon as she got it home and never even put it on.

'Aha! Here we go. Sexy too.' He risked a cheeky smile, but she clamped her lips together and looked away.

He laid it on the bed, still messy with sheets crumpled and twisted after their passionate night together. 'Chrissie, look at me.' His tone turned serious. Her head still facing the other direction, she slid a wary glance his way. 'I'll wait outside while you put it on. Take your time, and when you're ready, come on out. I'll be with you the whole time. We can just go to the water's edge, dip your toes in, and if you can't handle it you can go back inside. Do we have a deal?' His raised eyebrows waited for her response.

She was about to say 'no way' when her voice paused. Drew's soft and sparkling eyes sent a caring glance her way, his arms hung gently by his side, his face saying 'please, just try.' She looked at the costume lying limp on the bed... it could either be the key to her recovery or the trigger for a major panic attack. Experience told her it would be the latter.

'One step at a time, remember?' he whispered. 'Costume on, walk outside, toes in water. That's all. You can do it.'

She knew that tomorrow life would return to normal, Drew would be gone, and she'd be doing the same old school morning routine with Kai. If she didn't try doing this today, she feared she never would.

She swallowed and cleared her throat. 'Okay.' Her response was barely audible.

'Okay? Good. Great. I'll be waiting outside.' He brushed past her and closed the bedroom door behind him.

Chrissie examined the costume first with her eyes, then her hands, the soft synthetic fabric cooling her fingers. She stood in front of the mirror, holding the costume up in front of her. It would still fit. Her fingers grasped the price tag and brand label, and with one swift tug, ripped it off, the popping sound symbolically breaking the tether to her past.

Breathing deeply, she stripped off and stepped into the costume, pulling it up over her hips, and feeding her arms through the straps. She adjusted the straps and smoothed her hands down over the fabric, its smoothness not too different from that of some of her yoga outfits. *Okay, step one — achieved. All I have to do is go outside and touch the water.*

She hesitated near the bedroom door, as though she was forgetting something, feeling naked and exposed. She turned back and peeked through the window at the gentle rolling waves tumbling into the shore. *I have showers, I can do this. It's just water.*

Her mind turned to a memory of Danielle on Christmas morning, when she'd given Chrissie one half of the *sisters forever* bracelet. 'I found it in a gift shop,' Danielle had said. 'I thought if we both wear one, it'd be like we're always together no matter where we are.' They'd had their fair share of sibling rivalry, but most of the time they enjoyed each other's company. Danielle had been quite mature for her age, so she'd been like an equal to Chrissie, despite their two year age gap. She remembered when Danielle had put the bracelet on Chrissie's wrist, then held her own up close to it. Her eyes had sparkled almost as much as the silver charms. How she longed to look into her sister's eyes again, feel that sisterly bond...

Chrissie approached her jewellery box and opened it, retrieving the bracelet she'd lodged in the corner — Danielle's half of the bracelet. She held the charm up in front of her, the word 'sisters' engraved on it engraving a deep absence in her heart. Then, as though Danielle was here right now, she hung the bracelet over her wrist and hooked the clasp together. Knowing the last person to wear this was her sister, almost twenty-five years ago, at this very location, sent a chill up her spine.

'I miss you, Danielle,' she whispered. 'How I wish you were here right now.'

Her skin cooled where the bracelet hung as she turned the doorknob and stepped tentatively out and into the living room, past the kitchen, and towards the veranda door where Drew stood waiting.

His soft smile greeted her, and he slid his hand in hers. 'You did good.'

Chrissie's breath quickened as she let him lead her outside, onto the grass, and then onto the sand. The warm particles spread under her feet, adding to her feeling of instability yet, in a way, preparing her for the looseness of water. *If* she made it that far. Her heart rate sped up, the dull pounding in her chest making her lungs suck in more air with each step forward.

'You're doing well,' Drew said, his hand gripping hers firmly and Chrissie gripping it harder in return.

She stepped onto wet sand and gasped at the change in texture under her feet.

'It's okay. Just breathe,' Drew's voice calmed her.

Her toes tightened together as she took more steps forward onto the wet sand, knowing that at any second a curved remnant of a wave would meet her toes. She forced her breathing to slow, each breath loud in her chest.

'That's it, keep going.' Drew's eyes were on her, but she couldn't look at him, could only allow her gaze to blur and go distant in an effort to cope with what was coming.

Cold water tickled her feet and her legs wobbled. 'Oh God, I don't know if I can do this,' her voice shook.

'Yes you can. You're already halfway there. Just keep breathing slowly, like you taught me, keep holding my hand, and step forward.'

More water lapped around her ankles, the sensation both familiar and unfamiliar, swirling long gone memories around in her mind. When the next wave came and threatened her balance, she panicked, grabbing Drew's arm with her other hand. 'I can't do it.'

He didn't listen, guiding her further forward. 'You *are* doing it, Chrissie, look.'

The fuzziness in front of her cleared as she refocused, glancing down at her legs, the water now up to her knees. She *was* doing it. She was in the water, and she was okay. The panic that had risen a moment ago subsided at her small achievement. She could go back inside now, having fulfilled Drew's demand, or she could keep going. Go further and end the debilitating fear once and for all. Or at least make a huge dent in it.

'Don't let me go, Drew,' she said, still gripping his arm.

'I won't.' He stepped forward with her, and when another wave tumbled into them he wrapped her in a supportive embrace. 'I've got you.'

Weightlessness lifted her feet from the sand for a moment as her body buoyed itself in the rhythmic dance of the ocean, Drew letting one arm go to tread water. She mimicked him, her arm creating arcs in the water, and when the next wave rolled in she let go of him, water surrounding her completely. 'Oh God,' she said. 'Oh God.' Adrenalin rushed through her, keeping her afloat, and strangely, a smile stretched across her cheeks. She was swimming, she was okay, and so was Drew. She locked eyes with him as water moved their bodies up and down, and he smiled so widely she thought he might burst open with happiness.

'Drew, I'm doing it, I'm really doing it,' she said. 'After twenty-five years.' She moved her arms around and swam closer to him, her slippery hands meeting his under the water. They moved closer to shore, putting their feet on the ground, their bodies closing in and wrapping around each other along with the water's embrace lapping at their waists.

She buried her face in his chest, pulling him close to her, and tears spilled from her eyes. 'Goodbye, Danielle,' she cried.

His hands rubbed her back, up and down, soothing her like nothing else could. It had started, the dam holding all her grief had cracked open and the pent-up emotion gushed out, releasing itself in healing sobs. He held her close for a long time, her tears falling from her face onto his chest, into the sea, merging with it, the cleansing salt water washing them away.

When her sobs became exhausted sighs, she eased her head off his chest and looked at him. Drew's eyes were glossy, and a lone tear slid down his chiselled cheekbone. She brought her hand to his cheek, stroking it and caressing the face of the wonderful, beautiful man who'd helped her more than she thought she could be helped.

'Thank you,' she said, her gaze connecting intimately with his. 'Thank you.'

He leaned forward and his soft lips cushioned hers, kissing her gently and tenderly, before they moved to her forehead and the top of her head as he cradled her head against his chest. His hands ran down her arms, bringing her hands up to his face, and he kissed them too, one finger at a time as though they were a lost treasure he'd finally found. His kisses stopped and he focused on her right hand. He lifted her wrist and eyed the bracelet. 'I haven't seen you wear this before, it's yours?'

'Yes. This is the first time I've worn it. It was my sister's.'

'Danielle's?'

She nodded. 'She gave me one of my own not long before she died, and each had half of a silver heart-shaped charm. Except I lost it.' She sighed. 'They went together, a matching pair, except, while hers said *sisters*, mine said—'

'*Forever*,' Drew whispered, his eyes wide.

'Good guess,' Chrissie said. 'How did you know?'

'It wasn't a guess.' A small smile floated onto his face. 'Come with me.' He pulled on her hand and led her out of the water. 'Go lock up, then come over to Serendipity with me.'

'What? Why?'

'Just... come on.' He smiled.

She dried off and wrapped a sarong around her waist, then grabbed her phone and keys and followed Drew to the private side entrance of the V.I.P. quarters.

He dashed up the stairs, Chrissie behind him, and when they arrived at his bedroom he said, 'Close your eyes.'

Curiosity creased her forehead but she closed her eyes, trusting him implicitly. She expected him to say, 'Now, open your eyes,' but he didn't, as something else prompted them to open. She felt his hands near her wrist, then the familiar cool touch of metal, and the click of a clasp.

Her eyes snapped open and she looked at her wrist as he held it up.

Another bracelet. Exactly the same as Danielle's, only the charm had the word *forever* on it. Her free hand flew to her mouth to meet her gasp. Drew held both charms together, two halves of the heart forming a whole, displaying the words, *sisters forever*.

'Where did you get this? It couldn't be mine, could it?'

'I believe it is.' His smile grew wider.

'But how? Where?' She could hardly believe what she was seeing.

He patted the bed and she sat next to him. 'Let me tell you a story.'

Chrissie's fingers fiddled with the bracelets as he spoke...

'When I was thirteen, I met a cute girl on the beach, here in Tarrin's Bay. She had just been for a swim and had set her towel on the sand near mine. The beach was packed, it was January — tourist season — but she stood out from the rest. Her hair glowed under the sunlight and her smile was infectious.' Drew's eyes glazed over, as though lost in the memory. 'As I was sunbaking, something bright glinted towards my eye as it reflected off the sun and I had to shade my face. It was the girl's bracelet. That's when I first saw her.' He grasped Chrissie's hands. 'I said to her, "What are you trying to do, blind me?" and she laughed. When she sat I shuffled over next to her and took a look at the offending item. The half-heart said *forever* and I teased her about it, asking if her true love had the other half. I was surprised when she said her sister had the other half and together the bracelets said *sisters forever*.'

Oh my God. No way. Chrissie's mouth gaped.

'I went for a swim and when I came back she was gone. I lay in the sun for a while, fell asleep and got really sunburnt, and when I woke and most of the crowd had cleared the beach, I gathered my things to head home. But something glinted in the sand. I picked up the bracelet that the girl had left behind.'

Chrissie's heart felt about ready to topple over.

'I tried to find her, asked around, but I didn't know her name or if she was a local or just here for the holidays.' Drew took a deep breath. 'So, for some reason I held onto it, in case she showed up again. I hooked it onto the tuners of my guitar, and from that moment on it became my lucky charm. I went in an amateur talent show the next day and won, and hung it from my guitar every time I performed somewhere. I've had nothing but success ever since.' He smiled. 'And I thought that if I ever saw her again she'd have to fight me for it.'

Tears welled up in Chrissie's eyes, even though she thought she had none left to cry, but instead of upsetting her, they brought joy.

Drew cupped her face in his hands. 'It was you. All those years ago, it was you!' He shook his head in amazement.

'I remember,' Chrissie said, 'I remember you.' She grasped his face too, looked deeply into his eyes, as though trying to see the boy who resided in there more than two decades ago.

'How did you lose it in the first place?' he asked, his hands stroking her hair in wonder, reunited after all this time.

'I didn't realise till I got back to Aunt Felicia's. The bracelet had a wonky clasp and would sometimes unlatch and fall off. I remember it got caught on the fringing of my towel that day on the beach and I yanked it free, but it must have loosened the clasp and fallen off later without me noticing.'

'Ah yes, it happened to me too, fell off my guitar, but I fixed the clasp for you.' He smiled with accomplishment.

'And you've hooked it on your guitar ever since?' she asked.

'Yep, not on a day to day basis, just before I perform, it's become kind of a ritual to quash my pre-performance nerves.'

The man had no reason to be nervous, his talent was outstanding, but knowing that he did get nervous and had created his own lucky ritual only reinforced the humility that she found so endearing. 'That's incredible. I can't believe it. You found it, found me, and now it's back with its other half!'

Drew's grin was unfading. 'Makes you wonder...'

'Wonder what?'

'If there is such a thing as fate.' His gaze locked with hers.

'Maybe there is.' She smiled. 'Maybe there is.'

It was close to five o'clock by the time Chrissie left Drew's room at Serendipity, her hand holding onto his until the last moment when she stepped out of the door and it fell from his grasp like a feather. Kai was due home any minute and she had to get back.

The day had been a mixture of tears, laughter, reminiscing, and pondering. Pondering the meaning of life, the way they'd been brought together, and how life had its own process of serendipity that was beyond all imaginable understanding. Drew had ordered up a gourmet meal for lunch, and after eating and drinking and talking and laughing, they'd made love all afternoon beneath the soft breeze that wafted in through the windows, and the low afternoon sun that cast a golden glow on their bodies.

When it had come time to leave, Drew had said, 'I have a lot of things to think about, a lot of plans to consider, and a lot of decisions to make. I don't know what the future holds just yet, but I know that somehow, sometime, somewhere, I will see you again.'

That was enough for Chrissie. They had only known each other for one month; one sweet, spectacular, mind-blowing month, but they needed to be apart now, reassess their goals and where they were headed on life's journey.

Drew had given her a gift, the gift of belief. Belief in herself, in her ability to raise Kai, and in the fact that life was not to be feared. She could step forward, face her challenges with confidence, knowing that everything would be okay and would work out the way it was meant to.

She'd kissed him one last time, slowly, deeply, savouring every second, and she'd asked him what he would do now without his good luck charm hanging from his guitar. 'I'll be right,' he'd said. 'It's time for you to have some good luck. And besides, the memory of you, your face, your smile, that's my good luck charm now.'

And so she'd left him there, at Serendipity where they'd first met, and walked back home. Not to Felicia's house, but *her* house. She still planned on selling it so she could find a place to start anew, but for now, it was a place to call home.

CHAPTER TWENTY-EIGHT

The following morning, a tapping sound tore Chrissie from a dream in which Kai was performing on stage with a guitar, and when the audience applauded she handed him a packet of potato chips as a congratulations gift and he took it off her as though it was a coveted Grammy Award. *What the?*

She rubbed her eyes, straining to open them, especially as the sun wasn't quite up yet and her room was still dark. The tapping changed from low and heavy sounding to light and sharp, and closer. It was on her window. She slipped her fingers between her blinds and pried them apart a little, her eyes jumping open at the sight of Drew on the veranda outside her window.

Chrissie moved to the right, stumbling over her shoes, and dashed quietly to the door so as to not wake Kai.

She unlocked the door and opened it, a fresh breeze rushing in and sprouting goose bumps on her arms. 'Drew, what are you doing here? Don't you have to catch your plane?'

His face was bright and lively, like he'd had fifteen hours of sleep. 'I'm on my way, a car's waiting out front for me, but I had to see you first. Your phone was turned off and I don't have your landline number.'

'But Drew, I thought we agreed that yesterday was our goodbye, I didn't want to have to say goodbye all over again.' If she had her way she'd pull him inside and drag him back to bed with her.

He held the sides of her arms. 'It's not a goodbye. It's a see you later.'

'Huh?'

'I'm going back to the States, yes, but then I'm coming back, in July.'

'For another month-long holiday?'

His wide eyes shone with certainty. 'No. For good.'

Chrissie was sure her heart had stopped beating. *For good?* Was she still asleep and dreaming all this? 'Are you serious?'

'Absolutely. I had planned on thinking everything through when I got home, talking to my manager about some options he'd been telling me about, weighing up my next steps, but last night... last night, I couldn't get you out of my head.' He brought his hand to her face, moving her matted bed-hair from her cheek and tucking it behind her ear. 'I realised that for once in my life I needed to put my personal life first. No more fitting everything else in around my career. I decided it was time to rearrange my priorities.' His grasped her hand, his fingers gripping hers as they entwined. 'And you. You're at the top of my list.'

'Drew,' she stepped closer to him, his words and revelation shaking all sleep from her body. 'What are you saying? You're moving here from L.A.? What are you going to do about your career, your tour schedule?'

'I'm still doing the concerts in late March, and I'll still do the odd tour, but I've cancelled my plans for later this year. It's time to do things my way, more slowly, more in sync with the life I want to lead now. No more hectic schedules and saying yes to every offer or demand.'

His words were like candy, every word a sweet lick of bliss, giving her an increasing rush.

'I've accepted a job I've been mulling over. I'm going to be a judge and mentor for the contestants on *Search for a Star*, in Sydney. It's like things have come full circle. I'll be giving back to the show that gave me my big break. Shooting starts in July, and I'll only be a ninety-minute drive away from here.' His smile was infectious, her lips slipping into a wide grin.

'Oh my God, I can't believe it! You're really coming back. Are you sure?'

'One hundred and ten percent sure.' He slid his arms around her waist. 'I can stay with my parents for a while and help them pack up their house and move somewhere new, be around when Sarah has her new baby, give Gemma a helping hand here and there, and most importantly, be with you. If you'll have me.'

She rose up on her toes and pressed her lips onto his. 'What do you think, Williams?' She teased a smile over his lips.

'I think that's a yes.' He teased her too with his lips.

Chrissie laughed with relief, and shook her head at the surreal situation that this was. 'And you'll really be able to make things work, living here, without being where all the action is?'

'I'll make it work. It's *my* life, *my* career, and I'm in the fortunate position of not needing to do something just to make money. I can go at my own pace, follow my own rules, and I want to do it from here. I need a home base I can truly feel connected to.' Enthusiasm and certainty oozed from his voice. 'I want to make Tarrin's Bay my home again. I love it here, and...' He pulled her in close, 'As crazy as it sounds, I love *you*.'

Each of those three little words landed smack bang in the centre of her heart, like Cupid had shot his arrow and achieved a perfect ten score.

'If that is crazy,' she whispered, her breath floating next to his ear, 'then I am too. Crazy, madly, utterly in love with you.' She kissed the smooth skin on his neck, just below his ear, and a small sigh slipped from his mouth. He turned his head and met her lips, enveloping them in his, his hands running through her hair and all over her back.

When she pulled away from him, footsteps sounded behind her. She turned around.

'Why are you up early, Mum?' Kai rubbed his eyes, his hair stuck up in all directions. 'Oh, painting man's here.'

'G'day, mate. Sorry to wake you.'

'Kai, honey, go back to bed, I'll be in with you in a minute, okay?'

'Okay.' He turned around and offered a tired wave from behind. 'Bye, painting man.'

'See you again, Kai.'

Chrissie chuckled. 'So, you know we're a package deal, right? Me and Kai, you're happy with that?'

He took her in his arms again. 'I couldn't be happier.'

She said 'see you later', watched him disappear around the side of the house, and waited for the sound of the car's engine to fade in the distance before she went back inside. She filled a glass with water, squeezed some lemon into it, and went back outside to watch the sunrise over the beach, realising this was the first day she'd seen it since she'd moved in. Today was the first day of March, the first day of autumn, and most importantly, the first day of a new and exciting life that was better than anything she could have imagined.

CHAPTER TWENTY-NINE

TEN MONTHS LATER

'C'mon, Kai, time to get out of the water!' Chrissie shaded her face from the morning sun.

'But, Mum, can't I swim for a bit longer?'

'Not now, it's moving day, remember? Drew's waiting for us.' She glanced over at the beach house where Drew stood on the newly built deck, leaning his elbows on the railing and flashing a gorgeous smile.

'Okaaay,' he said, trudging through the water and stepping onto the sand, his shorts stuck to his lanky seven-year-old body like they were shrink-wrapped.

'You can swim again once we're at the house. Grandpa Geoff and Grandma Susan can keep an eye on you while Drew and I unpack all the essentials.'

'Can we still go to the Wishing Festival later on?'

'If you get a move on we can. We'll head down there for a short while, long enough to make a wish or two, but then we'll have to get back to the unpacking.'

Being the 4th of January, crowds had gathered in Miracle Park for the annual festival, but Chrissie wasn't fussed one way or the other about going. Her wishes had already come true. Big time.

As Kai walked up to the house, Chrissie glanced at Drew who blew a kiss her way, and she returned it, the sun casting a sparkling glint on the ring on her left hand.

Kai dried off and put on a T-shirt and shoes, then went through each room in the house and said goodbye to what had been his home for the last twelve months. All going well, the next time he moved would be when he was over eighteen. Chrissie looked forward to staying put, setting down roots, and revelling in the freedom that came with having her own place, *their* own place.

Chrissie locked up and scanned the house as Kai and Drew got into the car, packed to the brim with the last of their belongings. Felicia would be pleased with the final result. It looked brand new, yet still had that homely, welcoming feel to it. The buyers loved it, and Chrissie had smiled when she'd overheard them during their second inspection saying where they would put their furniture and how their extended family would be visiting every chance they got to stay in the spare rooms. The couple had a young daughter, with another on the way, and Chrissie was glad that the house was going to people that would appreciate it and fill it with happy new memories and new life.

'You ready?' Arms slid around her waist from behind, and she turned to her fiancé.

'I'm ready.' She nodded and smiled, hopped into the car, and watched the house get smaller until it was no longer in view as they drove down Dune Road, past Serendipity, and towards their new life.

Several minutes later they turned into the driveway of Honeydew House, an excited giggle surfacing from Chrissie's lips. 'It's all happening! I'm so excited.'

Drew rubbed her thigh. 'Me too.'

'And me too!' Kai called from the backseat.

They unloaded the car with the help of Susan and Geoff,

who'd lost about ten kilograms, and put the boxes and bags in the appropriate rooms. The unpacking and sorting would take a while, but they'd do it gradually. She wasn't due back at Serendipity until school resumed at the end of the month, and then she'd get a week off again in February over Valentine's Day for the wedding and honeymoon. The Serendipity staff had taken to calling the health retreat the Love Nest after hearing the story of how Drew and Chrissie came to be together. Not that they knew the details, only that they'd bonded and agreed to reconnect after he returned from the States. They didn't know what went on in that yoga studio, Drew's bedroom, or at the beach and the rocky hill, and never would. It was their little secret.

'Mum, can I swim now?' Kai asked, already ripping off his T-shirt.

'I'll take him,' Susan said, holding out her hand for Kai.

'Just for a while, then we'll sort out some of your room before we have lunch and head down to the Wishing Festival.'

Kai dashed off outside to the pool, Susan following.

'Can we walk for a bit outside?' Chrissie asked Drew. 'I want to remember this moment before we get busy with unpacking.'

'Sounds good.' He crooked his elbow and she hooked her arm through it.

'I'll set up your cookware, if I may?' Geoff asked. 'Gotta make sure the essentials are unpacked so I can cook our feast for tonight.'

'That'd be fantastic, thanks, Geoff.'

Drew's parents had moved into their new place, a modest two bedroom house in walking distance to the shops, beaches, main street, and medical clinic where Dr Sylvia Greene was keeping a close eye on Geoff's health.

Chrissie shaded her eyes as she took in the awesome, expansive view of the ocean in the distance, framed at the sides by the lush green hills that Honeydew House sat on. It was paradise.

They walked over to the concrete imprints of Drew and Sarah's childhood feet. 'We should put Kai's in there too,' Drew said.

'Good idea,' Chrissie replied. 'And as soon as Daniella can stand, her footprints too.' She smiled as the cute little face of Sarah's four-month-old baby popped into her mind. Her smile lingered at the fact that Sarah had wanted to honour Chrissie's sister by giving her baby a variation of Danielle's name. It was the nicest thing anyone had done for her, apart from all the nice things Drew had done for her.

'Hmm, I think we should have the ceremony over there, beside the trees with the hammock.' Drew pointed. 'Great view and plenty of room for guests.'

'Hang on, what about over there?' She pointed in the other direction to the mature garden area with paving and water fountain. 'Don't I get a say in the matter? I do own half the place, you know,' she teased, nudging him in his side. Although Drew had the means to buy the whole place outright from his parents, Chrissie had refused. She'd wanted to have an equal share in the house and fulfil her goal of buying a property. The sale from Felicia's place had been just enough to cover half the price of Honeydew House, and Drew had paid the remainder.

Drew hung his arm around her back. 'I don't mind where we get married, as long as we do.'

She slid her arm around his back. 'I can't wait to start planning the yoga retreat business. I keep pinching myself, but it's really happening.' Chrissie looked forward to the idea of teaching yoga to celebrity guests, and sitting by the outdoor fireplace at night while Drew sang for everyone. By the looks of things, Kai's childhood was going to be quite cultured and unique, and who knows, maybe he would pick up the guitar himself one day. But for now, he was happy being a water baby after regular lessons had taught him how to have fun and stay safe in the water.

'It is exciting, that's for sure,' Drew said. 'And we better get to it right after the honeymoon, you know I already have some people ready and waiting to be our first guests.'

A ripple of anticipation rolled through her body. The V.I.P. yoga retreat idea had been a great one, and when Drew had spread the word about their plans to associates in the entertainment industry, quite a few had jumped at the opportunity. When it was all up and running, she'd most likely leave Serendipity for good so she could focus purely on the retreats. When she'd told Damon her plans, he said he'd have to throw her an *Adios* Party. She asked why it couldn't be a *sayonara* party, and he'd said he'd make it an *adios, sayonara, ciao, adieu,* and general farewell party to cover all bases.

'It's going to be a great partnership, this,' Chrissie said.

'Are you talking about the yoga business or us?'

She turned to face him. 'Both.'

'Can you believe that this time last year we didn't even know each other?' Drew said.

'I know, it's crazy.' She slipped both arms around his waist. 'And last February was just amazing. Up and down like a rollercoaster, but amazing.'

'It looks like this February is going to be amazing too.'

'I hope the *amazingness* continues into March this time,' Chrissie said.

'Oh, it will. And April, and May, and June...' Drew picked up her hand, kissed it, and caressed the heart-shaped charms on the bracelets, 'And forever.'

THE END

288

BONUS

Drew Williams' long awaited 14th album:
Back in The Bay

February or Forever
Breathe
The Best Day (duet with Barry Reynolds)
Serendipity
Coming Home to You
From the First Touch
Seeing Stars
Lightin' up the Night
I've got a Secret
Dance with Me
Soulmates
Bonus songs (Live & Local from Café Lagoon):
A Good Start
Fired Up

ALSO BY JULIET MADISON

ACKNOWLEDGEMENTS

Thanks again to my editor Belinda Holmes for her enthusiasm for my work, and to the Bloodhound Books team for republishing this novel.

I'd also like to thank my family, friends, and the writing community for your support and encouragement, and my mum for reading the first draft of this novel and getting excited about it.

Thanks to author Nicola Marsh for recommending the nifty little writing machine, the Alphasmart NEO, which helped me write this book faster than I thought possible and without distractions from the internet!

Thanks also to author, Kate Belle, for suggesting the name 'Serendipity' for the health retreat in this book, which perfectly fits not only this story but my books in general, and a special mention to Jessie Chapman's book *Yoga Postures for your Body, Mind, & Soul* (Harper Collins 2000), which was a great help to me many years ago when I first got into yoga, and which I revisited while writing this book to help with the yoga scenes between Chrissie and Drew.

And thanks to all the wonderfully talented singers out there who inspire people with their music every day, and inspired me to create the character of Drew.

ABOUT THE AUTHOR

Juliet Madison is a bestselling and award-nominated author of books with humour, heart, and serendipity. Writing both fiction and self-help, she is also an artist and colouring book illustrator, and an intuitive life coach who loves creating online courses for writers and those wanting to live an empowered life.

With her background as a naturopath and a dancer, Juliet is passionate about living a healthy and positive life. She likes to combine her love of words, art, and self-empowerment to create books that entertain and inspire readers to find the magic in everyday life.

Juliet lives on the picturesque south coast of NSW, Australia, where she spends as much time as possible dreaming up new stories, following her passions, being with her family, and as little time as possible doing housework.

You can find out more about Juliet, her books, and her courses at:
http://www.julietmadison.com
And connect with her on social media at:
Facebook http://www.facebook.com/julietmadisonauthor
Instagram http://www.instagram.com/julietmadisonauthorartist

A NOTE FROM THE PUBLISHER

Thank you for reading this book. If you enjoyed it please do consider leaving a review on Amazon to help others find it too.

We hate typos. All of our books have been rigorously edited and proofread, but sometimes mistakes do slip through. If you have spotted a typo, please do let us know and we can get it amended within hours.

info@bloodhoundbooks.com

www.ingramcontent.com/pod-product-compliance
Lightning Source LLC
Chambersburg PA
CBHW061522210726

48287CB00006B/1790